His voice was gruff, stimulating a heat deep inside of her.

She looked up. His eyes blazed with warmth and something else . . . She was achingly aware of how closely they sat pressed together.

The silence in the carriage grew thick, the air electric with unspoken longing.

His lips were so smooth, so enticing. They drew her. His gaze fixed on her mouth, searing her as if touched.

"Tess . . . " His hands gripped her arms, as if unable to decide if he wanted to push her away or pull her closer. She didn't give him the chance.

She pressed her mouth to his, wrapping her arms around his neck.

He tore his lips from hers. "Tess," his voice cracked. "We . . . have . . . to . . . stop."

She blinked as reality crashed into her consciousness.

Other AVON ROMANCES

DESIRE NEVER DIES *by Jenna Petersen*
GOOD GROOM HUNTING *by Shana Galen*
MISTRESS OF SCANDAL *by Sara Bennett*
NIGHT OF THE HUNTRESS *by Kathryn Smith*
THRILL OF THE KNIGHT *by Julia Latham*
TOO WICKED TO TAME *by Sophie Jordan*
WILD AND WICKED IN SCOTLAND *by Melody Thomas*

Coming Soon

THE DEVIL'S TEMPTATION *by Kimberly Logan*
WILD SWEET LOVE *by Beverly Jenkins*

And Don't Miss These
ROMANTIC TREASURES
from Avon Books

AND THEN HE KISSED HER *by Laura Lee Guhrke*
CLAIMING THE COURTESAN *by Anna Campbell*
TWO WEEKS WITH A STRANGER *by Debra Mullins*

SARI ROBINS

When Seducing A Spy

AVON BOOKS
An Imprint of HarperCollinsPublishers

AVON BOOKS
An Imprint of HarperCollins*Publishers*
10 East 53rd Street
New York, New York 10022-5299

Copyright © 2007 by Sari Earl
ISBN: 978-0-06-078248-1
ISBN-10: 0-06-078248-X
www.avonromance.com

First Avon Books paperback printing: April 2007

Avon Trademark Reg. U.S. Pat. Off. and in Other Countries,
Marca Registrada, Hecho en U.S.A.
HarperCollins® is a registered trademark of HarperCollins Publishers.

Printed in the U.S.A.

10 9 8 7 6 5 4 3 2 1

For Marilyn and Normie,
We love you always

Acknowledgments

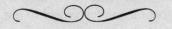

I will be eternally grateful to my family and friends, especially my mother, who continue to enthusiastically champion my efforts. I want to specially acknowledge the following people for their wonderful support: Susan Grimshaw, Frances Drouin, Dorothy Rece, Bill Eubanks, Laura Goeller, Jennifer and Steven Linowes, JR Mayhew, Ann Rawn, Marilyn Simes and Digitalinstincts.com, Laurie Ann Goldman and Blair Ross, Willa Cline, Barb and everyone at RF Designs, The Paradies Shops, Deb Brink, Becky Rose, Martha Jo Katz, Nicole Kennedy and Kathleen Adey, Nancy Yost, Robyn Freedman Spizman, George Scott, Esther Levine, Julia Quinn, Emily Cotler at Waxcreative Design, Georgia Romance Writers, and The Beau Monde.

My gratitude to the incomparable Avon books team, including but not limited to: The two Brians; Donna, Judy, and the entire Merch Sales Team; Mike, Carla, and the whole Field Sales Team; International Sales, Foreign Rights, and Sub Rights. My heartfelt appreciation for Pam, Buzzy, and Adrienne!!! Thank you!!

Tom, Gail, and Patricia—thanks for my gorgeous covers. Special thanks to Carrie, May , and most especially Lyssa!

Finally, I am thankful for my husband and children, who make every day more meaningful for me.

Your support means the world to me.

When Seducing A Spy

Prologue

London, England
1810

"**W**hat are you reading there, old boy? You seem positively mesmerized." Puffing on his thin cigar, Sir Lee Devane lowered himself into the creased leather armchair, his stiff legs an irksome reminder of his almost seventy years.

Tristram Wheaton acknowledged his former superior at the Foreign Office with a mild grunt, his eyes not leaving the newspaper. With his corpulent belly, snowy white hair, and shiny pink cheeks, Wheaton could easily pass for Father Christmas, an ironical exterior for the cunning, cold-hearted master of spies.

After a few moments, Wheaton looked up, a calculating gleam in his blue gaze. "Have you read this?" Leaning forward, he handed the broadsheet to Sir Lee, his gray superfine coat straining to accommodate his movement.

The thin paper crackled as Sir Lee held it open and

read, "Sifting Truths: The Power of Rumor and the Art of Discernment." Sir Lee looked up. "No, I haven't. But I don't usually read the *Girard Street Crier.*"

"Nor do I, but that scandalmonger Mr. Norton pointed it out to me. Apparently this article has tongues wagging. And well it should. It sorts through the whole Brinkley affair and separates fact from innuendo and misinformation."

"Misinformation that you planted."

"Quite right." Tapping his finger against his meaty lips, Wheaton's eyes narrowed as they usually did when he was deliberating a strategy. "This author, what's his name . . .?"

"Deiniol."

"This Deiniol fellow managed to slash through my carefully constructed web of lies quite neatly."

Sir Lee leaned forward, concerned. "Do you think someone's talking?"

"No. The information here was puzzled together and clearly didn't come from us."

Setting the broadsheet aside, Sir Lee leaned back into the soft leather and puffed on his cigar, enjoying the pungent flavor and the fragrant cloud floating in the air around him. "Then I would ignore it. The periodical will be hearth ashes before the end of the week and the gossips will find other fodder."

Motioning to a passing waiter for a glass of port, Sir Lee nodded to Lord Bertone, but the man didn't approach. Club members at Brooks's knew that when Sir Lee was with his former protégé, no one came near unless specifically invited.

Wheaton reached for the glass of port on the table beside him and sipped. "The intelligence reflected in this article is too good, too well considered to ignore. I must find this fellow wherever he is and enlist him."

"Do you have any thoughts on who Deiniol might be?"

Pursing his lips, Wheaton nodded. "A gentleman, no doubt. He knows the territory too well not to have been born into the upper classes."

Sir Lee raised a brow. "Are you sure you want to recruit a civilian, from the upper classes, no less? We're at war and this is not child's play."

Wheaton set down his glass so hard, it clanged on the wooden table and the liquid swirled inside. "I'll use anyone, in any way, to fight Napoleon." He waved a meaty hand. "Besides, you know as well as I that I can curtail his activities, keep him useful and yet out of harm's way."

"Hmm." Sir Lee opened the newspaper once more and read, "Sifting Truths: The Power of Rumor and the Art of Discernment," by Deiniol. Skimming the article, he nodded. "This is quite good. You may have something here."

Wheaton leaned back, with a crafty smile. "If I don't yet, I will shortly. And this Deiniol fellow will soon learn that there's more to be gained from sifting truths than merely seeing one's name in the newspaper."

Chapter 1

Two and a half years later

"There you are, Aunt Sophie!" Entering the drawing room of the Society for the Enrichment and Learning of Females, Tess Linowes, Lady Golding, smiled.

Lady Braxton looked up from the tome lying open on the desk before her. Her dove gray eyes were filled with delight. "Tess! What a pleasant surprise. How are you?"

"I went to your house and your butler directed me here," Tess explained, setting a kiss on her aunt's cheek.

"I find my house a bit too quiet for comfort these days." Aunt Sophie's moon-pale face was melancholy as she set her place with a band and closed the book. She'd lost her husband of twenty-five years to a lung ailment last summer, and Tess could hardly imagine her grief. Her aunt's already graying hair had completely turned slate, as if washed in a cloud of her sorrow.

"I like it here." Aunt Sophie sighed. "The Society for the Enrichment and Learning of Females has been a salvation for me. I wonder that you don't utilize your membership at the society more frequently, since there is such a premium placed on books and learning."

Tess busied herself with her gloves, unable to explain that if she associated much with the society's members, she'd be duty bound to spy on them for her supervisor at the Foreign Office, Mr. Tristram Wheaton, a task she'd been putting off for months. Wheaton had insisted that Tess join the society since he was worried that it was a potential vessel for discord.

Tess had joined, but had quickly concluded that the members represented what was best about English society and were simply seeking a refuge to study and enjoy each other's company. She could hardly imagine the founding members, Lady Janelle Blankett, Lady Edwina Devane, and Lady Genevieve Ensley, being traitorous in any way. Thus far, Tess had seen no reason to impose on their privacy, and she prayed that it remained so.

Adjusting her cambric blue gown, Aunt Sophie stood. "Shall I call for tea?"

"That would be wonderful."

After speaking to the footman, Aunt Sophie reclined into one of the armchairs by the low-burning hearth, and Tess dropped into the seat facing her. Aunt Sophie's eyes seemed sad and her lips were pinched.

Tess reached over and squeezed her aunt's hand. "Are you having a difficult day?"

"A bit."

"His birthday?"

"This is about the time when I would start planning the festivities." Staring into the fire, her smile was bittersweet. "Chocolate layered cake. A pheasant. Fine brandy . . ."

"I think . . ."—Tess bit her lip.—"that we should still have the party."

Aunt Sophie's brow furrowed. "You do?"

"Uncle Jack liked nothing better than a good party. What better way to celebrate his wonderful life?"

Aunt Sophie's eyes grew shiny with unshed tears. "A party for Jack." After a long moment, she nodded. "He would like that."

"Although we must make it smaller. No Uncle Hayden. Or Cousin Christopher. He's a sweetheart but he always has the most atrocious flatulence."

Aunt Sophie's lips lifted. "You're dreadful, Tess."

She smiled, glad to see the light in her aunt's gaze. "True or not?"

"True."

"And he doesn't seem embarrassed by it in the least."

"True again." Aunt Sophie sighed. "Thank you, Tess. I think it's a brilliant idea. I'll start planning right away. Will you help me?"

"Of course. Though I am dearly looking forward to that chocolate cake and brandy, I don't give a fig about the rest."

As she tilted her head, Aunt Sophie's gaze was admiring. "You're always so—oh, I don't know—

industrious. You always have a plan or an idea. I'm so envious of your ability to strike out with such confidence, Tess."

Tess thought about her nightmares, the sleepless nights, the days when her insides felt so twisted with anxiety that she feared being too far afield from a chamber pot. She stared into the fire. "I have my moments, just like everyone else."

"From the way you act, one would never know it. You have this air of resiliency, of"—Aunt Sophie shrugged—"I don't know . . . perseverance about you. And you're always so cool. I remember when Jack died and my world was falling apart, you were like an anchor steadying me. I knew that if you were around I would be taken care of."

Tess lifted a shoulder, uneasy with the praise. "I'm glad that I was able to help."

"But it's not supposed to be like that. I'm older. Your mother's sister. I'm the one supposed to be helping you."

"You do help me."

Aunt Sophie's look was disbelieving. "I can't recall the last time you allowed someone to help you. And I have no idea where this independence comes from, certainly not my side of the family."

"Talking to you is an inordinate help to me. It keeps me sane when I'm feeling less than rational. Aunt, niece, it doesn't matter, what I like about our relationship is that it transcends assumptions. The best of family."

"Indeed we're family, yet somehow I don't feel toward any of my other nieces or nephews the way I feel about you. Perhaps it's because none is nearly as nice to me as you are."

Tess had nothing to say in her family members' defense; often she understood them as well as she understood the whims of "fashion" that called for new colors and new lines every season. As if everyone had extra gold lying around just waiting to be spent on a new wardrobe.

Aunt Sophie's lips pursed and her eyes were amused. "You've courted favor with the wrong aunt, Tess. Aunt Matilda is the one with the large bank account, not me. As your sister Vivian has made inordinately clear."

Tess had some choice words for her opportunistic sister, but didn't see the point in giving them air. "Vivian doesn't mean to be so . . ."

"Calculating? Or obvious about it? Vivian could take a lesson or two from you in keeping her intentions close to her chest." Picking a speck of thread from her blue skirts, Aunt Sophie straightened. "But I don't wish to speak about Vivian, I want to talk about you. And your intentions."

"My intentions?"

"Yes." Aunt Sophie licked her lips. "Paul Rutherford came by to see me."

Tess looked away. "Oh?"

"He wishes to know, well, he asked me if I thought you would ever be interested in marriage again."

"Oh." Tess exhaled. Rutherford was a sweet cousin, but she could never see him *that way*. But Tess had sworn never to be swayed by passion again; that's what had gotten her into so much trouble with Quentin. She had mistakenly thought that desire had equaled love. A very big miscalculation she would never make twice. Would she be better off settling down with a sweet but boring man like Rutherford?

Aunt Sophie bit her lip. "You are an independent woman, Tess. You don't need a man as some women do. But I confess, I think that you are missing out on one of the greatest rewards in life, that of being a mother. Have you ever considered that your time for babies will soon be past? You are not as young as you used to be."

Rearranging her skirts, Tess brushed away some imaginary dust. "Thanks to my mother, that is a fact that I am very well aware of."

"I know you're afflicted enough by my sister's badgering that you don't need me doing it. But all I'm saying is that if you wish to be a mother, and I know that you will make a wonderful one, then you need to consider the fact that your opportunity is waning."

"I'm twenty-four, Aunt, certainly not decrepit."

"You're almost five-and-twenty, Tess. Your birthday's after Jack's. Rutherford is interested, available, and is a wonderful man . . ."

Was her time for children passing? Were her opportunities for a real life dwindling like grapes on a winter's vine? Then there was Wheaton. Somehow Tess couldn't imagine him just letting her stop working for the Foreign Office. Even if she was pregnant. But once she'd had a child? Tess had to withhold a snort. Even if she had ten babes, Wheaton would try to keep his "asset" functioning.

Then there was the issue of the father of the child. Even though many women did it and Tess did not begrudge them their choices, she didn't feel right about using a man for his seed.

And it wasn't as if she didn't have any choices left in life. Or perhaps she was so deluded, she didn't realize that her prospects were bleak. The thought was depressing enough to make her belly ache.

"Did you call for any sweets?" Tess eyed the empty doorway.

"Don't try to change the topic."

She exhaled, trying not to wonder if fruit tarts or scones would be coming with the tea. And if they were scones, would they be accompanied by clotted cream or preserves. Strawberry or—

"Rutherford, Tess," Aunt Sophie chided.

Lifting her hands, Tess tried to sound regretful. "Now is not a good time. It would stir up sleeping dogs better left quiet. The scandal business would gain a whole new life. I'm not quite ready to face it yet."

Aunt Sophie scowled. "I still cannot believe that anyone in their right mind can blame you for Quentin's descent into depravity. You certainly weren't standing at his side, forcing him to toss the dice or cheat at cards."

Tess could only imagine what she would have done if she'd been a front-row spectator to her husband's throwing away her inheritance like yesterday's trash.

"They don't allow ladies like me in gaming halls," she tried to quip, trying not to recall the painful time.

"And for good reason, we're too *damned* smart."

"Aunt!"

Aunt Sophie lifted her chin. "I can blaspheme when I wish to. I'm a widow now. There must be some small benefit."

"If there isn't, there *bloody* well should be!"

They laughed.

Aunt Sophie raised a brow. "Rutherford is exceedingly interested, and with the right encouragement . . ."

Tess stood and walked over to the window. She crossed her arms, staring out into the sunlit street. "Cousin or no, I find it hard to fathom that Rutherford has somehow forgotten that I was supposedly the cause of Lord Berber's death and consequently my husband losing his will to live."

"You and I both know that it's all stuff and nonsense. Lord Berber never should have engaged in that dangerous race, and he was drunk, no less. You *saved* Quentin's life by not letting him sail that boat that day. He would have joined his best friend in death when it capsized, and no amount of seamanship could have saved them."

"Tell that to Lord Berber's family, Quentin's, all of society, for that matter. According to them, had I not had Quentin tied so tightly by my apron stings, Berber would have lived, he and Quentin would have won the race, and Quentin would not have turned to drinking and gambling to make up for the loss of his dearest friend. They attribute the duel to me as well, for not giving my husband solace during his grief."

Sophie made a noise of disgust. "Every boat went down that day. That channel was too hazardous to traverse in those conditions and Berber was drunk, for goodness' sake! Quentin was caught cheating at cards! Cheating! And the duel was your fault? Those people are disregarding the real facts."

Tess pressed her lips together, trying to ignore the pain. "Facts are hard to discern when there is so much rumor and innuendo." She laughed, but it was not a pleasant sound. "I never told you the other twist on the tale. That Berber and Quentin had been lovers, and after Berber perished, Quentin engaged in the duel as a fancy bit of suicide."

Shaking her head, Tess looked down. "There's no truth to any of it, but that doesn't stop some people from talking. I just can't allow it to make me cease caring or stop trying to protect those I love."

Aunt Sophie stood. "I think you should consider Rutherford's interest."

"Why? Because he's the only one *with* any interest?"

"Not at all. He's simply willing to overlook your past. He says that a respectable marriage will go a long way toward helping with your tarnished reputation."

Tess gritted her teeth and held her tongue. No matter that she knew it for truth; she resented the implication that she was a charity case.

"As you are well aware, many gentlemen wouldn't be so forgiving . . ."

"Don't deign to do me favors," Tess muttered.

Aunt Sophie sighed as if greatly put out. "I know it's not ideal. Certainly not a love match. But see how you fared with love the last time around?"

"Don't remind me."

"And think of the children. Your children. I know you want them. You always have. This is your best chance."

A war was waging inside Tess. On the one hand, there was nothing more appealing than the idea of being a mother, having babies, and making a life somewhat akin to what she'd always envisioned as a girl. On the other, she had too much pride, too much self-respect, to submit herself to Rutherford's ideas about a wife and mother, and if she made one wrong move, she'd be hearing about her "tarnished" reputation or her "overlooked" past.

Then again, would marrying a respectable man actually help her reputation? Wouldn't it be lovely to move out from under the shadow of her past? Would Wheaton ever let her go? Did she *want* to stop her intelligence activities for the Foreign Office? She took great pride in being useful and in helping her country. Would she have to give up the book business that Wheaton had set her up in, but that she'd come to love?

Part of her loathed the idea of being dependent once more. She'd grown accustomed to being an independent lady, to some extent anyway. The other part of her longed for a time when she wasn't obsessed with bills, accounts, making ends meet, and answering to Wheaton.

It was all too messy, too complicated, and too many emotions were involved for her to grasp.

Tess pushed it all aside and turned. "I'll think about it." She realized that it was a lie as soon as the words had left her mouth. She had no intention of ever letting Rutherford within a mile of her bed. Whether for children, her reputation, or anything else, she simply couldn't do it.

Aunt Sophie clapped her hands. "I'm so glad to hear it. I think that I should have both you and Rutherford over for dinner. How's next Tuesday?"

Tess bit her lip. "Ah . . . Tuesday?"

A servant entered, carrying a salver. "A note for you, Lady Golding." He stopped before Tess.

Glad for the interruption, Tess quickly scooped up the folded letter. "Thank you." She immediately recognized her assistant Fiona's handwriting.

Aunt Sophie clutched her hands together. "Is it bad news?"

Tess looked up. "No, thank heavens. Fiona's just having a bit of a problem at Andersen Hall Orphanage. We're assessing Headmaster Dunn's book collection. I must go home and change into a more serviceable gown, then head over to see what's amiss. Her notes are always so vague; it's hard to tell what's happening."

"Must you go, really? You work so hard . . . Well perhaps we can see each other on Tuesday, then?"

Leaning over, Tess kissed her aunt. "I'll let you know later. For now, I must go. Duty calls. Love you."

And she was off, happy for a new problem to draw

her attention away from the discussion and the disquieting emotions it had evoked. She didn't need a man or even want one.

A ghost of a whisper threaded through her soul. If she did, would she ever find a man she could trust with her heart?

Chapter 2

"**A**ndersen Hall would never sell these books!" Fiona Reed sputtered, indignant. "They are a memorial of all that Headmaster Dunn cherished!"

Even though only six years separated them, Tess felt ages older than her eighteen-year-old assistant. Part of it was Fiona's naiveté, the rest was the fact that Tess had lived in a darker world since her husband's death three years before.

Scanning the magnificent collection of books lining the shelves, Tess sighed. "Headmaster Dunn cherished swathing a child's cold bare feet in winter and filling hollow bellies in need of sustenance. There are more important things than written pages, Fiona."

"Your callousness appalls me." After selecting another book, Fiona turned, sending her raven curls bouncing with her indignation. "I can't believe you intend to sell even one of these wonderful volumes." If it was up to Fiona, Tess wouldn't make a farthing in her business, for each book was a precious favorite, never to be parted with.

It was likely her mother's influence as a teacher that guided Fiona's outlook. It had certainly swayed Tess's decision to hire the young woman, who had been barely sixteen but sorely in need of funds since her mother had fallen ill. It had been a good choice; Fiona took great care of the volumes, maintaining their value in a way a less scrupulous assistant might not. Moreover, she was not particularly shrewd when it came to people's behavior, and had no notion of Tess's other vocation.

Tess opened a volume from the pile on the desk. "Look at this. A collection about the bats of warmer climates. One of three such sets." Closing the book, she jested, "Andersen Hall has enough pests catching the children's hair not to need five treatises on them."

At the look on Fiona's face, Tess groaned, "I was joking, Fiona. Mrs. Nagel keeps the children cleaner than most, God bless her. And yes, I know it's only a myth about bats being drawn to hair." She pursed her lips. "Yet, somehow I still duck whenever I encounter one . . . Human nature, I suppose."

Fiona's russet eyes were troubled. "Upon my honor, I still cannot tell when you're joking. In fact, I don't understand you at all. You engage in the book trade, so you must love literature, yet often you treat the books like a butcher selling swine at market."

"It's called the book *trade*, Fiona, because it's about doing business so we have funds to live on. And I do enjoy it." It wasn't completely untrue. The business that had been foisted upon her had turned out to be surprisingly rewarding.

Scratching her chin, Fiona scowled. "But you profit from people's grim situations. Yes, you help people who are in dire straits procure funds, and when you are with the clients you are compassion personified. Yet there are times when you speak so coldly it gives me chills. It's hard to tell if you're a rescuing angel or a greedy bones."

Inwardly Tess sighed. For all the pleasure of the nice camaraderie that had developed between them, it seemingly meant Fiona was comfortable asking a lot more questions. She'd certainly been more challenging of late, not a comfortable thing for Tess, who didn't want anyone to know she gathered intelligence for the Foreign Office. Was it time for her and Fiona to part ways? Tess certainly hoped not. She liked the young woman and knew that Fiona didn't have many prospects that would pay as well.

Mayhap Fiona was asking more questions because Tess was acting prickly of late. Even though Tess hadn't wanted to dwell on it, this job was particularly difficult for her. Headmaster Dunn's death had been so sudden and tragic, his loss painfully felt. Tess had met the man about two years ago at a lending library, and she'd come to admire him greatly. She enjoyed his gruff humor, his obvious devotion to his charges and to Andersen Hall Orphanage, and his delightful obsession with books. It was his passion for the written word that had helped Tess embrace her book business and really begin to take pleasure in it.

Dunn had been tenacious, sending her books every two weeks to ask for an opinion or make a recommendation. He was one of her best customers, but she never charged a fee. She could not take money from a man who rescued orphaned children for a living.

The funeral had been devastating . . . the faces of those grief-stricken children . . . the many diverse people who had loved Headmaster Dunn. She'd felt so sad, and so impotent. The world was a darker place for his loss.

When Headmaster Dunn's daughter-in-law, Mrs. Marcus Dunn, had asked for Tess's help in assessing Headmaster Dunn's private collection, Tess had been all too willing to assist. Again, she'd refused to charge a fee, averse to take even a shilling from the institution. In some small way, she felt her efforts paid tribute to Headmaster Dunn.

Stepping forward, Tess held open her hands. "I apologize if I seem unfeeling, Fiona. This is hard for me. I loved Headmaster Dunn well. It is easier for me to pretend to be all business about this, than to bear the grief of his loss. Even though it's been months since his passing, I miss him still. He was an extraordinary man."

Fiona blinked. "Oh, I hadn't realized . . . Forgive me."

"It's my own fault; I'm not one to wear my emotions on my sleeve. My mother says it's a downfall of mine." *Wheaton at the Foreign Office says it's one of my best assets.* "So please try not to read too much from my conduct, Fiona."

Tess gathered up the books she'd set aside the day before. "Regarding the rest of my clients, if it's any comfort, I only work with people who request my assistance with their collections and always try to engage in fair business dealings."

A look of horror washed over the young woman's face. "I did not mean to be impertinent, Lady Golding. Nor did I ever question your integrity!"

"Of course not."

With her hands clasped together, Fiona stepped forward. "Please, Lady Golding. I want you to know how much I appreciate my job working for you. You always treat me fairly, pay me promptly, and even give me extra time off when my mum has one of her episodes. I don't ever want you to think that I'm not grateful."

"I do know that, Fiona. And I appreciate your hard work. It's a nice arrangement for us both." *For the moment.* "I'm going to take these volumes outside for a better look in the light. Some of the markings have faded." A little separation from Fiona was not a bad idea, either. "Do you think you might be finished cataloging that first row of books today?"

"Yes, I do." Turning so that her perfect black curls bounced, Fiona removed a book from the half-empty shelf. The young woman had the loveliest raven locks, unlike Tess's which were so rusty she'd always suffered the hints and slights associated with "the devil's" hair. Since her husband's death, she'd been particularly sensitive about her provocative mane, always keeping it covered with a wide floppy bonnet, today in sea blue to match her serviceable blue gown.

Fiona turned. "I hope to complete two rows of books, at least."

"Excellent. I'll be on the porch if you need me."

Carrying an armload of books, Tess headed down the musty hallway toward the exit, thinking about Fiona's recent rash of inquisitiveness. Wheaton had told Tess to report if anyone began asking a lot of questions.

She bit her lip, wondering if it was even worth mentioning.

No. She shook her head. Fiona was merely enjoying the new rapport that had developed between them. It was a very natural thing for two women working together for so long.

Tess shook her head once more. She didn't need her supervisor at the Foreign Office embroiling himself with Fiona. She shuddered just to think what he might do.

Tess suddenly realized that she'd been so lost in thought that she must have made a wrong turn. She was in a hallway that she didn't recognize and stopped, trying to regain her bearings.

The cries and foot stomps of many children reverberated through the walls like the rumblings of thunder off in the distance. A door slammed somewhere nearby. At least it had sounded nearby. The faint scent of fuller's earth, used to clean the floors, marked the air. Tess began walking, knowing at some point she would either find her way or encounter someone who could direct her.

As she turned a corner, two boys came racing toward her.

"Excuse me . . ." she began.

But the lads were in such a tear they charged right past her so that she had to spin to get out of their way. The top book in Tess's arms went sliding and she careened forward, trying to keep the book from toppling. But her toe caught on her skirts, tripping her and sending her pitching forward with the prized books hurling airborne before her.

"Oh no!" she cried as the books tumbled in a series of thuds just as she landed hard on all fours, her palms and knees smarting.

"Are you all right?" a male voice inquired from down the hallway, accompanied by footsteps approaching fast. "Can I help you?"

"I'm fine," Tess replied, not bothering to look up at the owner of the large black Hessians now standing before her. Her only thoughts were for the volumes splayed open and the fear of bent pages. Grabbing the closest books as quickly as possible, she checked and righted the wounded pages.

"Tess? Is that you?"

Tess's head jerked up. She found herself staring into a face so achingly familiar, her stomach lurched. "Heath?"

His thick hair had grown longer since she'd last seen him, hanging just past his squared jaw and around his white collar like dark ribbons. He had whiskers now, thin though, almost as if someone had skillfully painted them on the underside of his pronounced cheekbones. His skin was a shade darker as well; lost was the sallowness that had haunted his flesh when he'd fought whooping cough as a child.

As a lad, Heath's features had been pleasant, with his attractively sloped nose, pink even lips, and steely dark eyes. In manhood, well, "a biscuit" was what Tess's friend Bonnie would call Heath Bartlett if she met him today. "A biscuit" dressed as if he'd shopped on Bond Street his whole life, even though Tess knew better.

Lowering her head, Tess continued collecting the books, although now her mind wasn't on the injured pages but on the wounded remains of her life.

"Uh, hello. Uh, what are you doing here?" She didn't mean to sound so tetchy, but she hadn't expected to see Heath. Hadn't expected to face him for years, if ever. He was a part of her past better forgotten. Buried, only to be examined in her later years, when she would revisit her mistakes, and he would be but one of many. But to run into him now, when she was on her knees dressed like a scullery maid? Somewhere the gods were laughing, and inside Tess cursed their delight.

"It's good to see you, too." Heath crouched down and retrieved the books farthest from Tess's reach.

She kept her eye averted from his handsome face and found her gaze drawn to his gloveless hands. His long, slender fingers gathered the old volumes with astonishing gentleness. Watching those cream-colored masculine hands somehow roused a warm, tickling sensation deep in her middle.

Tearing her gaze away, Tess swallowed. "Ah, sorry.

I just didn't expect to see you. And especially not at the end of a graceless tumble."

"You always did prefer four legs to two."

Frowning, she straightened. "How dare—"

"Deiniol, wasn't that your mount's name?"

Tess blinked, tensing as her fingers curled around the hard-edged books. "I can't believe you remembered. That must have been over . . . ten years ago."

His burly shoulders shrugged. "He was a fine steed, and how can I forget when he dropped you in the pond? You were soaked from head to toe."

Tess relaxed; Heath plainly was not referring to her article in the *Girard Street Crier*.

Heath smiled, exposing white, even teeth. "I'll never forget how your skin stained to the same color as your raspberry riding dress."

Talking about their childhood, before things had turned sour, eased something inside Tess. Still, she couldn't meet his eye. "You look well . . ." *Handsome as sin, actually.*

"I'd like to say the same for you." He touched the tip of her bonnet. "But I can hardly see you beneath that balloon on your head."

Shoving her floppy bonnet out of her eyes, she muttered, "You must charm all the ladies."

"I'm certainly more of a gentleman with them, that's true. But I'll remedy that at once." With one arm, Heath encircled Tess's waist and lifted her off the floor and onto her feet.

Trying to recall the King's English, she sputtered breathlessly, "Ah, I, ah . . ."

They stood side by side, like dancers preparing for a reel, yet so scandalously close, they'd be barred from any decent assembly. Tess was achingly aware of his earthy male scent, the breadth of his shoulders, and the heat of his skin. Her heart was racing, her face overwarm, and for once, she was bereft of words.

Awkwardly they parted, each stepping a few inches away, not enough to seem as if they were repulsed by the other, but enough to send the message that this was just *wrong*.

"If you would?" She motioned for him to give her the books.

"I'll carry them for you."

"That's not necessary. Please just place yours on top of mine."

"No, really, I would like to help—"

"Please do as I ask. I prefer it that way."

"That I can see." He set the books in her arms.

"So, ah . . ." Heath cleared his throat. "I'm sorry about your husband."

"Me, too." She looked away. "But thank you all the same." The topic of her ne'er-do-well, cheating mate layered tension atop the already uncomfortable atmosphere. "How's your father?"

"Very well, thank you. Still tutoring. With a family in Southampton, actually."

"Oh. How nice. Please send him my regards . . ." Not that Mr. Bartlett would want them, but it was the proper thing to say. Biting her lower lip, she told herself that it was unimportant as she asked, "And you? Are you . . . ah, married?"

She held her breath.

"I hope to be shortly."

Her stomach clenched. "So you're engaged?"

His jaw tightened and his eyes narrowed as if ready for a fight. "I'm in discussions and am hopeful of a positive conclusion."

"Sounds so romantic," she muttered under her breath.

"I'm a barrister now, Tess. I work for Solicitor-General Dagwood himself. Some count me a fine catch." His tone was defensive.

She looked up. "That's not what I meant—"

"In fact, I have an important meeting to attend, the Andersen Hall board of trustees, and don't have time to stand around and reminisce. I know I've certainly not spent *one moment* dwelling on times better left forgotten."

"Forgotten?" Even though minutes ago she'd thought the same thing, she frowned. "Really, Heath—"

"Good day, Lady Golding." Smartly, he bowed.

Her spine stiffened. They had agreed never to use anything other than their Christian names. And to use her husband's!

He spun on his heel, but then stopped and turned. "I suppose it will be another ten years before we see each other again."

Pasting a false smile on her face, she cooed, "Mayhap twenty, if we're lucky. Don't want to waste time reminiscing over nothing, do we?"

"Until then." Bowing once more, he marched down the hallway, turned a corner, and was gone.

Tess fumed, until she realized that she still had no idea where she was. Hugging the books so hard they dug into her ribs, she turned her back on the direction Heath had gone. She'd be damned if she'd follow him. She'd rather walk in circles until she expired from lack of food and drink!

Making her way down another corridor, she seethed and ranted in her head, until she suddenly realized that unshed tears burned the backs of her eyes and her heart ached with the sadness of dreams lost forever.

She hated feeling this way; it reminded her of when she'd been married to Quentin, and all those dreadful years after.

"I won't see him again for years," she muttered to herself, wondering if she believed it, wondering why she cared, and wondering who the woman was who'd captured Heath Bartlett's heart.

Chapter 3

"**M**r. Bartlett," the butler announced as Heath entered the femininely-appointed rose salon of Lord and Lady Bright, the people he hoped to call "family" soon.

Miss Penelope Whilom, the focus of his aspirations, sat in a floral chair before the open window, an embroidery in her gentle hands. She looked up, and a shy smile lit her pretty face.

The tightness that had been strangling Heath's chest ever since seeing Tess eased a dash.

Penelope is the right lady for me. Sweet, gentle, and mannerly.

Unlike the flame-haired shrew he'd encountered this afternoon.

Penelope was going to be a good partner to him. A gentle mother to his children, an asset to his career. He could only imagine the impact on his job prospects if he married the widow of a cheating snake . . . Oh, he'd heard the rumors that people blamed Tess for her husband's descent into debauchery, but Heath didn't

buy it. A man was his own master, especially one born
to power and privilege.

How could Tess have married that knave in the
first instance? It was probably the fact that the man
had been a baron. What good was respectability when
there was such a premium attached to "Quality" even
if the man had had no redeeming qualities to speak
of? Having lived with nobility on and off for most of
his life, Heath had had a taste of how differently he
could be treated simply because of his father's rank
in a household. He also had had his share of noble-
men warning him away from their daughters, as if
he wasn't good enough and never would be. There
was always that trickle of doubt that they might be
right.

"Oh dear, what have I done?" a soft voice broke
into his musings. "You're looking at me as if you're
frightfully angry with me."

Shoving aside his thoughts and smoothing his features, Heath bowed. "Pray forgive me, my dear, I had
my mind on . . . an incident at the orphanage." Penelope didn't need to know about Tess; she tended to
discuss everything with her officious mother. Where
was Lady Bright, anyway? She always chaperoned
these twice-weekly visits. Was she finally appreciating the fact that Heath wasn't about to debauch the
lady he intended for his bride? He couldn't imagine
doing any such thing to Penelope; she was too kind,
too sweet, an innocent in a world filled with worldly,
cunning women who wanted a man only for what
they could get from him.

"Was it one of the children?" Her hazel eyes were tinged with worry.

Stepping forward, he smiled and grasped her hand, a little boon to Lady Bright's absence. "Nay, just some business matters. Nothing to worry over."

Her face relaxed. "Oh, good. I'm so pleased that Solicitor-General Dagwood asked you to serve with him on the board of trustees. It's quite a feather in your cap."

"He's been very good to me and has guided me well." It had been Dagwood's suggestion that Heath pursue Penelope as a bride. Her family was inordinately respectable, and since her three older sisters had all married nobility, her parents might be inclined to accept a well-favored commoner with good prospects. Everyone knew that Law Officer of the Crown was a steppingstone to still higher judicial or political preferment. Since Dagwood was well on his way, and Heath was modeling his own career in Dagwood's style, the future looked promising, indeed.

Dagwood couldn't have been more encouraging toward Heath. He'd taken Heath under his wing and had even gone so far as to intercede on his behalf with Lord and Lady Bright. Penelope's parents had been skeptical at first, but with Dagwood's persuasion and Heath's quiet dedication to proving himself, they seemed finally to be coming around. They'd claimed that only the death of Lady Bright's mother barely six months ago was standing in the way of the announcement.

Mindful of public perception, Heath understood the

need to wait to go public with the news. It was *practically* official, but there was that tickle of doubt that Lady Bright liked to nurse within him. A well-placed *if* in a sentence, a look of question shot Penelope's way as if the judgment was still under consideration. He wished that Lady Bright didn't perceive how badly he wanted to put his past behind him and to secure a better future. She was like a bloodhound when it came to sensing weakness.

Penelope removed her hand sooner than he would have wished and adjusted her lavender gown. "Mama says that he was married once. And quite well."

Heath blinked, bringing his mind back to the conversation. "Who?"

Penelope's face was the epitome of patience tried. "Mr. Dagwood, of course. Mama says he was once married to the Viscount Benbrook's daughter. But after she died there was some sort of terrible falling out. Do you know what happened?"

"We don't speak of such matters." It was partially true. They spoke of Heath's private life, but never of Dagwood's. Heath had heard snippets about Benbrook, but the topic was clearly unwelcome, and Heath respected his superior's privacy. "Work seems to be his passion."

"I'm talking about marriage, not passion."

His astonishment must have shown on his face, for she offered a quick smile. "I'm jesting of course. Mr. Dagwood's affairs are none of my business. We are here for our visit, so let us sit, we have but a few moments together before Mama arrives."

Deciding that it was easier to accept her assurance than dig into the matter further, Heath sat.

Gracefully lowering herself onto the edge of the opposite settee, she clasped her hands in her lap. "Mama will be along in a moment. And then we'll have tea. But I must warn you, she is late because she is dreadfully upset and had to lie down."

Lady Bright allowed herself to be dreadfully upset about a multitude of things, but in this instance, Heath didn't mind. "How are you doing with your painting? Is it coming along as you'd hoped?"

Penelope's golden brow furrowed. "Don't you wish to know what's bothering Mama?"

Inwardly Heath sighed. "If you wish."

"Our cousin George has been swindled and Mama intends to see the vile thief suffer. She called upon Solicitor-General Dagwood this morning and—"

"She went to my superior without discussing it with me?" Heath interrupted, straightening.

Penelope eyed him as if he was being obtuse. "Mama always goes to the person with the most influence. It's the only way to get things properly done."

"Person with the most influence . . ." Heath held his irritation in check. Would Lady Bright go to the Prince Regent if she had an issue with not being able to purchase embargoed wine? Probably, if she managed to get close enough to bend the prince's ear.

Penelope folded her hands before her. "Don't feel badly about her not going to you for help. You see, you work for Mr. Dagwood, so for you to be of assistance, you need his acquiescence. This avoids that unnecessary step."

Heath didn't like that his future mother-in-law considered him unnecessary. "I don't have to beg for his indulgence to investigate a matter. But that is neither here nor there, since the solicitor-general is the Law Officer of the Crown. He advises and answers only to the Crown. Any matters he takes up are within strict bounds."

"Mama says that Solicitor-General Dagwood will help us because . . ." Suddenly her cheeks tinged pink. "I . . . ah, well, this is a grave injustice . . ."

Heath tried to ignore the clench in his gut. Lady Bright felt that she could impose upon Dagwood because he'd interceded on Heath's behalf.

"She should have at least waited and spoken to me about it today." Heath stood and walked over to the window so that Penelope couldn't see how irritated he truly was. Dagwood shouldn't have to suffer for aiding Heath's cause with Lord and Lady Bright. "Moreover, this is probably a case better handled by a Bow Street Runner than a Law Officer of the Crown."

"Mama says that Mr. Dagwood investigates matters that interest him. Like that dreadful Beaumont affair, even though he mauled that one so terribly."

Staring blindly at the branches swaying in the wind, Heath gritted his teeth. "The evidence was well positioned to mislead. But that aside, Mr. Dagwood has ensured that the true culprits paid for their crimes."

"You needn't be so tetchy," Penelope stated, moving to stand beside him and thereby providing him a whiff of rosewater perfume. "Your Mr. Dagwood told Mama that he would discuss the matter with you this afternoon during your customary call. So between the two of you, I'm sure you can find a way to help Mama. And me, of course. For I can only be happy if my mama is."

So Dagwood was coming here today. Heath nodded. Knowing his clever superior, Heath surmised that they would somehow turn this "favor" to their advantage. He was inordinately pleased.

Turning to Penelope, he smiled down at her. Her golden hair gleamed in the pale afternoon sun. She was angelically pretty, like a porcelain doll, and he hoped that their daughters would take after her. Regardless, he knew that they were going to wrap him around their little fingers, and he likewise knew that he wouldn't mind in the least. "I will do everything in my power to make you happy . . . Penelope." It was the first time that he'd used her Christian name. He waited for her reaction.

She blinked, and then smiled shyly, making him glad. "I know that you will. Mama says that you have good character."

That was very nice to hear. Emboldened by the privacy after so many chaperoned visits, he stepped closer, leaving only a couple of inches separating them. Her skin flushed pink and she inhaled a shaky breath, but blessedly, she did not step back. Reaching for one of her golden curls, he smoothed it away from her face. "What do *you* think of my character, Penelope?"

She swallowed, her hands fluttering about like nervous butterflies. "Uh, Mama will be here in a moment . . ."

"But she's not here now, is she?"

"I think . . . I think . . . I think that we should call for tea." Hastily she stepped over to the bellpull and jerked on it, her eyes trained on the floor.

Though disappointed, Heath smiled; she was too sweet, too innocent even to flirt. A rare find in today's London, and an excellent contrast to sophisticated, flame-haired widows.

A flurry of silk swooshed behind him as a high-pitched voice intoned, "Mr. Bartlett."

Hiding his smile, Heath turned and bowed. "Lady Bright."

Heath took it as a good sign that the lady had put off her full-black mourning garments, but in this instance the new color did not favor. Layers of spinach green ruffles with black lace were a decidedly unflattering style for a woman of her heavy girth and did not compliment a female with graying blond locks and yellow-toned skin.

Distantly Heath worried that Penelope might someday become like her mother. It wasn't her physical properties that bothered him; Lady Bright seemed fit and had given birth to five healthy children. It was more the lady's tendency to control every conversation and refuse to consider alternative viewpoints. That, and her airs. He pushed aside the thoughts, realizing that he was being critical because he was annoyed that his future mother-in-law had tried to snub him. Once more he sent silent thanks to Dagwood for being so savvy.

Pressing a white-gloved hand to her forehead, Lady Bright exhaled noisily. "I must sit. I am overcome."

Heath grasped her extended hand and eased her to recline on the chaise just as a servant rushed to place a footstool under her lifted feet.

Adjusting her spinach green layers, Lady Bright was careful not to expose even a hint of ankle. "Thank you, Mr. Bartlett. Your consideration is appreciated."

He smiled, trying to ignore the overpowering odor of roses wafting around her. "Think nothing of it, madame. Pray tell, what ails you so?"

"My cousin George. Poor, poor George. He's been undone. Completely and utterly undone." She pressed a lacy black handkerchief to her nose and sniffed. "He's been swindled, cheated, robbed. And just when he was finally getting serious about marriage. Oh, it's dreadful."

"What was stolen?"

"All of his funds. The very living that he depends upon. Some jewelry. Everything. Oh, how is it to be borne? How can he survive? How can he go on living like . . . well, living like . . . a common person?" Her shoulders shook, making her bosom shimmy like undercooked pudding. "He's a Belington, for heaven's sake! It cannot be endured!"

Heath's brow furrowed. "This surely is a serious matter. If it's true, we need——"

"If it's true?" Lady Bright screeched, sitting up. "Of

course it's true! How else could someone take every-thing that George has to his good name?"

Heath could think of a thousand things that may have happened, but George was going to be part of his family, and losing everything did warrant a full accounting. "I agree, this is a matter of the utmost importance."

"Solicitor-General Dagwood," the butler announced, quickly followed by Dagwood's powerful stride into the chamber. Except for the streaks of silver at the temples of his short black hair, the attorney had a youthful vitality that emanated from his every movement. His motions were purposeful as he removed his black hat and gloves and handed them to the butler, advanced into the room, and accepted Lady Bright's proffered hand.

Heath stood.

"Madame." Dagwood bowed, then his dark eyes fixed with Heath's in silent communion. In that instant, Heath knew that his superior had a strategy for turning Lady Bright's request in their favor. "Greetings, Miss Whilom, Mr. Bartlett."

"Sir." Heath nodded, feeling the powerful sense of solidarity that he always felt when he and Dagwood were striving toward the same goal.

Heath could not admire the man more. He was politically astute and maneuvered through the ranks like a commanding general seizing territory. The fact that he'd lifted himself up without the aid of family connections to be one of the most powerful men in England inspired Heath as no other model could.

"Please sit down and join us for tea, Mr. Dagwood," Lady Bright intoned, shooting the butler a commanding glare. The servant nodded imperceptibly and strode from the room, obviously intent on that tea service.

Arranging his impeccably cut Weston coat, Dagwood sat with his long legs stretched out before him, his cane resting alongside.

Adjusting his own coat, not a Weston, but decent enough, Heath reclined into the opposite chair.

Lady Bright sighed. "I was just telling Mr. Bartlett here about the terrible wrong my poor cousin George has suffered."

"A travesty." Penelope's lovely face was troubled. "One that must be righted. Especially since he has finally agreed to consider marriage. Why, Mama's been after him for years, but now, only after Grandmama's death, and the terms of her will—"

"That's enough dear," Lady Bright interjected with a meaningful glare. "There's no need to bore these men with unnecessary details. They simply need to understand the significance of this injustice."

Nodding sagely, Dagwood set his quizzing glass to his eye. The man had the most astonishing way of focusing on a person, making him feel, for good or ill, that his commanding attention was completely trained upon him.

Penelope leaned toward Dagwood. "Mr. Bartlett said something about you only handling matters pertaining to the Crown."

That's not what I said, Heath thought, but correcting Penelope would earn him no credit.

Peering through his monocle, Dagwood pursed his lips. "Mr. Bartlett is quite right that I'm assigned the task of representing the Crown on legal matters. This can entail serving a function in the courts, providing legal advice, questions involving public welfare. Law officers are consulted for intricate legal matters involving debts to the Crown, thefts from the Crown . . ."—he smiled, and Heath knew this was his trump card—"exceptional prosecutions . . ."

"This is extraordinarily exceptional!" Lady Bright declared. "This Jezebel should be prosecuted to the full extent of the law! She should be hanged!"

Jezebel? This was a new twist.

Tilting his head, Dagwood held open his hand. "One cannot make accusations without evidence. We must be very clear on the facts before making a case for exceptional prosecution."

Dagwood would be careful about this, especially after the Beaumont affair. Penelope had been right about one thing: it had been a wretched bungle. Although the evidence had seemed unambiguous and had pointed directly at Beaumont's guilt, the real culprit had designed it to be so. Dagwood had arrested and tried to convict the wrong peer of the realm, very publicly, and very aggressively. When the truth had come to light, it had been a terrible embarrassment to their office and to Dagwood personally.

Since then, Dagwood had asked Heath to review every case with him and to assess every matter with a critical eye. Heath had been more flattered by this task than any other in his short career.

"But this thief cannot act with impunity!" Lady Bright shook her fist, making the lacy handkerchief flutter.

"I'm not saying she or he will get away with it." Dagwood waved a hand. "I'm simply saying that the matter should be investigated thoroughly before one arrests anyone, or even goes about declaring another person's guilt. One wouldn't want to be sued for slander, now would one?"

"No . . . certainly not . . . but she couldn't . . . could she?" Lady Bright frowned, the conversation obviously not going as she'd anticipated.

Dagwood shrugged, noncommittal. Then he turned to Heath. "And what have you to say on the matter, Bartlett? You have a knack for prosecutions."

Heath rubbed his chin. "I believe that a full investigation is in order. To see if a crime has been committed." His gaze moved to Lady Bright. "And to protect those who are interested in seeing justice properly done. Slander can be a wretchedly messy affair and can be avoided by a detailed inquiry."

Lady Bright nodded so vigorously her chins jiggled. She obviously included herself in those to be protected by Heath and his office, a nice twist in their relationship.

"Excellent notion." Dagwood smiled. "I will leave it in your capable hands, then."

Heath inclined his head. "As always, I am at your disposal."

Dagwood motioned to Lady Bright. "I do not wish to be presumptuous, but may I surmise by your costume that the period of mourning for your dear mother has ended?"

Lady Bright's cheeks tinged pink. "Yesterday. And not a day too soon; I could not stand to wear all black any longer."

Heath withheld his smile as Dagwood moved to the next question, "Then shall we all be celebrating an auspicious occasion soon?"

Lady Bright sniffed. "I pray it be so. But at the moment, I can think of nothing but my poor cousin George. How can we go about our business as if nothing has happened? Nay, it cannot be borne. Not until justice is done."

Dagwood shot Heath a telling glance. This lady was going to press her advantage for all she was worth. "Then we must start the investigation at once. Lady Bright, if you would introduce Mr. Bartlett to your cousin and to all of the pertinent parties?"

Lady Bright smiled, a calculating gleam in her eye. "Of course."

Masking the fact that he felt like Hercules with his twelve tasks, Heath asked, "And the alleged thief?"

"Lady Golding."

Heath felt as if he'd just swallowed a hunk of powdery coal. "Lady Golding?" he croaked.

"Are you all right?" Penelope leaned forward, her gaze concerned.

Coughing into his fist, Heath motioned to his throat. "A tickle . . . nothing . . ." Trying to regain his composure, he coughed once more. "The baron's widow?"

Glowering, Lady Bright snorted. "The very same

Jezebel. I should have known that any lady who would drive her husband to kill himself—"

Heath suddenly felt sick, but he pasted a smile on his face. "Wasn't . . . he killed in a duel?"

"Driven to it, I've heard. And who can blame him after his wife caused his dearest friend's death? Well, the lady is a . . ." Lady Bright scowled. "I cannot say such things in front of my virtuous Penelope, but you know of what I speak."

Pressing his lips together, Heath inhaled a deep breath, trying not to get too much rose perfume.

"Can you get started today?" Dagwood asked, keen enough to note Heath's discomfort.

Standing, Heath nodded and stepped over to the window. He stared blindly out at the garden, wondering what tricks destiny was playing on him to set Tess in his path twice in one day after so many years apart. "Yes, of course. I will see justice done and the culprit duly punished." And he meant it. If Tess had done the crime, she'd suffer the consequences. It was as simple as that.

Then again, when it came to Tess, nothing was simple.

Chapter 4

Tess was careful to keep her face fixed and her body positioned in a relaxed pose as she tried to keep her eyes locked with Wheaton's icy blue gaze. Wheaton disdained weakness, and she wasn't about to give him the impression that he unsettled her, even if staring into those eyes was like looking into the bleakest winter frost.

Withholding a shiver, she smiled, casually allowing her eyes to drift away, and they invariably fixed on the odd ghouls that her supervisor kept on his mantel. Tess couldn't fathom why anyone would want a porcelain collection of miniature goblins and ghouls. With their beady eyes, rapacious mouths and thorny talons, they seemed enthralled by the goings-on in the gilded chamber of Wheaton's house.

The room was warm, yet, as usual, Tess was chilled, feeling no effect from the crackling flames in the hearth. The pleasant scent of cloves filled the air. Tess liked how Wheaton added spices to his grate; at Christmastime her superior always sent her a bag of cloves so that she could do the same. It was a nice gesture, one that reminded Tess that Wheaton was capable of being a shade warmer than a cold-blooded shark.

"It was a stroke of good luck unearthing that informant at the harbor," Wheaton declared, leaning back into the seat facing hers. "Now we know of a link in Séverin's intelligence network. If we can compromise that link, we can impair the frog's access to information in London. Let us see Napoleon cause mischief without eyes and ears here."

When he was excited about a matter, as he was at the moment, Wheaton's face grew flushed, his bulbous nose reddened, and his thick jowls shuddered with each animated breath. When he was like this, Tess couldn't help but be astounded by Wheaton's striking resemblance to Father Christmas. Today his snowy white hair was tied back at the neck and his big bushy brows were a little neater than usual, but the likeness was there still. Tess liked imagining Wheaton with sprigs of holly in his long white mane. It helped her see him in a warmer light, something she found necessary to continue working with him.

"Aside from naming the countess, did the informant have anything more to say about her connections?" Tess asked, feeling that the information was less than solid.

From his perch behind Wheaton's chair, Mr. Reynolds, Wheaton's wiry "secretary," added in his nasal voice, "He was a tough nut to crack, but once he did, he was almost done for. He gave up little else."

Tess shuddered. No matter Mr. Reynolds's quaint title, Tess knew he was never near a quill or foolscap. The coldness he exuded was far different from Wheaton's. Wheaton was matter-of-fact about the brutal side of his occupation; Reynolds, on the other hand, seemed to take an unnatural pleasure in his work.

Adjusting her sleeves, Tess took pains not to look Reynolds in the eye. The secretary's piercing brown gaze was disturbing, like a foul itch that Tess wasn't allowed to scratch. Tess had yet to understand why Wheaton relied on the man so heavily.

Wheaton looked up at Reynolds, castigation in his icy gaze. "You're going to have to work at keeping the buggers alive longer if they're to be of any use. You can't let your zeal get the best of you."

Zeal? Tess licked her lips, trying to ignore the revulsion budding up within her. She often lay awake at night haunted by visions of Wheaton and Reynolds setting their ruthless hands on anyone she might know or hold dear.

Inclining his head, Reynolds pursed his reedy lips. "I'll try to do better next time."

Turning back to Tess, Wheaton nodded. "See that you do."

Tess swallowed, pasting an easy smile on her face. *They're patriots. Their work is necessary to safeguard our homeland. They would never harass a fellow countryman or an innocent. They are in the service of good, and as such would not hurt anyone I love.*

Wheaton's eyes narrowed. "Don't get thin-skinned on me now, Tess. You understand that these are traitors—threats to the Crown and a danger to everyone and everything that you cherish."

"Is there ever the possibility . . ." Tess cleared her throat. "That you . . . get the wrong person?"

"Never." Wheaton made a cutting motion with his hand. "To draw my attention, one has to intend to do harm or actually inflict injury on our land. You know as well as I that only someone up to no good draws my ire."

Exhaling, Tess forced herself to believe him. Aside from the fact that she felt too tied up with the Foreign Office to extricate herself, she took great pride in the work that she did on behalf of her country.

Wheaton spared Reynolds a glance. "Leave us."

Reynolds hesitated a moment, and Tess felt his disturbing gaze on her as if he wanted something. She refused to meet his eyes, feeling guilty about it and yet justified. If it weren't for Wheaton and the work she did, she would never associate with such an odd man.

Without a word, Reynolds slipped from the chamber.

Tess's shoulders dropped slightly with relief. Wheaton alone was bad enough; with Reynolds she felt as if she was constantly under that unsettling scrutiny.

Leaning forward, Wheaton enclosed Tess's hand in his warm, meaty grasp. "You are a sharp lady, Tess. Sharp enough to comprehend that the Reynoldses of this world have a place, as do you. Each of us does our part to the best of our ability, keeping in mind the greater good."

"Yes, of course. I just——"

Squeezing her hands, Wheaton smiled in a grand-fatherly way. "And to protect the greater good, we must dirty our hands a little. A necessary evil, so to speak, but one we did not choose. Were it not for Napoleon's voracious thirst for power and England's steadfast resolution to stop him, we would not be at this place and we would not be forced to do the things we do."

Tess knew she was being worked on, but didn't mind. She wondered if all of Wheaton's assets needed a bit of bolstering now and again.

He sighed. "We are simply doing what is necessary to protect ourselves, Tess. I shudder to think what Napoleon and his dog Séverin would do if their merciless reach came over our dear land. The French are animals. Without honor or thought for the innocents in this game. They sent a lady here to infiltrate London society. A lady, for heaven's sake! This is not a game of lawn battledore! Men use knives and firearms, not paddles and shuttlecocks! It's a dangerous business. No place for a lady."

It was reassuring that Wheaton deemed her intelligence gathering as so low risk. Yet he failed to consider the wreck and ruin that might result to her already tattered reputation if anyone knew that she was passing along information to the Foreign Office. Wheaton held society in disdain, and did not care one whit about its favor. Tess wished she could be so cavalier; whether accepted or reviled, it was her world and she couldn't help but care.

Wheaton scratched a snowy whisker. "Could you

imagine what Séverin would do if he ever learned of you? I don't think he would appreciate the innocuousness of your efforts on my behalf."

Tess doubted that *all* the information she passed along was completely harmless. A little fact about a looming debt or a cousin in France could lead to further questions and deeper secrets still. But that was not her purview, and Tess chose to believe Wheaton's little lie, for she could not bear to dwell on the truth of it.

Wheaton's bushy brows rose. "Can you imagine how he would treat a little flower like . . . what is your assistant's name? You know, the one with the pretty dark curls."

A chill slithered up Tess's spine.

He shrugged. "I'm simply giving an example."

Tess willed her heart to calm. She felt like one of those newfangled lanterns, the ones with the many mirrors reflecting the inner light. With different people she showed different aspects of her personality, but none of them was the whole picture.

Now, with Wheaton, she was the appearance of calm indifference, but she listened, hard. Nuance was her specialty; hidden meanings, his.

Removing her hand from his, Tess coughed into her balled fist to adjust her voice to an even tone. "Is that something you anticipate?"

"What?"

"Exposure."

"I must anticipate every move our enemies might make. Even the most repulsive." Again that grand-fatherly smile. "But this is all conjecture. There is no danger that I foresee. To you or to your assistant."

Tess met that icy, all-too-innocent gaze. She realized that it was a mistake to try to paint Wheaton as anything but the cold-blooded viper he was. Better to appreciate the dangers than to get bitten by the hand that supposedly fed her.

He sniffed. "I am simply reminding you how important the work that we do is to all that we hold dear."

"I wouldn't be doing the work if it wasn't important."

"May I remind you that it was money that led you to sign on in the first instance. Not patriotic duty."

Looking down, she made a point of examining a fingernail. "You seem to forget the fact that you were threatening to tell everyone that I'd written the article on the Brinkley affair in the *Girard Street Crier*."

"Would it bother you if people knew?"

She shrugged. "Not so much anymore. But at the time, yes, it was quite incendiary. And staying anonymous did greatly influence my decision—"

"There's no need to discuss matters long forgotten," he interrupted, holding up a hand. "I'm simply hoping to encourage your efforts where they have been less than forceful."

She looked up. "When have my efforts been less than required?"

"When it comes to that society for females."

Tess smiled. "I would think that you have more important things to engage your valuable time—"

"That's why I'm the one who *thinks* and you're the one who simply gathers the information."

Tess licked her suddenly dry lips, waiting for him to drop his coup de grâce. Wheaton's gaze was too self-satisfied; he knew something, for sure.

"Countess di Notari made application for membership at your society yesterday. Something you would already know if you were investigating the society as I'd asked you to."

Tess willed her cheeks not to warm. "I spend a considerable amount of time and energy at the society—"

"On those wretched 'good works' projects, not on the members' activities. What can you learn of use if you whittle away your hours at Marks-Cross Street Prison?"

"Other members volunteer with me. But that's not the issue. So what if the countess the informant mentioned has applied for membership? That doesn't paint the entire society as seditious."

"But it's telling."

"Perhaps. Or perhaps she wanted an easier entrée into London society."

"How telling her membership application is will be for you to discover. As part of that process, you will investigate the society and its members and find out all I wish to know."

"When did the countess arrive in London?"

"Last week."

Exhaling, Tess considered it a long moment. "And she already made application for membership at the society. That is a bit hasty, considering setting up house, retaining servants, entering society . . ."

Wheaton smiled. "There's a girl. Get the scent."

I'm not a hound. But Tess knew that this was a compliment, coming from Wheaton. She nodded. "I'll get started straight away."

"I have a golden opportunity for you."

"Do tell."

"The president of the society, the Earl of Wootton-Barrett's daughter—"

"Lady Edwina Devane."

"Yes, her. Well Lady Devane has asked for a volunteer to oversee the new applicants and evaluate them. Lady Janelle Blankett has expressed interest in the position, but you will ensure that the job comes to you."

Her brows furrowed, evidencing her surprise. "How do you know all this?"

Leaning back, Wheaton smiled. "Oh, I have my sources."

"If your sources are so good, then why do you need me to look into the society?" And who was providing Wheaton with such information? But whoever they were, Wheaton clearly wanted more than they could provide. Tess wondered if it was one of the servants.

"Stop challenging me on this, Tess, and do what I'm paying you for. You shall use the cloak of office to learn everything about the countess. Where she calls, with whom she eats, with whom she corresponds, and most especially with whom she shares her bed. At the same time, you will ingratiate yourself into the upper echelons of leadership in the society and get to know all of the members."

"I'm still working on Searles and Jacobs. And then there's the Hogsworth matter." She didn't bother to mention her work at Andersen Hall since Wheaton clearly disapproved of her good works.

"Put everything off. This is more important. The countess takes full priority."

"As you wish." Tess rose, anxious to be free of Wheaton. She didn't mind the work, felt good about aiding her country, was proud of her efforts and her independence. Yet she wished that she could collaborate with people a little less . . . zealous, as Wheaton put it. Then again, a wilting lily would make a dreadful spy.

"I'll report to you next week, sir."

Wheaton stood. "Report to Reynolds."

Tess ignored the drop in her belly. "Not to you?"

"No."

"Is this . . . is this a permanent arrangement?"

His smile was noncommittal. "Nothing's permanent in our game, except for the fact that our enemies are dogged and so are we."

Nodding, Tess absorbed this new twist. She of all people knew that if a situation had the opportunity to worsen, it would.

"He prefers a report every third day."

She straightened. "Every third day? Even if there's nothing to report?"

"That's what he's asked for."

"What a waste of time! I can do more good gathering information than making arrangements for clandestine meetings with him." Pulling on her gloves, she shook her head. "No. I'll contact him as soon as I have some intelligence to share."

"He will not like it."

"Then I'll report to you."

He tilted his head. "I'll be traveling a bit."

"But you will be back in London."

"Off and on, perhaps. But I still want you to report to Reynolds. He's asked for more responsibility, and I want to see him rise to the occasion."

"You think he has the necessary skills?" She was unable to keep the doubt from her voice. Reynolds was a muscle man, not a tactician, and she couldn't believe that Wheaton couldn't see that.

He smiled. "We'll know soon enough."

Chapter 5

"**G**ood day, Joe." Heath stepped into Tipton's tavern and nodded to the barkeep. "How're you faring?"

Joe, a bald, wizened chap with a lame leg and a sharp eye, shook his head. "Better than yesterday. The damp's a killa on the ol' leg."

Allowing his eyes to adjust to the dimmer light, Heath removed his hat. "Then it's your good luck that it looks like we're in for a spot of sun."

Spitting into a glass and wiping it with a gray cloth, Joe grinned, showing some vacancies for teeth. "An' none too soon." He jerked his head to the left. "Bills is in his usual spot. I'll 'ave Ursula bring yer beer."

"Thanks." Heath headed toward his old friend.

William Lawson Smith, know to his chums as "Bills," had been Heath's best friend since they were green-heads joining Middle Temple in the hopes of being called to the bar. While earning their education at the Inns of Court, Heath had done everything to be inconspicuous, and his academics the only thing noteworthy. Bills had done exactly the opposite. He'd been a loud, cocky bugger, and as was his habit still today, had dressed like the most foppish dandy in London. Heath had tried to avoid the brassy chap at first, but ultimately he couldn't resist Bills's zest for life, that and his astoundingly astute political mind. The man was always one step ahead of the next chap and glad to take his friends along with him. He'd kept Heath safe while navigating the invisible strata at the Inns of Court, and had helped him land his first legal position. He'd also guided Heath in obtaining his current post, for which Heath would be eternally grateful.

For all his political skills, Bills wasn't particularly ambitious and had refused many coveted positions. He preferred the softer life, he'd say, answering to no one but himself and his clients. So he'd set up shop with a few other fellows and was content breezing by.

Today Bills's King's yellow coat and pea green waistcoat were in marked contrast to the muddy walls and brown tables of Tipton's tavern, his favorite haunt.

As he closed his broadsheet with a crackle of paper, Bills's smooth lips split into a wide, white smile. "Heath, old boy. So glad you could join me." As was his style, he wore his blond hair slicked back with pomade and his whiskers thick but short beneath his cheekbones. His nostrils flared as he inhaled deeply. "Can you smell Winifred's mutton? You're in for a treat."

Just over the scent of beer, the air smelled enticingly of roasting fat, meat, and potatoes.

Grabbing the opposite chair, Heath sat. "Why else do you think I'm here?"

The barmaid, Ursula, ambled over, flashing a saucy grin. "How are ya, Mr. Bartlett? It's been a while." She slapped a tankard down before Heath, froth dripping in rivulets down the glass and splashing onto the table. She was a pretty thing, well rounded, with buxom breasts and a plump end, and she stood close enough to Heath to give him an eyeful of her offerings.

From the bar, Joe called, "Yer ma needs ya in the kitchen, Ursula!"

Not bothering to turn, she yelled. "Leave me be, ol' man!"

Joe kept an eagle eye on his daughter, not that it did either of them much good; nothing seemed to lessen Ursula's appetite for men, and her father's nagging was a splinter in their already fractious relationship.

Heath busied himself removing his gloves and setting them with his hat on the bench. "Thanks."

She leaned forward, so that her loose blouse gaped open providing an ample view of curvy white flesh. "Stayin' long?"

"Ursula!" the barman warned, laying his palms on the bar.

"He's no longer in the market, Urs," Bills supplied, sipping from his beer. "The poor sod only has eyes for Miss Penelope Whilom." Pressing the back of his hand to his forehead, he sighed. "Oh, Penelope, Penelope, wherefore art thou, my Penelope."

"Lemme know if ya change yer mind." Shrugging, Ursula turned and walked toward the kitchen. "See ol' man. I wasn't doing anythin'."

Heath sipped his beer; it was earthy and warm, just as he liked it. "How are you, Bills?"

Bills's pale gray eyes were stormy. "Devil's to pay."

"So your mother's in town."

"Along with her blasted sisters. They're worse than the witches of *Macbeth*."

"You're hiding out where you know they'll never dare to tread."

"What else am I to do? Listen to their constant harping? 'She's a lovely girl,' 'good breeding in that family,' 'her uncle's a member at Serjeants' Inn,' and so on. It's like a pig-squealing contest, but I don't get to eat the swine."

As if on cue, Winifred, a woman who looked like her daughter but wore her years in the many lines on her face and the hunch on her back, brought over two bowls of mutton stew and set them on the table with a loaf of bread.

Bills gave his most dazzling smile. "Thank you, my dearest Winifred. With just a hint of the aroma of your fine fare you could bring me back from the dead. Swear to me you'll bring a bowl to my funeral and I'll hop right out of that coffin and give you a kiss."

"I'll be dead long before you, and mutton's the last thing I'll want ta be smellin'." Though she scowled, her dark eyes glowed warmly as she cleaned a few crumbs from the table with the cup of her hand. "Eat up, now." She took her leave.

They ate a few moments in silence. Heath liked the hot stew, although he found the meat a bit chewy.

Bills wiped his mouth with his handkerchief. "So what's bothering you?"

Heath smiled; his friend knew him well. "A ticklish issue, one that cannot enter public discourse."

"Duly noted. I shan't tell a soul."

"George Belington claims to have been swindled."

"The man's a gambler, he gets what he deserves. Besides, why should the Office of the Crown care?"

"Because he's Lady Bright's dear cousin."

Bills leaned back, clapping his hands together. "I love it! A hero in the making!"

"Don't start blasting the horns just yet. I need to build a case against the alleged culprit—"

"Gamblers are all cheats, it shouldn't be that hard. Besides, he's a swell, and most of the fellas he probably deals with are far from innocents."

"I'm astounded at your cynicism. The legal process can only work if each person is judged on the merit of his actions as it bears on the particular crime. Otherwise we'll have the good men, the bad men, and a sliding scale of depravity, judged by whom?"

Bills sniffed. "You, my dear friend, would fare appallingly well in such a system. I can't recall the last time you bedded a wench or got foxed with me. Where's your sense of morality, man?"

"I suppose I left it at Lord and Lady Bright's."

"Come on, admit you miss it."

Heath smiled. "I do. But that doesn't mean that I'm not ready to be more serious—"

"Heaven forbid!"

"I want respectability——"

Bills covered his ears. "Pray, say no more!"

"A family——"

"A death sentence!"

"Just because some of us are ready to marry doesn't mean you have to be such a naysayer, Bills."

Bills wagged a finger. "You'll be sorry, my friend. You have a rosy image of marital life but all you'll get is a life sentence with *Macbeth*'s witches in the form of Lady Bright!"

"Don't start picking on them again." Heath frowned. Bills didn't hold his sharp tongue from any topic. Yes, Heath recognized their shortcomings. Lord Bright was a bit of a boozer, Lady Bright had her self-absorption and dramatics, but that didn't mean he wanted those flaws aired. Heath knew the damage wagging tongues could cause from his experiences with his own father.

Bills sipped from his drink. "I still can't believe how you allow that dragon lady to use the engagement like some sort of leading string."

"As I told you before, it's barely six months since Lady Bright's mother died. Propriety calls for us to wait to announce it." He wasn't about to admit that Lady Bright was using the investigation as yet another hurdle.

"But public or not, is the engagement official?"

Heath gritted his teeth. "Will you help me figure out my problem or not?"

Bills's gaze was assessing as he sipped his drink. "Leading you again, is she?"

"Bills," Heath warned.

Burping loudly, Bills waved a hand. "Of course I'll help you. Tell me the obstacle in your grand quest to capture the fair maiden's dragon lady of a mother's heart."

"The alleged culprit has been inaccessible to me."

"Inaccessible how?"

"Well, my first issue is that I cannot make the suspect aware of the investigation."

"The Beaumont affair has your hands tied in a knot, I'd say, and with good reason. So it's a tacit inquiry and you need to approach your target unseen."

"Yes. Dagwood insists upon it. He does not want any possibility of a scandal or any possibility of a suit for harassment."

"Very prudent of him. But then, again, Dagwood is no fool."

"Hardly. He wants me to be discreet, and not have the suspect know that she is being investigated."

"She? Now it's getting interesting." Rubbing his chin, Bills smiled. "And why has *she* been inaccessible to you? Is she married?"

"No."

"Are you afraid she'll think you're interested?"

Heath snorted. "Not in a thousand years."

"Why? Is she a hag?"

Picturing Tess's crimson curls, her milky white skin,

and those eyes that flashed blue fire, Heath shook his head. "That's not the problem."

Wagging his brows, Bills grinned. "Oh, a dazzler eh? Now I'm really intrigued! So what's the trouble? An overzealous guardian?"

"Nay, she's a widow. An independent lady in her own right."

"Ugh. I can't stomach those 'I'll stand on my own' ladies. They have no respect for the roles our Heavenly Father delineated for male and female in the Good Book."

Heath chuckled. "I must have missed that passage."

"But if she's independent, without a man standing in your way, why can't you see her?"

"I'm hindered because she spends every waking moment at the Society for the Enrichment and Learning of Females."

"Blast the woman! How dare she associate with her own kind! The nerve!"

"She's been selected as the new membership chair. So she's in charge of events, screening, and all things related to the new member applicants. To my great irritation, she takes the role exceedingly seriously. She's there day and night."

"Have you attempted to call upon her at the society?"

"Under what pretext?"

Bills made a face. "I see your point. 'Ah, hello, I'm here because I'm interested in getting educated in the arts of knitting and gossip.'"

"I thought about trying to use our history as a reason for a connection—"

Leaning forward, Bills interrupted, "History?"

"My father was once her family's tutor."

"Let me guess. It ended badly with your father being sacked."

Heath looked away. "Yes."

"I swear I don't know how your father keeps getting new positions."

"I do. A lot of charm and a golden reference from the Duchess of Medford."

"But doesn't she know about his antics?"

"Of course, and she considers them amusing. She's very indulgent where my father's concerned."

Bills shook his head. "So why not use the past connection with . . . who are you investigating?"

"Lady Golding."

Bills's whistled, and his brows lifted almost to his hairline. "No wonder you need to be circumspect."

Heath shifted in his seat. "Don't believe everything you hear." Still, Tess had managed to marry Lord Golding, the cheating knave, and there was that terrible scandal surrounding Lord Berber. Heath wondered what the truth of it might be. And now Tess was being accused of theft. So perhaps she had changed from the good-natured girl he'd known? Stranger things had been known to happen.

Still, he was disappointed. She'd been so sweet, a bit timid, perhaps, but always kind to him when others had been less than pleasant to the tutor's son.

Shaking off the memories, Heath continued, "But as I was saying, I ran into her recently and she wasn't especially friendly. I don't believe that I can play upon our prior acquaintance. And Lady Bright wants results, as does Dagwood. Some serious political coin weighs in the balance, not to mention my prospects as Penelope's future intended."

Squinting his gray eyes, Bills tapped a finger against his mouth as he always did when thinking.

Heath waited, knowing that his friend never disappointed. Bills's ability to maneuver around people or issues was legendary, which was why, despite a dislike of work, he did astonishingly well in his legal practice.

Bills licked his chops. "I was just thinking, I would love to be a fly on the wall in that society."

"Why?"

"What is 'female enrichment' anyway? If not stuff about our superior gender?"

"You believe that the society members spend their time discussing men?"

"What else do they have to interest them?"

"A little self-centered of you, don't you think?"

"Don't forget, I grew up with the likes of *Macbeth*'s witches. Still, I'm sure there must be something interesting to the place, if not the possibility of being the only bull in the running."

Heath straightened. "What are you saying?"

"I'm saying I'm astoundingly brilliant and I have exactly the means for you to achieve all of your goals and then some."

An uncomfortable feeling began to grow in Heath's gut. "How?"

"You make application for membership to the Society for the Enrichment and Learning of Females."

"Have you gone round the bend? That's the crankiest idea I've heard since you ran off with Sir Arthur's prized grays!"

Bills grinned. "What a grand day that was! But this idea is far better."

"How the blazes so?"

"You want to get close to the lady who has no choice but to spend an inordinate amount of time with the applicants for membership. This will force her to do so, and she can't do a thing about it."

"You forget one very pertinent point—I'm not female."

"I find it hard to believe that the society has any particular rule in that regard."

"Because no one would think it necessary!"

"A fact in our favor."

Heath ran his hand through his hair, appalled at Bills's suggestion. "I can't believe that you would even propose such a course. Here I am seeking advice and you offer the one answer that would ruin everything for me."

"How?"

"Lord and Lady Bright would be horrified."

"Not if they think you are moving heaven and earth to help them. Nobility like nothing more than someone who will go the extra mile for them. Mark my words, they'll be delighted."

"My reputation—"

"Will be enhanced. We'll put out the story that you undertook the challenge on a bet. You'll be the most popular gent in town. The man who had the guts to enter a sacred domain closed to his sex. Every man will want to know what you learned, every woman your own secrets. It's bloody brilliant, if I do say so myself."

Heath's eyes narrowed. "Why else are you suggesting this? You have another reason, I can tell."

Bills stared over at the bar a long moment. "You're quite right. I confess that I think this will be a first-rate path to you understanding the terrible mistake you're making."

"You have that dim a view of women?"

"And of the nuptial yoke. There's a reason they call it wed*lock*, getting leg-*shackled*, the parson's *mousetrap*—"

"Enough, I grasp your point." Scratching his chin, Heath considered the scheme and all its ramifications. "You really want me to do this?"

"Actually, yes. It's a once-in-a-lifetime opportunity on so many different levels. Hell, if nothing else, it'll be a blazing good time."

"I'll consider it, but I'll need your help."

Bills smiled, obviously delighted to have won. "Anything whatsoever for you."

"Anything?"

"Unconditionally, my friend," Bills replied, obviously well pleased with himself.

"Then you must do it with me."

Bills straightened. "But——"

"It's a once-in-a-lifetime opportunity," Heath mimicked Bills's own words. "A blazing good time. If it's good enough for the goose . . ."

"Then it's good enough for the gander. All right, my friend, I'll join you. But let's make this really interesting." Bills raised his glass. "A wager. That I change your mind about marriage."

Heath raised his glass. "I accept. And bet you that I change yours about women."

They clanked glasses. "May the best man win." Smiling, they drank.

"We'll have two more, Joe!" Bills called to the barman. "And keep them coming! My friend and I are about to get foxed, and then we're going into the henhouse to pluck some hens!"

Chapter 6

Tess climbed the stairs leading to the red-painted door marked 183A, the entrance to the Society for the Enrichment and Learning of Females. She felt drained by her meeting with Reynolds. She hated how he belittled her efforts regarding Countess di Notari, acting as if she'd been lax in her duties.

Granted, she hadn't learned much, except for the fact that the countess had taken up residence at 45 Linden Square and that she was sleeping with Lord Barclay, but it had been only a few days since she'd begun the investigation.

First Tess had had to convince Edwina, the president of the society, that she was the best choice as the new membership chairwoman. Janelle Blankett had put up a mighty fuss, and after much negotiating, Tess secured the role of chairwoman with Janelle as her vice-chair.

Tess was not so pleased to be working with Janelle. The lady had a scalding tongue and often had no sense of diplomacy. Tess found her to be a bitter woman, something she attributed to the facts that Lord Blankett was an oft-absent husband who was obsessed with horses and that Janelle's son was a well-known drinker and gambler, a disastrous combination in anyone, but especially in one's child. Poor Janelle, and anyone who had to spend an inordinate amount of time with her.

But Tess would make do, as she always did. To her anything could be dealt with as long as she was a player and not a passive observer as she'd once been. Growing up, she'd been overshadowed by her sisters, bullied by her brother, and often ignored by her parents. She hadn't really minded being on the outskirts of it all since her house was so full of noise and color.

Then Quentin had stepped into her life, waking passions she'd never known existed. For all his faults, he'd been entertaining and funny. Living with him had been a whirlwind of pleasure. But looking back, it was still all about what Quentin had liked and the amusements he'd preferred. Between the sheets he'd taken his pleasure and had assumed that she'd enjoyed it.

Their activities about town mirrored the bedroom; he took his enjoyment as he pleased and assumed that she'd get hers in the meantime. She may have liked opera, but he preferred plays, so they went to plays. She may have loved art, but he had no taste for it, so they never once visited a gallery or museum. She loved nothing more than to snuggle before a warm fire, go to bed, and rise early in the morning ready to enjoy the day. He preferred late nights out and long days slept in. So Tess struggled to keep up, often still rising early and feeling like the dead.

Then after Berber's death, Tess's desperation to please had become almost like a sickness. She'd ached for her husband's grief, and felt stunned when the blame for the terrible accident was laid at her feet. So she'd toiled to show Quentin, and the world, that she was a good wife, a good friend, and would never harm anyone she cared about.

All that changed the night Quentin had confessed to her that he'd gambled away their future. He'd explained, without a shadow of remorse, how he'd emptied their bank accounts, pawned her jewels, and placed liens on their properties. He'd blamed it on a run of bad luck, the rules of the gaming hells, the poor sod who'd played next to him. He'd had a share of blame for everyone. Except for himself.

He'd pecked her on the cheek and left her then, off to "win back" their money. He'd only told her so he could pawn her wedding band, which, in her shocked stupor, she'd blindly handed him.

The taking of her ring and Quentin's betrayal together broke almost every last desire in her to please.

Quentin's treachery had happened over the course of months, but when the reality of it sank in, it was like a scythe slicing through the thin fabric of their marriage, leaving it in tatters.

After that, Tess's only focus had been on how to restore some semblance of a future to their lives. She'd begun making lists, placing the household on a budget, and had even gone so far as to talk to Quentin's parents about his obsession with gambling. Oh, what a terrible encounter that had been! Tess shuddered simply recalling the ugly accusations and the rampant denial. Quentin was perfect, anything amiss was her fault entirely. She'd learned later that his gambling had been a problem for years, which was why he'd needed a well-heeled bride.

Exactly ten long, fearful, acrimonious, tear-filled days after his world-altering confession, Quentin was caught cheating at cards and issued that stupid challenge. He was dead by the next dawn. Tess's world had fallen apart around her as the reality of Quentin's death, the debts, the loss of her home, and the magnitude of the scandal sank in.

Then her father had given her the unjust choice—marry her cousin or go without. Quentin had been barely two months' cold. Her father had wanted to save face and show the world his family's disdain for the lying cheat. Tess marrying so quickly after his death would do that quite admirably.

Tess clearly recalled that moment standing before her father's great black desk, as he'd puffed on his cigar and shuffled his papers, not once meeting her eyes. He'd considered the matter decided, and he was only pretending that she had any option. Tess's brother had stood by the window staring out at the garden, his back to her as if unwilling to witness the distasteful exchange.

Standing there, she'd blamed herself for allowing them to think that she was so malleable. She'd been like a seashell swept up in the current, crashing against the rocks, again and again. All her life things had happened *to her*, and in that moment she swore she wouldn't be that passive child ever again.

Then she'd given them her answer.

Her father's shuffling had stopped, her brother had turned, and in that reaction Tess had tasted the exhilarating power of making a choice . . . and suffering its consequences.

For all the grief she'd experienced, the yelling, the ultimatums, the barred doors, the creditors, when she looked back on that dark time, she appreciated that it was the severity of her situation that gave her rebirth. And she was thankful for it.

"Good day, Lady Golding." A grim-faced butler dressed in a purple uniform with marigold lapels had opened the door.

Tess blinked, brought back from the past. "Ah, thank you. Good day to you, too, Deering."

As she stepped inside the vestibule, she noted that the adjacent door leading to Edwina's house was closed, a situation that was happening more frequently now that Edwina was pregnant with her first child. Dr. Winner had prescribed limited activity for Edwina, forcing her to lessen her involvement in the society. She had tried to resign her post as president, but no one would have it, and Tess was glad. She liked the ebony-haired, dark-eyed lady; she was smart, and driven to do good works. There was no way on earth that she was involved in anything nefarious, and Tess was going to see that fact proven without doubt.

Tess had a new perspective on her covert activities at the society; like a surgeon with a scalpel, she would carve out the countess and ensure that no shadow of blame besmirched the society or its members. In addition to protecting king and country, this was her newest goal.

Tess handed her gloves to the butler and allowed him to remove her cloak.

"They're waiting for you in the library, ma'am."

Waiting for me? "Who?"

"Lady Blankett and the two gentlemen."

Tess raised a brow, wondering what was up, but the butler had already begun walking away and Tess was not one to chase servants; it brought too much attention to the inquiry.

Smoothing the line of her navy wool dress, Tess adjusted her floppy bonnet and headed up the stairs.

The door was open as she approached, and Tess allowed her steps to slow so she could overhear the goings-on inside the library.

"This is most extraordinary! Most extraordinary!" Janelle sounded vexed.

"We can say no, can't we?" It was Ginny's sweet voice. Lady Genevieve Ensley, known to her friends as Ginny, was a rosy-cheeked, gray-haired matron, a founding member of the society, and Janelle's dearest friend. "It's not taken up in our charter—"

"And why would it be?" Janelle cried. "It's positively ludicrous! Ginny, will you please read Lucy's note, I am too upset to read it myself."

Mrs. Lucy Thomas must have written a communication. The dark-haired, doe-eyed beauty had lost her husband to a terrible wasting disease, and when her dying husband had lost his ability to speak, inexplicably, so had she. Despite being mute, she was a very active member of the society, and was on the membership committee with Tess and Janelle. Tess liked her, even though she could be a bit shallow. She would write little notes that bore no import, like one yesterday asking if Tess admired her new gloves.

Ginny read, "It says, 'They're playing us for fools.'"

Intrigued, Tess squared her shoulders and feigned nonchalance as she crossed the threshold. Two gentlemen sat on the couch facing the ladies standing before the hearth; one had blond, slicked-back hair, the other was dark-haired and square-shouldered.

Even with the dark one's coat designed to enhance, she could tell that those muscular shoulders were not made of cloth padding. The man's body was strapping indeed, but what was most remarkable was that Tess was taking notice of such masculine attributes, and twice in a handful of days.

Tess caught Janelle's eye, and the storklike matron cried, "Oh, thank the heavens you are here! Lady Golding is the chair of the committee, and she will decide what to do with you."

Tess hid her smile. After weeks of fighting for authority, Janelle was suddenly very quick to abdicate it.

The men stood and turned.

Tess's heart lurched. "What the devil are you doing here?"

Heath had the audacity to smile and bow. "So good to see you, too, Tess." His chocolate brown superfine coat matched his dark eyes and blended with his long hair held back with a leather tie. He wore a white linen shirt with a high, pointed collar that almost met his thin, dark whiskers, and although he was clean shaven, she could almost see the shadow of dark striving to grow through.

Her traitorous cheeks suddenly burned and her insides warmed, probably because she was so infuriated to see him again. That was the only thing that could explain the stirring he inspired deep inside her.

Tess lowered her eyes, only to notice that Heath's bulging thighs made his caramel-colored breeches as if like they were layered on, like sugar on flan. Tess swallowed, as her mouth was suddenly bone-dry, and she forced her gaze from those curving muscles down to his black Hessians. Heath's boots were so shiny as to have been polished by a valet, a valet for heaven's sake! Who would have thought that the rambunctious son of a tutor would turn into such a gentleman dandy?

Befuddled by his presence and his unsettling effect on her, Tess turned to the stranger. "Who are you?"

The companion's pale gray eyes widened, but then he smiled, bowing. "Mr. William Lawson Smith, at your service."

The fair-skinned, blond gentleman was about a hand's width shorter than Heath, but Heath had always been tall, a full head and shoulders above Tess. Mr. Smith wore a royal blue coat, double-breasted, just like Heath's, but whereas Heath was the epitome of lean, broad musculature, his companion had a bit of a pot belly, as evidenced by the colorfully striped waistcoat jutting out.

"You know this man?" Janelle barked, motioning to Heath.

Tess frowned, having trouble tearing her eyes from Heath's broad shoulders. "I can claim a slight acquaintance."

Heath flinched, raising his hand to his heart. "Slight? You wound me, madame. We've known each other for over fifteen years."

Looking away, Tess folded her hands together before her. "But not recently and not well."

"You're cross with me, and I don't blame you after our last meeting. I shouldn't have called you what I did."

"What did he call you?" Janelle asked, a speculative gleam in her eye as her gaze flitted from Heath to Tess and back again, as if she were watching a tennis match.

Tess looked away, uncomfortable explaining the source of her anger, especially since it seemed so volatile where Heath was concerned.

"I referred to her by her married name," Heath supplied, stepping forward. "After we'd agreed as children always to be friends, never to be so formal as to not call each other by our Christian names."

"That was a long time ago," Tess bit out.

"Did you forget?"

Tess wished she could lie about it and pretend it didn't matter, but he'd broken the promise first and she wanted him to know it. "No."

"Then I am sorry and it will not happen again."

Her gaze met his. Something familiar and yet wholly foreign glistened in those chocolaty brown eyes, as if he was the lad he'd been, yet now there was heat and invitation and hidden mystery . . . Her heart began to pound and her belly fluttered. Her cheeks warmed and she licked her lips, ripping her gaze from his. "What . . . what are you doing here?"

Moving around the sofa, Mr. Smith grasped her hand.

Tess started, assaulted by the surprising but gentle touch and by the scent of Eau de Cologne.

Mr. Smith scratched his chin. "I understand that you are in the rare book trade, Lady Golding. As a lover of fine books, I have an extensive collection that I would like to expand. Is there the possibility that we might discuss the matter?"

Heath's face darkened. "Bills . . ."

Mr. Smith smiled at her, amusement gleaming in his pale gray eyes as he spoke to his friend over his shoulder. "Don't worry, Lady Golding is far too smart to fall for a slick-tongued lout like me."

Raising her hand to his lips, Mr. Smith murmured, "Unless, of course, I can convince her to become my mistress . . ."

Ginny gasped, her blue eyes shocked.

Heath took a menacing step forward.

" . . . of membership, that is," Mr. Smith continued. There was deviltry in his voice and gaze. "Wouldn't that be fun, Lady Golding? Having me and Bartlett at your beck and call day and night. Testing us, challenging us, evaluating our mettle?"

Despite herself, Tess was amused. There was something oddly charming about this pudgy man. Even though Mr. Smith's cambric shirt was full of frills and lace and his cravat wound so tightly on his neck one wondered that he could breathe, there was something devilishly droll about him.

"What are you talking about, Mr. Smith?"

"We wish to apply for membership to your society," he cooed, his breath warming her hand.

"To what end?"

He shrugged a shoulder. "Call it a challenge."

Heath stepped between them, breaking Mr. Smith's grasp. "Enough, Bills. I think this was a mistake."

"Of that there's little doubt." Tess crossed her arms and stepped away from the earthy scent Heath emanated. It was far preferable to the cloying colognes most gentlemen wore, but it was disconcerting just the same. She didn't want to catch Heath's scent, any more than she wanted to spend another moment in his presence. He was like glaring sunlight in her eyes the dawn after a night of revelry, and she just wanted to lower her lids and have him be gone. Again, she wondered at that searing gaze when their eyes first met, but she was better off not knowing. Better off staying away from Heath, and keeping her past locked away.

Janelle tilted her head. "I'm curious as to why the two of you would even consider making application to a society for females."

Mr. Smith's smile was apologetic. "It was a bet, actually. Heath here was bemoaning the rhetoric of independent ladies these days. He believes that women live to serve men. That this whole notion of 'self-reliance' is merely a cry for attention."

Tess felt her eyes widen and her ire rise up like a goddess incensed. The jackass! "Oh he does, does he?"

Heath raised a hand as if in surrender. "That's not what I said——"

Mr. Smith interrupted, "He was also of the opinion that, as inferior beings, females cannot hold a solid thought in their heads. As such, he posed the question, what could women possibly have to learn, or better yet, how could they possibly be enriched?"

Crossing her arms, Lucy stepped beside Tess, with Janelle and Ginny following close at her heels, her limp barely slowing her down. All four women lined up, facing the men.

"Don't twist my words, Bills," Heath warned, watching all the women but keeping his eyes on Tess.

Tess lifted her chin. "Then why don't you inform us of your opinion on the topic. I am dying to hear the pearls of wisdom that drip from your split, I mean silver, tongue."

"I believe . . ." Heath's dark brown gaze flitted over to his friend, who was looking on innocently as if to say, *You boiled the soup, now you swallow it scalding hot.*

Squaring his broad shoulders, Heath tilted his head. "All I said is that I am curious as to what you learn and how you wish to be enriched so I can better understand the female mind."

Mr. Smith slapped Heath's back. "So that's the story you're sticking by, my friend?"

Heath glared at Bills. "You're the one who said that the ladies have nothing better to do than sit around talking about men."

Janelle huffed. "Of all the idiotic notions!"

Ginny shook her head, indignant. "We have lots of things to talk about—"

"That's what I told him, I did!" Mr. Smith intoned, with a dog-eyed look. "But he would not listen. So we made a bet. If he was right I had to pay him one hundred pounds. If I was right, then he must give me one hundred and fifty."

"Why would you have to pay more?" Tess asked.

Mr. Smith's face was sheepish. "It's the odds, Lady Golding. Odds favor he's right."

Another jackass. Tess didn't know the last time she'd been this angry, and about something so inconsequential. She didn't care what Heath Bartlett thought of her! So why was she so furious? On behalf of her sex, she supposed.

Tess looked to her comrades in arms. "Ladies, I believe that we have two new applicants to consider for the society."

"But they're men!" Ginny shrieked.

Tess raised a brow. "Nothing in our charter states explicitly that a man cannot join. I think that these two chaps need an opportunity for some enriching, don't you agree?"

Janelle's greenish-blue eyes met Tess's, and a sense of communion flashed between them. Janelle might be a bit harsh and somewhat of a shrew, but she was also quite sharp and a good ally to have. "I like how you think, my dear."

Turning to the men, Tess smiled. "But let's make this really worthwhile. I propose a new wager."

Scratching his chin, Mr. Smith nodded. "I like this club already."

Shooting him a silencing glance, Heath crossed his arms and looked to Tess. "We're listening."

"We will bet you two hundred pounds that you cannot make it through the application process to graduation day."

"Each?" Mr. Smith asked, his eyes twinkling, his pale cheeks flushed with excitement. "Are we in this as a team or do we stand alone?"

"We're in this together." Heath slapped his friend's back. "If he goes, I go. But how can we be certain that you will judge us fairly?"

Tess smiled. "You'll have to trust us. Those are my terms. Do you accept?"

"I do." Heath grinned.

All eyes trained on Mr. Smith. He clapped his hands

together. "Oh, I'm in. I wouldn't miss this for the world! Hundreds of pounds on the line, and someone here is going to eat their words! I love it!"

Tess smiled sweetly at Heath. "I do hope you like the taste of parchment, for you'll be eating it before the month is out."

Heath's eyes narrowed. "Don't bet on it."

"I already did."

Chapter 7

The next afternoon at the Society for the Enrichment and Learning of Females applicants' meeting, Bills eyed the ladies assembled in the drawing room. He leaned forward and whispered to Heath, "You said Lady Golding was a dazzler; you didn't mention that she's sharp as a tack!"

"Sharp-tongued, you mean." Heath stared at Tess's back, a decidedly flattering view of curves and slopes encased in robin's-egg blue cotton, a lovely enhancement to her crystal blue eyes. Every time her gaze met his, he recognized the challenge within, and all he wanted to do was *conquer* her. He was unused to such primitive urges, but supposed that it was her defiance that drew his anger. Or could it be that she'd grown up to be a sophisticated siren who was too appealing for her own good?

Could she truly have engineered George Belington's financial downfall? Had they been intimate? Had she used her feminine wiles to convince him to part with much more than he ought? Images of the hoggish, hairy-nosed Belington with Tess made Heath's stomach churn, and he couldn't quite believe how far Tess could have fallen from grace.

Belington had had to leave town on business, to save the last remnants of his fortune, his letter to Heath had said. But he'd left behind a duly authenticated affidavit setting forth the particulars of his allegations. That, along with a power of attorney granting his cousin, Lady Bright, full authority to act on his behest. And act she was, ordering Heath this way and that. Investigate the book business, she said. Look into her membership at the society, she demanded. Heath didn't mind, though. It made Lady Bright beholden to him, a situation he welcomed, for he still needed her blessing for his marriage to her daughter.

The first claim in the affidavit had been overly broad, asserting that Tess had taken undue advantage of him. This was no help at all, so Heath had focused on the next two claims. First, that she'd stolen jewelry allegedly worth hundreds of pounds, in particular a special collection in which each piece was designed to favor a bird with fine-colored gems. The next allegation was that Tess had pirated his entire library collection, allegedly worth thousands of pounds. Belington had thereafter stated that these thefts left him in dire straits.

Heath couldn't quite imagine how a landed gentleman could have his last bits tied up in jewelry and books. But it was not for him to judge. His role was to investigate a crime, then sniff out and bare the lavender-scented thief.

Bare? Hastily Heath took a sip of tepid tea. He was going to have to be exceedingly careful where Tess was concerned; she was too pretty by half. He'd always had a weakness for redheads, ever since he was a lad. Crimson hair and milky white skin that looked smoother than cream had a way of making his body warm in decidedly uncomfortable ways when he was in public. It was one of the reasons he liked Penelope—she was the kind of woman whose influence would be very appropriately limited to the bedroom.

Bills watched Tess with a decidedly assessing eye. "She's not the typical well-bred lady, I'll grant you that."

Heath straightened. "There was nothing wrong with her rearing. She was brought up in the manner befitting her station." Heath had not liked her parents, but he respected the education they'd provided their children. Before the "incident," his father had been in charge of the children's instruction, and for all his faults, Heath's father was a gifted tutor. If only he could respect the lines of propriety drawn for him.

Bills sipped from the dainty teacup. "That's not what I meant. It's simply that she's not particularly transparent. She's not as easy to read as the typical English lady. She doesn't flutter or flirt."

"Nay, not Tess." But she had that mutinous streak that was far more beguiling. When had that happened? As a child she'd avoided confrontation at every cost, easily granting whatever anyone else wanted. Tess had been one of most biddable people he'd ever known.

"Nor does she have a withering tongue or use all of those wonderful double entendres. She's one to hold her cards close to her chest. Lovely chest that it is."

Scowling, Heath straightened.

"Don't pretend you haven't noticed," Bills charged. "You can't seem to pull your eyes from her figure."

As he leaned back, Heath's gaze happily settled on Tess once more. "I'm investigating her, I need to watch her." Lush curves, milky white skin, and all. She moved as if unaware that she was so enthralling, but he knew that any woman that alluring had to be well practiced in the art of seduction.

"So was she always so sphinxlike?"

"No." Heath shifted, recalling a time when he could read every emotion on Tess's face. Aside from her expressive mouth, her blue eyes had dipped when she was sad and crinkled at the corners when she was pleased. Often, even without the benefit of seeing her, he could tell by her footsteps if she was happy or upset about something. As a child she'd tended to skip when she was joyful. He could hardly imagine that girl had grown up to be the inscrutable woman standing across the room from him today.

Her pretty face was closed, unreadable, her blue eyes hooded from view. Even her body gave little hint as to what she was thinking. She was poised, but other than that she was no open book for anyone's perusal. But oh how he would love to peel open those pages . . .

For the investigation, of course.

"You didn't really speak of your history overmuch."

Tearing his gaze from Tess's lush rear, Heath

coughed into his fist to clear his suddenly dry throat. "I hardly recognize the girl I knew." Anxious to shift the topic, he nodded to the newest entrants to the room. "Who are those two?"

"A countess and a friend. That's all I know. Lucy told me that they are making application for membership, too. No doubt that's the countess on the left."

"No doubt."

Not only were her silken skirts, heavy diamond necklace and earrings indication, but the lady's bony shoulders were squared back and her hawkish nose lifted high with a decidedly authoritative air. She stood a full head shorter than the storklike Lady Blankett, yet seemed taller for some reason. Her dark curly hair piled atop her head like a beehive might have added to the effect, in great contrast to Lady Blankett's tight graying blond chignon.

Heath blinked, as realization dawned. "Lucy? You mean Mrs. Thomas? You're on a first-name basis?"

"We need to keep an eye on that one," Bills commented, his eyes fixed on the brown-haired young lady dressed in black bombazine. In addition to the costume, there was an aged sadness in her doe-like eyes that let everyone know that she was in mourning.

"The widow? The one who doesn't speak?"

Smiling, Bills nodded. "Oh, she gets her message across when she wishes to."

"I can't believe you're taken with a woman who's still grieving for another man."

"I'm not taken," Bills huffed. "More like curious. Why would a woman suddenly lose the ability to speak? It's unnatural; women live to hear their own lofty opinions."

"You mean she wasn't born mute?"

"It happened when her husband was ill. When he lost his capacity to speak, so did she. Very odd."

"What's odd is that you know so much about her when we've been here less than an hour."

"While Lady Blankett was interrogating you, I had a lovely chat with Ginny. What a dear."

Heath blinked, amazed by his friend's natural charm. "Ginny?"

"Lady Genevieve."

"Are you on a first-name basis with everyone in the society?"

"Not with your Tess. She's kept away from us, ostensibly to visit with some of the other applicants, the countess and some others. Or hadn't you noticed her absence?"

Of course, he'd noticed. Heath seemed aware of Tess at a very elemental level. He knew where she stood, when she drank, when she was present, and he felt, more than saw, when she departed. It must be having her under investigation that caused such sensitivity to her actions. For there was no other good reason to be so concerned with a woman he hardly knew, and he was the last man on earth to succumb to her feminine wiles.

As Lady Blankett murmured in the countess's ear, the lady's brown gaze flitted over to him and Bills with interest. The woman next to the countess, a stout lady with mousy brown hair and a round, jolly-looking face, turned to them, making no secret of her examination. The lady murmured something to Lady Blankett, then Tess entered the conversation and a heated exchange ensued.

"What do you think they're talking about?" Heath wondered aloud.

"My guess is that they're trying to decide how to include us in the normal course of things while ensuring that we feel excluded."

"They don't have to work very hard at making us feel out of place," Heath murmured, sipping from the delicate teacup. "Between the paper-thin china and dainty furnishings, I feel like I'm walking on eggshells for fear of inadvertently crushing something."

"We may be bulls in a china shop, but as I said, we're the only bulls in the running. Not a bad way of things." Straightening, Bills smiled as Tess, Lady Blankett, the countess, and the stout lady approached. The widowed Lucy moved over to a group of young ladies by the window and motioned for them to join her at the secretary.

By the lines creasing around her blue-green eyes, Heath supposed that Lady Blankett had to be about fifty years of age. She motioned to the new duo. "Mr. Smith, Mr. Bartlett, may I present Countess di Notari and Miss Gammon."

The men bowed and expressed the appropriate responses of honor and privilege.

Surprisingly Tess hung back, not saying a word. Yet her crystal blue gaze was watchful.

"Like you, I, too, wish to join the society." The

countess's musical voice betrayed her Italian origins. "Yet I am inordinately qualified. And you"—her smile was thin.—"are not."

"I don't see the trouble of it." Miss Gammon waved a chubby hand. There was warmth in her blue gaze, and her lips seemed to hover on the brink of a smile. From her accent and manner, it was clear she was English. "The more the merrier, as far as I'm concerned."

"Thank you, Miss Gammon," Heath intoned, liking the amiable lady.

Lady Blankett explained, "Countess di Notari made her application a few weeks ago, while Miss Gammon is new to us today."

The countess sniffed. "Miss Gammon is my new companion. I wish for her to be a member of the society as well."

"The more the merrier as far as I'm concerned," Bills mimicked with a smile.

Miss Gammon nodded. "Male or female. Why should the society exclude anyone based upon unreasonable grounds? Isn't that a founding principle of the place? These men could hardly help the sex to which they were born."

"And who wouldn't wish to be the fairer and sweeter." Tess raised a brow; her eyes fixed on Heath were filled with that irresistible challenge.

Heath smiled, ready to give it right back to her. "You're about as sweet as sour lemon drops."

Shaking her head, Tess set a hand to her shapely hip. "You really know how to charm the chairwoman of the membership committee."

He stepped forward. "I'd sooner charm the scales off a dragon."

Beaming falsely, she moved closer, and he got a whiff of lavender bouquet. "Are you sure you don't wish to give me my two hundred pounds right now and save us some wasted time?"

He beamed just as falsely back. "And miss your jovial company? Never."

Tess sighed deeply as if greatly put out, her lush breasts rising and falling. Heath's gaze strayed to those milky white mounds, and he had to wonder what it would be like to see more than just the hint of her wiles that her gown permitted. He imagined that her nipples were peach-colored to match her lips, and that the lush flesh of her breasts would mold perfectly into his hands.

"Very well, then. I suppose we must allow you to complete the process." Tess turned to Lady Blankett. "Janelle, if you would?"

Heath blinked, brought back to the conversation by Tess's self-satisfied tone. He coughed into his hand, forcibly leashing his wayward thoughts.

Lady Blankett nodded, a mischievous gleam in her catlike eyes. "It would be my pleasure."

Heath exchanged a glance with Bills, who was quick to inquire, "And what is it that would be your pleasure, Lady Blankett?"

"I'm going to show you firsthand the reform program the society manages." The matron beamed proudly. "Marks-Cross Street Prison."

Heath glared at Tess, knowing that she was behind this little stunt. "You're sending us to prison?" He would do what he needed to, but couldn't help but needle Tess. To not do so would be as unnatural as not petting a cute pup when it jumped at your leg.

Tess smiled. "Don't worry, it's only for the afternoon . . . this time."

"Criminal defense is not my specialty." Bills clasped his hands over his protruding belly. "And my friend Heath here cannot defend anyone as he is an adviser only to the Crown."

"This is not in your capacities as members of the bar, but as potential members of the Society for the Enrichment and Learning of"—Tess's smile broadened.—"Females. And given that this is a prison for females, and where we perform some of our good works, acquainting yourselves with it is an important component of the application process."

Though he knew he was going, Heath had to ask, "What, pray tell, could we possibly hope to accomplish visiting Marks-Cross Street Prison?"

Lady Blankett adjusted the lacy shawl on her shoulders. "You will witness firsthand how we select the women who truly wish to improve their lot, and then we will watch my maid Margo teach some of the women how to darn clothing. This shawl was knitted by one of our reformed women, a Mrs. Kent whose husband had gambled the family into debt and then quite considerately up and died. Now she makes garments for the extraordinary modiste Madame Clavelle."

Heath's eyes narrowed, fixing on Tess. "And where will you be while we're getting educated?"

"I am taking Countess di Notari and Miss Gammon to my home where they can meet some of the women who have successfully completed the program and reentered society as productive workers."

"That sounds very interesting." Heath scratched his chin, curious about where Tess lived. Was her bed-chamber painted crimson, her bedcovering scarlet and designed to entice? "We would——"

"You're not invited." Her eyes flashed blue fire.

"But I would very much like to meet some of these success stories."

"Perhaps another time," Tess interjected, leaving no doubt that she'd prefer that the time would never come.

Bills coughed into his fist. "I must respectfully protest, on behalf of my dear friend, that is. He cannot go to a prison for females."

All eyes turned to Heath as Bills continued, "Pray do not make much of it, but my friend here is working on, and is indeed, improving his lot in life. In that vein, he has gained a venerated position with the office of the solicitor-general and he is courting a young lady of a very respectable family of the *ton*." He lifted his brows with meaning.

Heath frowned. Bills made it sound like Heath was a grasping social climber trying to fit in with the *ton*. "That's not exactly—"

"I know I shouldn't be so plainspoken," Bills interrupted with a raise of his hand. "But you must consider how hard you've worked and how precarious your position can be."

Tess rubbed her chin. "I wonder how applying for membership in our society affects your reputation? Detrimentally, perhaps?"

Heath glared at Bills. "Not detrimentally in the least. And neither will going to a prison to perform good works."

Clapping her hands, Miss Gammon smiled. "Then it's settled. The prison is not a problem for any of us, and I'm as intrigued as the next person to see the inside. So we can all go together."

The countess shuddered. "You must be joking!"

"Oh, please? It'll be fascinating, don't you think?" Miss Gammon hopped about like an excited rabbit.

Tess stepped backward, her skirts swooshing around her ankles. "Although a wonderful idea, it's impossible. My coach only seats four."

The countess raised her hawkish nose in the air. "Mine seats six!"

Raising her finger with triumph, Miss Gammon grinned. "It's settled then! We'll take two coaches and we're all off to prison!"

Heath smiled at Tess, communicating that he'd won this little skirmish. Those crystal blue eyes narrowed, clearly unwilling to admit defeat. Heath was reminded once more how much Tess had changed. She was no longer the young chit ready to cave in at the first sign of resistance. She was more resilient, ready for a fight. She had a mutinous streak a mile wide, and it was alluring as hell.

Chapter 8

Marks-Cross Street Prison was a hulking gray building of stacked stones and ironwork perched alongside the Thames. It was a pile of proper strength and simplicity, and gave Heath the same grim and forbidding impression he always got when visiting an English prison. Birds squawked overhead, and the air was so cloyingly damp that the icy wind bit through even the thickest wool coat. It seemed that temperamental Spring had turned her back on London for a few weeks more, at least.

As the carriages rolled alongside the compound, twenty or so filthy, half-naked women reached through a grille along the wall begging alms from passersby. Their pitiful cries and calls were enough to twist even the most hardened heart.

Lady Blankett scowled. "Those poor women have to pay for their keep, from their food to having a blanket in this freezing cold!"

"Aren't we going to stop?" Heath asked, wondering how much coin he had in his purse.

Tess's gaze was lost to the scene outside. "Nay, we can do much more good inside. And for all the women, not just a few."

Heath nodded. He'd visited Newgate Prison and Tothill Fields' Bridewell a time or two for his prosecutions, where the accused was usually either well placed or wealthy and segregated from the prison population. While there, he'd always focused on his legal duties and had kept the visits short. Never had he concerned himself with the conditions of the general prison inhabitants. He realized now that he'd avoided them as much as was possible.

"Who's the warden?" Heath asked.

Tess turned to him, her assessing gaze showing that she was impressed that he understood how important it was. "Until a couple of months ago it had been Mr. Hurt. Now the papers patent belongs to Mr. Pitts."

Lady Blankett waved her fan about, seemingly trying to dissipate the scent of refuse permeating the air. "The extortion is outrageous. There's a fee for turning keys for taking irons off. Then another for a blanket and another for a pallet. Those without means are forced to beg."

Tess grimaced. "At least under Mr. Pitts's watch the women don't have to pay to keep the very clothes on their backs that they had when they entered the place."

Lady Blankett pointed her fan toward Tess. "Thanks to you. Our Tess has a way with Mr. Pitts. He's particularly open to her suggestions."

Heath shifted in his seat, uneasy about Tess having such rapport with a prison warden. What, exactly, had Tess done to ingratiate herself with the man? Did she use her feminine wiles to influence Mr. Pitts, just as she'd done with George Belington? That mutinous streak coupled with her crimson hair and shapely form were a fiery combination that could entice even the most contained man.

An odd spark of anger flashed within him, but he couldn't quite recognize at whom it was directed.

Lady Blankett waved her fan. "The reformers are at it again."

At the entrance to the wrought-iron gates, a crowd of ten or twelve fairly well-dressed men and women marched in a circle to the rhythm of their cries. "Prison reform, now! Prison reform, now!"

"They do have a point," Heath muttered.

Sniffing, Lady Blankett jabbed her fan like a weapon. "Which they should take up with the law-makers, not Mr. Pitts. They have a martyr obsession if I ever saw one."

Tess looked out the window. "They believe that since Mr. Pitts is the holder of the patent of this prison and he has control of every aspect of how it's managed, they can change things here and now."

"What do you believe, Tess?" Heath asked.

Her blue gaze was thoughtful. "The best way to improve the lot of these women now is to convince Mr. Pitts that it's in his best interests to do so. Chanting doesn't help, it only makes him nervous. He fears these reformers are trying to undermine his living. I wish someone would tell them that one gets more flies with honey than vinegar."

Lady Blanket snorted. "Even if you told them, they wouldn't listen."

Heath's brow furrowed. "Honey?"

"A fine brandy. Fresh baked goods. But coin seems to afford the best results."

"You bribe him?"

Lifting her chin, Tess shrugged. "It's all about the best effect we can have on the most number of people. We've had the stocks removed as a punishment, every inmate given an extra ration of bread, and even provided some meat at the evening meals."

Heath couldn't decide which surprised him more, that the daughter of Lord Wallingford would be so cool about bribing a warden, or that she would be involved in improving the lot of women so beneath her station.

His eyes fixed on Tess's lovely profile set against the dark gray walls. Her brow was furrowed and her peach-colored lips pressed together in a determined line. She was obviously moved by the goings-on here. Could the need for funds to bribe the warden have motivated Tess to rob George Belington? A valiant intention perhaps, but theft was theft and there was no good excuse.

As he stared at the prisoners begging through the bars, it struck Heath that whatever Tess's reason, Lady Bright was determined to see her among those women, in the direst straits possible. Involuntarily, Heath's hands tightened on his cane. He'd prosecuted many a case, but never did the consequences strike home as they did just now. He couldn't imagine placing Tess behind bars. But he must serve justice; he was a servant of the law.

As the carriage rolled through the wrought-iron gates and into the open courtyard, the sounds of hammers and shouts could be heard.

"Excellent!" Lady Blankett declared, motioning to the laborers dismantling the stocks. "The final ones are coming down."

"I need to commend Mr. Pitts." Tess nodded. Surprisingly there was no triumph in her gaze, only a sense of purpose.

Silently they disembarked just as the countess's carriage rolled into the courtyard behind them.

The countess made a big to-do about the odor and the biting cold, while Miss Gammon kept going on and on about the scant attire of the women begging at the grille. Still, she was a calming influence on the distressed countess, and soon they were all headed inside.

An air of tension blanketed the party as they made their way through the dank, ominous corridors.

"I'll catch up with you shortly." Tess extricated herself from the group and moved to speak with one of the guards.

Heath followed her. "Where are you going?"

"To see Mr. Pitts."

Grabbing her arm and setting it into the crook of his elbow, he smiled. "I'll join you." The lavender scent she wore was a pleasant contrast to the musty corridor.

Tess turned to the guard. "If you would give us a moment, please?" The man stepped out of earshot.

Removing her hand from his elbow, Tess looked up at Heath. Her face was closed and unreadable. "It's not a good idea for you to join me."

"You want me to see your good works . . ."

She gritted her teeth, and defiance simmered in her eyes. "That's not the point. Mr. Pitts will not take kindly to your presence."

"You're very opinionated, aren't you?"

"When I know I'm right." She crossed her arms, making her bosoms swell nicely beneath her navy blue cape. She really was shaped quite agreeably.

"You've just got the devil's charm, you know," he teased.

He liked how her eyes flashed blue fire and her cheeks flushed to a rosy hue. "So you've noticed I'm not trying to curry favor with you."

What he'd noticed was that he was enjoying looking at her and verbally sparring with her far too much. So instead he focused on the fact that she didn't wish for him to meet Mr. Pitts, which meant he was coming along whether she liked it or not.

He made his tone firm. "I'm here, I've heard a lot about this Mr. Pitts, and I wish to meet him. Let's stop discussing it and move along, shall we?"

She didn't budge. She had a will, this one. But then again, so did he. He didn't pull himself up from being the son of a tutor to a barrister with the solicitor-general's office by backing down at every obstacle.

"Shall we?" he asked once more, gently urging her forward.

Lifting her dainty chin a notch, she bit out, "Has it

ever dawned on you that Mr. Pitts might be intimidated by your presence?"

"Has it ever dawned on you that I might be of service? That my position with the solicitor-general's office could influence this Mr. Pitts more than any bribe ever could?"

She glared at him. "You'll do more harm than good, I tell you. People have long memories, and few wardens can forget what happened to T. L. Cambridge."

"T. L. Cambridge was a barbarian of the cruelest sort who deserved everything he got. He abused his power as warden and went beyond the bounds of human decency. He very rightly paid for the error of his ways."

"But he was a warden, Heath! A warden who went from being king of the castle to prisoner in the dungeon! Those are the only facts that will impress Mr. Pitts!"

"My position with the solicitor-general's office notwithstanding, I'm not here to start an inquiry, and I'll tell Mr. Pitts as much."

Unwinding her arms, she raised her hands in entreaty, as if he was the one being daft. "You assume he'll believe you! Fear is an astonishingly potent argument, no matter what pretty words you use in contradiction."

Setting his cane and readying to go, Heath chided, "Nonsense. As you said before, I'm here in my capacity with the society."

"Must you always be so starched and full of yourself?"

He blinked, surprised and suddenly hurt. Was that how she saw him?

She dropped her hands, and her face softened. "I'm sorry about that. You just keep reminding me of your position, as if I'm going to somehow forget how far you've come. And . . . well, you seem to bring out the worst in me. I apologize. I think it's wonderful that you've risen so high—"

"Your condescension is admirable," he retorted stiffly. "But false flattery will not change the fact that I'm coming with you."

"It's not false—"

"Can we go now, please?"

Exhaling in exasperation, Tess turned and motioned to the guard. The man led them down a dank, narrow corridor. Still, she kept her distance and did not accept his proffered arm.

The very air around Tess was a few degrees colder for her vexation. Her skirts swished with alacrity, and her boot steps resounded with a crisp *clip-clop*. Heath didn't mind; she deserved to be ruffled.

Starched and full of himself?

Hardly. He was proud. And well he should be. He'd worked hard for all he'd accomplished . . .

He recalled his words, *Has it ever dawned on you that I might be of service? That my position with the solicitor-general's office could influence this Mr. Pitts more than any bribe ever could?*

My Lord, I sound like a presumptuous prig!

Her indictment had stung so badly because it was true!

Inwardly he groaned, never imagining that he would be such an uppity stiff.

He supposed there was still a part of him that was the son of a humble employee hoping to impress the master's daughter. Ugh. He hated how he must have sounded.

With how many other people had he puffed himself up or driven to impress? Scowling, Heath straightened his shoulders, forcing himself not to dwell on it. There was naught he could do but simply stop being such a prig in the future.

Soon they came upon a swarthy guard standing before a tall, black-painted door. Upon seeing Tess the man knocked, poked his head inside, and muttered a few unintelligible words.

The guard swept open the door and escorted them into a large, whitewashed room with tall windows and a series of closed doors. Then he left and joined the other guard outside.

A large mahogany desk was the centerpiece of the room, with two straight-backed chairs facing it. To the left of the desk was a huge hearth, to the right, the closed doors. No doubt these were avenues to reach the different parts of the facility, and in an emergency, a means of escape.

Even with the fire blazing, the room had a dampness that chilled the bones. The scent of cloves filling the air was a pleasant contrast to the odors of the other parts of the prison. Yet this chamber was far from warm and cozy.

Mr. Pitts was a rotund man with a round face, bul-

bous nose, and lengthy jowls. Between his graying hair
and his thick gold spectacles, he had a professorial air
that was only emphasized by his old-fashioned attire
of knee-breeches and stockings.

Stepping forward, Mr. Pitts bowed. "Lady Golding, so good to see you again."

Extending her arm toward Heath, Tess nodded.
"May I introduce Mr. Bartlett. He is here to observe
the society's good works."

Mr. Pitts's smile waned. "Mr. Bartlett? The barrister?"

"Pleased to make your acquaintance." Heath
stretched out his hand, trying to sound jovial and not
priggish in the least.

Mr. Pitts's pale brown eyes flitted from Tess to Heath
and back again. "What, pray tell, brings a member of
the solicitor-general's office to my door?"

Heath's hand lowered, and he tried not to be irritated by the rebuff. "I am not here in that capacity. The
only reason for my being here relates to the society's
good works."

Moving to stand behind the desk, Mr. Pitts busied
himself with shuffling papers. "Our accounts are all
in order, I assure you."

Tess sighed, sending an "I told you so" look Heath's
way. Then, pasting on a sweet smile, she stepped forward. "I'm so glad that you're enjoying the scents for
your fire."

"Yes, they're very nice." Mr. Pitt's tone was distracted
as he shuffled more papers. "Our accountant is un-
available at the moment, since his office is not here on
the grounds. But I can call for him if need be."

"I have no interest in the accounts, Mr. Pitts," Heath tried to reassure, leaning on his cane in a relaxed pose. "I am, however, most interested in the Society for Enrichment and Learning's reform efforts."

"Reform?" Mr. Pitts gulped, his face draining of color.

"I mean their efforts to rehabilitate women so they can join the productive workforce."

The papers shuffled more loudly. Mr. Pitts's hands visibly shook. "Where are those accounts . . .?"

Exhaling, Tess stared out the window as if to say, *You're the cannoneer who fired the ball into this ship, you can bail the water*.

Heath stepped forward. "Honestly, Mr. Pitts, I don't see what's upsetting you so much."

Mr. Pitts straightened. "Upset? I'm not upset in the least! How dare you make accusations as if I have something to be upset about?"

For the next twenty minutes Heath tried every avenue to calm Mr. Pitts's fears, without success.

Finally, at Tess's urging, Heath and Tess quit Mr. Pitts's office.

Silently they walked along the corridors accompanied by the guard.

"I can't understand why the man wouldn't accept that I had no hidden motive." Heath strode alongside her, his frustration eating at him like a parasite. He was a barrister, for heaven's sake; he should've been able to convince the man of his honest intentions.

"He couldn't accept it because there's no good reason for you to be here."

"With the society—"

"My point exactly. There's no good reason for you to be making application to the society. It begs the question of what you are about."

"We've been over this ground before——"

"Not to my satisfaction, or obviously Mr. Pitts's."

"You both should accept my word as fact."

"Why? Because you say so?"

Stopping, he turned her to face her. "Unless you've something to hide."

Crossing her arms, she lifted her chin. "Don't assume Mr. Pitts is guilty of anything simply because he wouldn't swallow your every explanation whole."

"Maybe I wasn't speaking of Mr. Pitts."

Her eyes narrowed. "Then who are you—?"

"There you are!" Lady Blankett swept up to join them, her face flushed and slightly out of breath. "Some of the women aren't feeling well today. There's a fever going around, so we had to cut our visit short. The countess was most insistent that we not press the poor women further. She and the others are already in the courtyard." Her greenish-blue gaze flitted from Tess to Heath and back again. "Ah, how did it go with Mr. Pitts?"

Tess scowled. "Not well."

"The man was decidedly unreasonable—" Heath began.

Tess interrupted with a raised hand, "It's my own fault, really, Janelle. I should have told you this was a bad idea."

Heath straightened. "This was her idea?"

"Don't look so shocked. I'm not the only one who wishes you'll lose this bet. In this instance, however, our own machinations have harmed our good works. I had assumed that Mr. Pitts wouldn't find out your identity if we were here simply to meet some of the prisoners. Obviously I miscalculated."

"You can't expect me to play the obedient dog."

"And you need to appreciate that your little prank has consequences! You should quit now before——"

"Don't waste your breath. I'm no quitter. I'll see the process through."

"What I'm trying to figure out is what got you started!"

"Enough!" Lady Blankett raised her hands high. "This is neither the time nor the place."

Tess glared at Heath, but blessedly held her tongue.

"Come away, and we can figure this all out later." Lady Blankett urged them along like wayward children.

Heath shot Tess a triumphant smile. "Saved by the matron," he whispered for her ears only.

Her lip moved silently, *This time*.

Chapter 9

"I'd like to know how you manipulated this," Tess ground out staring out the coach window as the London streets passed by. She was irritated with Heath for being such a bullheaded, thickheaded . . . *man*. And irritated with herself for being so unsettled by him. She shouldn't allow him to unnerve her so! Yet when she was with him she wanted to . . . wanted to . . . knock some sense into him! Do him violence until he admitted the truth of what he was about. And confessed, of course, that he was completely wrong about women. The pigheaded jackass.

She did feel guilty about the "starched and full of himself" comment, though. He had risen high on his own merit and should be proud. Perhaps it was simply the contrast from when he was young; he'd been so unassuming and easy to be around. Now he was stiff, and that business about marrying up!

He can't go to a prison for females. He is courting a young lady of a very respectable family of the ton, Bills had said. She withheld a snort.

Heath didn't like her family. Not that she could blame him after what had happened. And she certainly wasn't "very respectable," unlike the lady he was courting. But she didn't care. Why should she? The Whilom girl was probably a snob, and the two of them could be eminently respectable and *boring* together.

Inwardly she harrumphed, feeling a mite better, but not really.

"Manipulated what?" Setting his hat on the seat beside him, Heath stretched his long legs out before him as his body swayed to the motion of the carriage. He was so large he practically filled the small space, making her feel crowded.

She crossed her arms. "How is it that you and I are alone in my carriage while everyone else is in the countess's?"

Those brawny shoulders shrugged. "The countess should ride in her own carriage with her companion, of course. Lady Blankett wanted to speak with Miss Gammon, and her friend Lady Genevieve wished to listen. Mrs. Thomas wanted to ride in a countess's coach, and Bills . . . well, Bills wants to be near Mrs. Thomas."

"Why would your friend wish to be near Lucy?"

"I'll leave that for Bills to say."

On edge, Tess recrossed her arms. "I don't understand this. I don't see you for over ten years and then I can't seem to get rid of you. What are you about?"

"As I've explained, it's about a bet."

"I don't believe you."

"What hidden motives could I possibly have?"

Turning away, she considered her worries about the Foreign Office. Could he know about her work? If so, what could it signify? Somehow she doubted that was it and feared his motives were far more personal. She'd been dreading this accounting for years, even though she knew it was long overdue. She owed him and she hated it.

She swallowed, feeling the gauntlet he'd laid like an iron locket around her neck. Still, *now* she was a woman who'd rather understand what she was up against than face the unknown like an ostrich with its head in the sand.

"Really, Tess. If I had any scheme, what could it possibly be?"

She bit her lip. "Revenge?"

He straightened. "Revenge? For what?"

"For getting your father sacked."

His body tensed, and his hands gripped the cane so tightly the leather of his gloves squeaked. "What are you talking about?"

She swallowed as the guilt that had burrowed itself so deeply into her psyche rose up to taunt her. "I got your father sacked. It was because of me that he was let go. That you had to leave Morganfield Hall."

Tense silence filled the carriage.

Tess felt the disappointment like a shaft of glass in her heart. "So you don't deny it. You're here to take your revenge."

Heath lifted his gloved hand and rubbed his chin, his dark gaze troubled. "What makes you assume so much responsibility for what happened ten years ago?"

"You know very well—"

"No, I don't."

Shifting in her seat, Tess shook her head as the images flashed in her mind, dredging up shame and guilt and an aching sense of loss. Why did the incident upset her still? Mayhap because she'd been so submissive. She hated recalling how she'd been, always remembering her passivity with a knot of shame in her middle.

"Tess?"

She blinked, brought back to the present.

"I think I deserve an explanation." His tone was gentle, making her feel even worse.

But she was at a loss for words to explain her fault. Distantly she had a flicker of sympathy for how Lucy might have lost her ability to speak; some things were too awful to release into the world.

Heath rose and moved to sit beside her. His body was like a wall of warmth as he grasped her hand.

"What happened, Tess?" he asked, his voice quietly urging.

She swallowed, then shook her head. "It's so stupid, really."

"Don't diminish it, just tell me what happened."

She stared down at her small hand encased in his larger one. They both wore the same color leather, chocolate brown, reminding her of his eyes. That was one thing about him that had not changed. That, and his ability to comfort her.

Suddenly she recalled the two weeks when as a girl she'd been confined to bed, miserable with fever, chills, and a terrible rattling cough. Most of the family had avoided her; even her mother had stood in the doorway to her room for barely a moment, making her feel like a pariah. Not Heath. Every day he'd come into her chamber, set a chair before her bed, and read to her. Her favorites, *St. George and the Dragon* and *The Glass Slipper*. While he read, often she would doze, but she still heard his soothing voice in her dreams.

They had been such good friends. The invisible barriers of being the opposite sex and of their respective stations were always present, but they'd shared a companionable friendship. But then, after Heath had been sent away, the memory of that relationship had haunted her, exacerbating the guilt of her culpability for having destroyed it.

How he must hate her. And she could hardy blame him. She could only imagine how difficult it must have been for his father to obtain a decent post after being dismissed without references.

Heath exhaled, his brow furrowed, his face troubled. "What happened that makes you think that you're responsible for my father being discharged?"

Her lips felt glued shut. For some reason even after all these years, she couldn't bear to face his hatred.

"At least tell me where you were when it happened." His tone was kindly yet insistent. "The garden? One of the drawing rooms?"

"The art room." It had been a lovely yellow-painted chamber with tall windows facing south. The sun had shone so brightly in the afternoons that one had to almost wear a hat. After the incident she had never gone back into that room. It had been locked up, anyway, and she hadn't lifted a paintbrush or a piece of charcoal since.

"What were you doing in the art room, Tess?"

"Painting."

"What picture?"

"The one of you reading in the garden."

His brow furrowed. "The one that you made me move five times for until the light was just right?"

Her lips almost lifted as she remembered. "Yes. I was adding some finishing touches."

"What happened while you were adding the finishing touches?"

Exhaling, she pushed away the feelings and just focused on the facts. "Father came in very upset."

"How did you know he was upset?"

She suddenly had the sense that he must be a very good interrogator when in court. He was encouraging, yet tenacious in going after the details. "His hair was mussed, his clothing in disarray." She looked up at Heath then, seeing the understanding in his eyes.

He nodded. "He never had a button out of row or a scuff on his shoes. He was always immaculate in his dress."

"But, even more distressing . . . that day . . . his eyes were wild."

"Then what happened?"

Inhaling, she shook her head. "He barged into the room, ranting, upset. So very upset. I couldn't understand why he was so angry with me. I couldn't think of what I'd done."

She swallowed as her distress rose up like bile. "He came over to where I was working and when . . . and when he saw the painting of you . . . he went crazy. I've never seen him like that. He was wild . . . he kicked over the easel and flung the painting to the floor. Then he trampled it, grinding his heels into it . . . all the while screaming . . ." Her brow furrowed and shame enveloped her, gripping her chest so tightly that it was hard to breathe.

He squeezed her hand, comforting and yet encouraging. "What did he say, Tess?"

"He screamed . . ." The words thickened in her throat, stuck there until she wrenched them out, " . . . about my lack of virtue, my immorality, how I'd forsaken every godly notion . . ."

She was lost in the memory of it, until he brushed the back of his hand across her cheek, to wipe away a tear. "Then what did he do, Tess?"

His calm urging gave her strength. "He struck me." Closing her eyes, she turned her head into his shoulder. "He punched me in the head. The next day . . . you were gone."

Wrapping his arms around her, he held her so closely she felt as if he was squeezing the pain out of her. His arms were so strong, so enveloping, his chest so wide and inviting. She leaned into him, relishing that wall of comfort he gave her to rest on. She inhaled his rich earthy scent, feeling a sense of safety that she hadn't felt in years.

She couldn't recall the last time anyone had held her like this. She'd missed it, had ached for it in a way that she hadn't recognized until this moment. It felt so good, yet bittersweet for the contrast to the loneliness and lack of comfort of so many years.

His broad chest lifted with a deep inhalation. "What a bastard. If I'd known . . ."

"There was nothing you could have done for it. You weren't there, and if you would have been . . . well, I'm glad you weren't."

Leaning back, he stared down at her. "You're protecting me now?"

"No, of course not . . ." Heath didn't need her protection; he never had. He'd always been one to curl his fists and roll up his sleeves rather than back down from a fight. How had that iron-willed lad turned into the refined gentleman holding her so scandalously close?

Trying to ignore the heat seeping from him and warming her in a way she hadn't felt in years, Tess bit her lip. "I've never told anyone." She'd been too ashamed of herself and, secretly, of her father. She couldn't quite face the fact that the father whom she'd admired and adored as a man above men could be as unjust and spiteful as every other poor sod.

"What happened after he struck you?"

"I ran away. I couldn't believe he'd done it, but I was in such shock, I simply ran, and ran . . ."

His arm tightened around her. "What a selfish, ignorant bastard!"

"It was a long time ago. I don't know why I even let

it bother me anymore. I suppose, seeing you, well, I've always felt guilty that it was my fault that my father sacked your father and that you were sent away."

"But it wasn't your fault, Tess."

"I know we'd never done anything wrong, but I suppose my father, well, he was upset about me growing up and nearing marriageable age and being so close to you . . . I tried to consider how he looked at things . . ."

His jaw worked. "I can't believe that you're actually trying to be understanding! The man struck you! For no good reason! And then left you believing that you were responsible for damaging my father's career!"

"You know . . ." She swallowed, relieved to have told him and yet sad just the same. "I've never been alone with my father since then. If there is ever a chance for us to be alone in a room together, I escape, run away like I did that day. Stupid, really; I'm almost twenty-five years old and I'm afraid to be alone with my father."

"You think he'll——"

"Oh, I don't fear that he'll raise a hand to me. I'd never let him do that . . . It's almost as if I'm afraid he'll actually want to *talk* about it . . . and that I just couldn't bear. I just want to forget about the whole thing. If I didn't feel so badly about your father . . . well, then I probably would have by now."

Heath exhaled, hugging her close. "My father didn't get sacked because of my relationship with you, Tess."

"You and I were too friendly. My mother had made comments, but I didn't listen. I suppose I didn't wish to."

"You and I had nothing to do with it, Tess. It was wholly unrelated. Your father was a knave to take out his anger on you, his perfectly innocent daughter who had nothing whatsoever to do with any of it. Shame on him, the stupid bugger."

Her brow furrowed. "Then why . . .?"

Anger darkened his features, tinged with sadness. "My father . . . had a terrible . . . lapse in judgment."

"Lapse in judgment, what do you mean? Your father was a very sensible man."

"Sensible most of the time, perhaps, but he made a stupid blunder. A falter in prudence that truly cost him. He painted a picture of your mother."

"So?"

"She didn't have any clothes on."

Tess pressed her hand to her mouth, and her eyes widened. "Oh my God."

"One of the maids found it and gave it to the butler, who brought it immediately to your father."

"How do you know this?"

"When I demanded to know why we had to leave, my father told me. He felt quite dreadful about the whole thing."

Tess shook her head. "No wonder my father lost his wits."

"I suppose in his anger, your father went to the 'scene of the crime' and thereupon came upon you and saw you painting a picture of me . . . and, well, it was too much for him." He scowled. "But he should never have laid a hand on you. He should have been man enough to be a proper father!"

Tess bit her lip as the realizations settled upon her. "I've been carrying this guilt for so many years . . . that I'd been inappropriate, not a proper daughter. I thought you hated me."

"No, Tess." His voice was gruff, stimulating a heat deep in her belly. "I don't hate you."

She looked up. His eyes blazed with warmth and something else . . . Hidden in those cocoa brown depths she saw a yearning, one that stirred something deep inside her. Tess was achingly aware of how close they sat pressed together. She was almost in his lap, his arms engulfing her, his lips mere inches from her mouth, so close that his breath became hers.

The silence in the carriage grew thick, the air electric with unspoken longing. Tess's breath grew heavy and her body alert to his every movement as they rocked and swayed in rhythm.

His lips were so smooth, so enticing. They drew her gaze like a parched man to water. She licked her lips, desperately wanting to know how he tasted.

His gaze fixed on her mouth, searing her as if touched. Could he be thinking what she was thinking? Nay, he was practically engaged. The thought sparked a rebellious urge within her.

"Tess . . ." His hands gripped her arms, almost as if he was unable to decide if he wanted to push her away or pull her closer still.

She didn't give him the chance.

She pressed her mouth to his, closing her eyes and savoring him, relishing the sweet contact, the taste of male and earthy delights. His lips were as smooth as they looked, yet firm in just the right places. She nibbled at those lips, urging, demanding more. He held himself back, but she gave no quarter. Pressing her hands to his face, she bit his lower lip and sucked, taking what he was too upstanding to give.

His mouth opened with a groan that she felt deep in her belly. Her body quivered, awakened to sensations that had long been relegated to memory.

Relishing the sweet victory, Tess shifted against him, wanting, yearning. His large hands roamed across her bottom, kneading the flesh, pulling her closer still.

With a moan of pure pleasure, she wrapped her arms around his neck, crushing her breasts against his broad chest, fanning the flames of her already spiking passion.

He tore his lips from hers. "Tess." His voice cracked.

"What?" Her head was swimming, her body aflame.

"The carriage has stopped. We . . . have . . . to stop."

She blinked as reality crashed into her consciousness like an icy spray. Quentin had once told her that a man could only refuse a willing woman if he was repulsed or if it would be too bloody awkward to get rid of her come morning.

Tess's cheeks burned. She'd been more than willing. And if Heath's roaming hands were any guide, he'd hardly been repulsed. What was it, then? The scandal business yet again? Did he believe, as so many others did, that she was the cause of men's ruin? Or was Heath Bartlett simply too worried about his precious reputation to be with her?

Whatever his reasons, she felt injured and the fool.

Heath stood and quickly moved to the opposite cushion as if she'd singed him.

Gritting her teeth, Tess willed her emotions to cool. The man couldn't wait to get away from her! She didn't care. Why should she? The kiss was unimportant. It was an odd, isolated incident. They had nothing between them. Hell, the man was courting another woman, and an eminently respectable one at that!

She turned away, blindly staring out the window. Talk about a lapse in judgment!

"I'm sorry, Tess."

Blast the man for apologizing! She'd be damned if she ever showed him how badly she wanted him. *Had* wanted him. It was in the past, better left forgotten. She had to stop her hand from rising to her lips, knowing the lie for what it was. She'd never forget that kiss. But the memory would always be tempered with the shame of knowing that he didn't truly want her.

A swell of injured pride swept over her. *He'll never have the chance to touch me again. Never!*

He raised his hand as if in offering. "I didn't mean—"

"Yes, well, neither of us did," she lied, adjusting her bonnet and not meeting his eyes.

"But—"

"Don't say another word. It's best forgotten."

"Tess—"

Squinting, she pasted on a smile. "We'd better go inside before anyone begins to wonder. You don't want anyone getting the wrong idea. I know how important your pristine reputation is to you."

The muscle in his jaw worked and his hands holding his cane clenched. "Now hold on one minute—"

Tess rose. "We'd best be on our way."

The door creaked open and the stool was set. The footman stood waiting outside. She disembarked, glad that her back was straight, her head held high.

He stepped down behind her. "You go inside. I need to walk."

"Whatever suits you." She sniffed.

"I'll see you tonight, then," he offered, as if to soften the blow.

She didn't even bother to turn. "Oh, yes, at the Countess's ball." Her tone sounded icy even to her own ears. Striding up the stairs, she didn't even grant him a backward glance.

"Until then," he called.

But she pretended not to hear.

Chapter 10

S itting before the oval mirror, Tess watched as her maid Anna entwined her hair into intricate coils atop her head. No floppy bonnets for her tonight. She wasn't going to hide herself as she usually did for fear of being judged poorly by the *ton*. She felt reckless, like a horse too long in the stable yearning to race the wind.

Whenever she considered the reason for this sudden onset of rebelliousness, her anger grew and she worked to push every thought of Heath Bartlett from her mind. She tried not to think of his ribbons of dark hair, his magnetic cocoa brown eyes, or his delectably brawny shoulders. She forced herself not to recall how sweet he'd tasted or how hard he'd felt. She definitely didn't want to think about how desperately she'd clung to him. Never that.

"Is it too hot in 'ere, ma'am?" Anna asked. "You seem flushed. I can open a window if ye like."

Clearing her throat, Tess felt her cheeks warm. "No thank you, Anna. I'm fine."

There was little use in thinking about Heath; he truly had to be relegated to her past. She was now free from the guilt for his father's sacking, and he was merely an applicant at the society, nothing more.

Perhaps that little kiss was a good thing. A reminder that she was twenty-four, not dead, and it was time for her to get back in the game. It had been two years since she'd been with a man. Two long years that she'd used to cool her ardor and douse any lingering yearnings for a man.

Recalling the mortification that had followed today's kiss and the nightmare after her last affaire, Tess reminded herself that she didn't need a man. But more importantly, men were more trouble than they were worth.

What was a hot, salacious kiss compared to having to actually talk to a specious man? She didn't want to deal with those irritating male needs and pigheaded behaviors! Heath was a jackass. He thought that women didn't have anything better to do than talk about men.

Or think about them, Tess added with chagrin.

With that final irritating thought, Tess once and for all barred Heath Bartlett from her mind.

I need to focus on tonight's goals.

It was surprising that the countess would host a ball so soon after coming to London, but apparently she wanted to make a splash and quickly introduce herself to society. Tess wasn't questioning her good luck; the ball was the perfect opportunity to search the countess's home. First Tess would explore the countess's chambers, and if there was additional time, the study, to look for anything odd or out of place that might give some hint of her activities. Additionally, the ball itself would prove interesting. Tess needed to see who attended and with whom.

Tess's blood surged as excitement and anticipation rose within her. How could a man compare to this kind of thrill?

Memory of that kiss washed over her once more like a perfume that lingered.

Would she and Heath dance tonight? Unless appearing with a scandalous lady such as herself might be a problem for his oh-so-precious reputation? Inwardly, she harrumphed.

Well, it was his nature to be polite and she was chairwoman of the society's membership committee, so he would probably ask.

Would she say no?

The power of that option was tempting.

But she knew she wouldn't do it. She couldn't stomach depriving herself of the chance for a dance. It had been so long since she'd attended a ball, and she pined for a whirl across the dance floor.

Not a waltz. It would raise too many eyebrows. There would be no thigh pressed to thigh, no hard body mere inches from hers. Oh, how she loved the feel of a hand in the small of her back, moving to a rhythm the body instinctively understood . . .

Nay, he would probably ask her for a country dance or a Scottish reel, not wanting to give her any false ideas. She withheld a snort. He should only be so lucky. Granted, he was inordinately handsome and had those astoundingly wide shoulders. And the man really knew how to kiss . . .

But really, who wanted to be with a man who prized propriety and status above all else?

She knew she was being a tad unjust, but it felt good all the same.

So they would be polite, distant, and dance not more than one very reserved and proper dance.

What kind of dancer might he be? He was so tall, his body strapping, and he carried himself with fluid grace. She bet he'd be a good dance partner. Really good. *He'd be a great lover, too.*

Tess's mouth dropped open at the outrageous thought.

Licking her suddenly dry lips, she pushed the unsettling reflection aside and forced herself to face the cold, hard fact that Heath was practically engaged.

Would his fiancée-to-be, Miss Penelope Whilom, be present tonight? Tess found herself hating the lady without even a morsel of a reason. Tess and Heath would never be. There was no future there, so why shouldn't he marry his perfect English rose? Achieve his perfect career and the perfect life?

Because life was imperfect, as she well knew. Rarely did one have a chance for perfection, and usually it lasted barely a breath, evaporating into mist. Most people pretended otherwise, but Tess knew better. She liked being clear-eyed about the nature of things; it made the disappointments all the less upsetting.

The problem was, she wasn't being very clearheaded

about Heath, and his effect on her was beginning to cloud her efforts. She wasn't so deluded that she didn't see he was interfering with her investigation. She was so busy striving to focus on the countess and *not* on Heath, while trying to fulfill her duties as new membership chairwoman, while also endeavoring to keep Reynolds satisfied about the society so as to not do anything rash . . . It was convoluted enough to give anyone a ripping headache.

"Am I pulling too tight, ma'am?" Anna asked.

"Uh, no. It's fine." Tess lowered her hand from her temple.

"There, it's done." Anna straightened and stepped away. "Ye look lovely."

"Thank you, Anna." Tess examined the crown of crimson tresses coiled around her head, with pearls interwoven throughout. She particularly liked the curls softening her hairline. "You did a wonderful job."

"If I may be so bold, ye should wear yer hair this way more often. Ye look beautiful. Like a princess."

Exhaling, Tess stood. "I don't have much call for such elaborate coiffures. Most days I'm working."

"That doesn't mean ye can't look yer best. My mama said every day ye should look yer best."

Tess smiled. "She used to say the same thing to my mother when she'd fix her hair." Suddenly a vision of her mother lying naked while Heath's father painted overcame Tess, and she frowned.

How could Mother have been so condemnatory about my marriage when hers clearly wasn't so trouble-free? Mother was very quick to lay blame in my direction when things started to fall apart in my union. How much culpability did she accept for her own marital trials?

"Shall I get ye the diamond necklace with the flower, ma'am?" Anna asked.

Tess blinked, shaking off the upsetting thoughts. "The necklace with the flower?" It had been ages since she'd worn the bauble. The necklace had been a gift from her parents upon her engagement to Quentin. She had been so happy then. So deluded. She'd thought that she was on the road to happiness, instead of the highway to ruin.

Turning to the mirror, Tess stared at the crimson-haired, blue-eyed lady looking back at her in the glass. She hardly recognized the foolish girl that she'd been then. And it was much more than the angles present in her once-plump face. There was a hardness in her gaze, a knowledge of the realities of a life no longer secure. She wondered if Heath saw the differences in her. He had to, and for some reason this made her sad.

She shook off the feeling. "Ah, let me have a look." She went into the dressing room, opened her jewelry drawer, and examined the selection inside. *Too gaudy. Too inconsequential. Not enough . . .*

She bit her lip, wanting something that would complement the aquamarine muslin gown with tiny flowers stitched around the sloping neckline.

"What about that bird necklace?" Anna asked, pointing to the dark blue satchel containing George Belington's jewels.

"Ah, no." Tess was upset that Anna even knew of the pieces that were kept deep in the dark recess of the drawer. "You're right. The diamond necklace with the flower will look well with this gown."

Standing before the mirror once more, Anna helped Tess put on the necklace. "Very pretty, ma'am."

Tess bit her lip. "This neckline is much lower than I'm used to. A fichu, perhaps . . ."

"Yer not showing nearly as much as most of the ladies these days, ma'am. Ye can do without."

"Anna . . ."

"What? I say yers are better to look at. Show them off."

A flash of defiance surged through Tess. "Very well then. I'll be fashionable, if a bit risqué. Fitting, given my reputation."

"You, risqué? I think not, ma'am."

Tess looked up, surprised.

"Oh, I know what the tongue-waggers say, but they don't know ye like I do. There's nar a flighty, indecent bone in yer body."

Somehow, Anna's words made Tess feel better than any fancy gown or coiffure could. Impulsively Tess turned and gave Anna a quick hug. "Thank you, Anna."

Gently the maid pushed her away. "Have yerself a jolly ol' time, ma'am. It's been forever since ye had any fun that I can recall. Show those fancy gents what yer made of. And if one of them is lucky enough, perhaps he'll win the favor of yer charms."

* * *

Standing at the top of the lofty staircase, Heath scanned the sea of colorful silks, muslin, and lace, looking for a familiar head of crimson curls. The crowd was thick and the air filled with expensive perfumes. Rose, musk, mint, carnation, French violet, and lily of the valley competed to overpower even the most discerning nose. And through it all, Heath longed for a whiff of lavender.

"Where is she?" he murmured aloud.

Stepping up alongside Heath, Bills peered through his quizzing glass down at the crowded ballroom. "I see her."

"Where?"

"In the far corner."

Heath could not discern Tess through the crowd, yet trusted Bills's keen eye. But instead of immediately marching down the stairs and confronting Tess about that kiss, coward that he was, he turned to his friend. "Will you join me?"

Bills blinked as if surprised, but then nodded. "Of course."

As they made their way down the grand staircase and into the throng, Heath knew he was being spineless, but that kiss had shaken him to the core. Everything he thought he'd known about himself and the gentler sex had been tested by that innocent little kiss. Well, not so innocent. It had been searing hot—a salacious mix of spice and heat and lusty desire with the hint of pleasures too tempting for any red-blooded man to ignore.

Tess had ignited a lust in him that he'd hardly recognized. He'd wanted to take her, possess her, claim her as no man ever had before. A beast had roared up within him, one without a care for consequences or propriety or anything beyond bedding the fiery woman in his arms. The desire had been terrifying in its potency.

If the carriage had not stopped, if the driver hadn't called out . . . it had taken every ounce of Heath's self-control to leash that thunderous beast.

Heath couldn't decide whether to feel thankful or thwarted.

Had it gone further . . .

It would have come to no good. I have Penelope to consider. Hell, my future to cement.

And Tess, well, she might be a thief . . . Although he was finding it harder to think of her as such now that he realized that she had been so guilt-ridden over his father's sacking.

But that didn't explain the nagging feeling in his gut that she was up to something. Then there was the money she'd needed for Mr. Pitts. And George Belington's claims. Oh, it was all so jumbled!

Perhaps Tess was enthralling him, using her feminine wiles, of which she had many, to trap him. Did she somehow know about his investigation? Was she trying to distract him? Disarm him? *Corrupt him?*

The thought shook him to his bones.

He had to see her. Talk to her. Understand what she was about. She'd been so cold when they'd parted. So unlike the woman who'd been melting in his arms just moments before.

"I've never seen you this impolitic," Bills noted beside him.

"What do you mean?"

"You just passed Lord Dresher and barely spared him a glance."

Heath blinked. "Oh, I didn't see him."

"For the ambitious fellow that you are, you seem to be racing on the outside of the track tonight. Is anything amiss?"

"Of course not. I was simply thinking about our visit to the prison today. I hear that Gardener—you know, the chap from our Henderson's chambers days—that he's doing free legal work for debtors."

"Free legal work. Why?"

"To try to help those who can't afford to help themselves. I thought perhaps to give a few hours of my spare time."

"You have so much extra these days." Bills's tone was sardonic.

"I meant after the investigation is over."

Bills raised a brow. "How very generous of you. I, for one, would rather spend my precious time at Tipton's tavern. Joe and Winifred need my support, too."

Heath lifted his head, scanning the crowd. "To each his own, my friend."

"Bartlett, old chap!"

"Mr. Bartlett!"

"I say, Mr. Bartlett!" Three gentlemen approached. One was fat with a wild, curly blond mane, the second was thin, hawk-nosed, and had hair that reminded

Heath of dirty wheat, and the third was short, ginger-haired, and had a face awash in freckles.

The ginger-haired man pressed his quizzing glass to his eye. "We must congratulate you, my friend! You broke the silken barrier!" The three men chuckled and shot one another knowing glances.

Raising a brow to Bills, Heath nodded. "Good evening, Mr. Brown, Mr. Newman, Mr. Heatherton."

Mr. Brown licked his lips and smacked his hands together with a hollow-sounding clap. "We want all of the interesting details!"

"Don't hold back on us now," Mr. Newman chided, smoothing his white waistcoat over his stout middle. "I've been curious about that society for females since its inception!"

Mr. Brown snorted. "You have not. You didn't even know it existed until I told you about Bartlett's bet."

"Since the inception of my knowledge of the place," Mr. Newman corrected. "Now I cannot contain my curiosity."

Motioning to Bills, Heath tilted his head. "Gentlemen, this is my friend Mr. Smith."

"The other applicant!" Mr. Newman cried. "I've been wanting to make your acquaintance ever since—"

"My inception?" Bills smiled.

The men guffawed heartily.

"Excellent show!" Mr. Brown beamed. "So we want all of the details."

Winking at Heath, Bills leaned forward and spoke in muted tones, "It's quite hush-hush and we cannot say."

Mr. Heatherton shook his cane. "You must tell us!"

"You must!"

Heath held up his hand. "Sorry, gentlemen, but my friend is right. We are sworn to secrecy. Honor demands that we keep our word."

"This is utterly dissatisfying." Mr. Brown sniffed.

Stamping his cane, Mr. Newman scowled. "Smashingly disappointing."

Wanting to move along and find Tess, Heath exhaled. "Sorry to disappoint, but we must take our leave. Society business, you know."

"This will not suit!" Mr. Henderson barred Heath's way with his cane. "You must tell us something!"

Looking to Heath, Bills shrugged. "We must give them a little."

At a nod from Heath, Bills leaned forward conspiratorially.

The three men moved closer, leaning in.

Bills whispered, "All I can say is that in applying for membership . . ."

Mr. Brown urged, "Yes, yes . . ."

" . . . we were required to go . . ."

"Where?" Mr. Henderson demanded.

" . . . to prison. Marks-Cross Street."

"Prison." Mr. Henderson nodded with a hum. "Very interesting."

Straightening, Mr. Brown scowled. "What's so interesting about prison?"

"Are you completely without a brain in your head?" Mr. Newman scoffed.

"I can't stand it when you call me stupid!" Mr. Brown stomped his foot. "I am no one's fool!"

Mr. Brown turned to Mr. Henderson. "You explain it to him."

Shooting Bills a glance, Heath extricated himself from the group and slipped deeper into the crowd.

Trailing behind him, Bills wagged a finger. "I told you this society for females business would be in our favor."

"That you did." Heath's eyes scanned the crowd, looking for those crimson curls once more. "Which way, again?"

"Over there! I see her near the corner of the room."

As they approached the place that Bills had indicated, suddenly a white diaphanous silk gown came into view. But instead of lush curves and flaming curls, the gown belonged to a slender young lady with golden blond hair and hazel eyes.

"Oh . . . Penelope."

Bills stopped and stared at Heath a long moment. "That wasn't who you were looking for, was it?"

Heath swallowed his disappointment. "Of course it was."

Stepping forward, he bowed to Lady and Lord Bright and Miss Penelope Whilom, all the while trying not to look over his shoulder for the woman who possessed peach-colored lips that tasted like Aphrodite's nectar.

Chapter 11

Pushing away all thought of Tess, Heath bowed to the Whiloms and introduced his friend.

Sipping from his champagne glass, Lord Bright sniffed. "A barrister, you say?"

"Solicitor, my lord," Bills corrected with a smile.

Lady Bright turned away, peering over Bills's shoulder at the crowd. "This must be a very special occasion for you."

Bills's face was impassable. "I am honored to be here."

Hoping to ease the tension, Heath turned to Penelope. "You look exquisite, my dear."

Her pale cheeks flushed pink. "Thank you, sir."

"May I have the privilege of a dance?"

Penelope's hazel eyes flitted to her mother, who nodded. "That would be lovely."

Bills made a movement like he was going to leave.

Wanting to impress upon Penelope that Bills's friendship was important to him, Heath laid a hand on Bills's arm. "Mr. Smith and I have been friends for a very long time."

Playing along, Bills turned to Penelope, smiling. "Since we were first introduced at the Inns of Court."

"Oh, how nice for you." She sipped her lemonade, her eyes veering away.

"And for me as well," Heath interjected, irritated that his friend was being dismissed. He wished that the Whiloms weren't quite so snobby, but recognized that nobility tended to accept their own, a lesson he'd learned a long time ago from Tess's family. "Mr. Smith is as good a friend as one could wish for."

"That makes two of us, Bartlett," Bills agreed, with a look saying he was willing to play along for only so long.

Still scanning the crowd, Penelope nodded. "Are you members of the same club?"

"Being my friend should be recommendation enough for anyone," Heath bit out. "Mr. Smith is—"

Clearing his throat, Bills interjected, "Oh, Bartlett and I may have a history, but for the most part, we move in different circles." His tone made clear he wasn't distressed by the fact. "We have very different ideas about our roles in this world."

Penelope's eyes were wide, but her meaning less than innocent. "So you probably don't have the occasion to see each other that frequently."

Heath was willing to do many things to win Penelope's hand, but slighting a friend was not one of them. "Sometimes we may move in different circles, but we will always be dear friends. Nothing"—his eyes fixed on Penelope's—"will ever change that."

Heath turned to Lord and Lady Bright. "In fact, Mr. Smith is helping me with your cousin Belington's investigation."

Three sets of eyes fixed on Bills as if he were suddenly a new specimen to be dissected.

"You don't say . . ." Lady Bright's gaze was calculating as she waved her lacy black fan.

"Mr. Smith made application to the society with me and is assisting with the story that the entire affair is based upon a wager."

"How very useful of you." Eyes narrowing, Lady Bright sniffed. "Do you work for the solicitor-general as well?"

"Only when he needs me." Bills's tone was self-effacing.

The Whiloms were seemingly impressed, and the air warmed a notch or two.

"How goes it, then?" Lady Bright asked in dramatically hushed tones. "Have you secured the evidence against that Jezebel?"

Heath tried not to be annoyed by the nasty label. Even if Tess had done the crime, it still seemed wrong to vilify her. "These things take time. Especially if we wish to protect those making the claims."

"Of course we must be protected!" She huffed. "If only it was as simple as locking her up and throwing away the key!"

Bills scratched his chin. "You are wise to have a care about making unsubstantiated accusations, Lady

Bright. To expose yourself to claims of slander creates an unnecessary risk to your reputations, not to mention your assets."

"Assets?" The matron's face paled.

Her daughter stepped over and grasped her hand. "Don't worry, Mama, Mr. Bartlett will take care of everything."

"I will do my utmost," Heath assured.

Bills's face was markedly serious. "No matter the sacrifice."

Heath glared at him.

"What?" Bills lifted his shoulder. But his eyes twinkled, letting Heath know that Bills considered being with Tess far from painful.

Turning to Lord and Lady Bright, Bills leaned forward. "I must warn you that the person who is the focus of our inquiry will be present this evening."

"Here?" Lady Bright screeched, her face reddening.

Penelope grasped her mother's arm. "It's all right, Mama."

"We must leave at once!" Lady Bright declared.

His brow furrowing, Lord Bright frowned. "It's a large ball with hundreds of people. We can hardly—"

"My delicate constitution cannot sustain it!" Lady Bright wailed. "My lord, please!"

Scowling, Lord Bright held up his hands. "What was I thinking? Of course you cannot stay. Penelope, please take your mother home at once."

"But . . . but . . ."

Lady Bright's mouth pinched. "Don't be so selfish, Wilbur."

"What's selfish? I promised Walworth I'd meet him for cards. Besides, that woman's presence offends you, not me. So why should I miss out on a wonderful evening?"

Lady Bright's nostrils flared. "One might argue that being with me was the only way for you to have a wonderful evening."

Lord Bright grimaced with irritation. "You're going to take a dose of tonic for your nerves and fall asleep. Besides, you're always complaining about me drinking alone. Here I'm surrounded by friends with whom I can partake. At home . . . well, there's little enough of *anything* for me to join in at home." His tone left very little to the imagination, and Heath looked away, embarrassed for them.

Lady Bright's face was flushed as her gaze fixed on Heath. "At least would *you* be a gentleman and escort us home?"

Heath understood that he had a chance to score some perfectly brilliant marks with his mother-in-law-to-be. Yet he didn't want to go, even for that. He told himself that it was for the investigation, but deep down he knew he wouldn't miss out on seeing Tess. Not tonight. Not after that kiss in the carriage.

Heath bowed. "I must remain, madame. To further the investigation. But I will gladly call for your carriage and escort you outside."

Her shoulders deflated. "Very well then. Penelope, we will go."

Heath swallowed, regretting his choice, if only a little. "I'd been hoping for the honor of a dance."

Penelope smiled at him. "Another time, then." She extended her hand. It was skeletal thin and cool to the touch through her white gloves.

"Your hands are cold."

Penelope shrugged. "They always are. Mama says it's from being so small when I was born. My blood doesn't move much."

Why had he not noticed that before? Perhaps because he was comparing her touch to another's. Inwardly he pushed away the notion. Penelope was nothing like Tess, and he was glad for it. Penelope was kind-hearted, sweet; she would be a good mother—all the things he wanted in a wife. Not a passionate hellion. Not a woman whose desire flashed and then sputtered as if doused in water. Who needed the headaches and heartaches that were endemic with someone like Tess? Not Heath.

He offered one arm to Lady Bright and the other to Penelope.

Bills bowed. "I wish you a quick recovery, madame. Miss Whilom. I am off in search of the card room."

Lord Bright gulped the rest of his champagne. "I'll join you. I hear it's upstairs."

Heath envied his friend's quick escape, but knew he was doing the right thing by his Penelope. Or the best he was willing. He motioned to a passing servant. "My good man. Would you be so kind as to call for Lady Bright's carriage? She is unwell and wishes to depart posthaste." The sooner his mission was completed, the sooner he could find Tess.

The servant nodded. "She's the third tonight. It's the crush, I think."

"Your haste would be most appreciated."

Lady Bright sent him a grateful glance. "Thank you, Mr. Bartlett. You truly have fine character."

He nodded, not feeling very gentlemanly at all. "It's my pleasure. I only wish I could be more of service to you."

"You are doing me a great service by capturing that dreadful witch."

"I'm simply doing my job, madame."

Oh, the games one played to secure one's future.

Heath returned to the ballroom even more tense than before. Securing the ladies into the carriage had taken a vexing half hour while Lady Bright had complained and fussed. Now free from the ladies, Heath felt wound up, like a cork ready to pop.

The sands of the hourglass were sifting away and he hadn't yet accomplished his goal. Seeing Tess. Talking to Tess. Finding out if he was enchanted, or going mad, or being duped.

Reaching over, he grabbed a flute of champagne from a passing servant's tray and gulped, trying to quench his sudden thirst. The orchestra played a minuet and the dancers moved in elegant procession. The murmurs of many voices accompanied the music, as did the clanking of glasses and the footfalls of many shoes on the marble floor.

Where was Tess? She had to be here by now.

A flash of red hair captured his eye. He snorted.

Nay, the owner was a stout matron awash in pounds of diamonds.

Bills came up alongside him and slapped him on the back. "There you are, my friend! So you've sent the ship sailing, have you?"

Heath didn't turn. "Don't start."

"I thought I had it bad with *Macbeth*'s witches, but Lady Bright gives a whole new meaning to the expression *self-absorbed*."

"She's upset—

"I can't wait to win my bet and save you from the clutches of that officious Whilom clan."

Heath exhaled. "I'm not asking to be saved. They're my future."

"*They* are? Not 'Penelope is'?"

Heath scowled. "You know what I mean. I would be privileged to have the benefit of such a clan."

"It's your death sentence. By the way, if you're looking for your Tess—

"She's not *my* Tess."

"Whatever you tell yourself, my good man. But if you're looking for her, she just headed out that door." He motioned to the entry to the left passage angled away from the stairway where they stood. "She was trying to be inconspicuous, but she seemed very intent, and I know she wasn't headed to the ladies' retiring room as it's in the opposite direction."

Peering through his quizzing glass, Bills raised his brows. "A secret rendezvous perhaps?"

Heath felt his anger rise. *She couldn't . . . wouldn't . . .*

"You didn't happen to have an assignation planned with the lady . . .?"

"Shut it, Bills."

"I suppose not."

Heath stamped down the stairs and pushed his way through the crowd, unmindful of whom he passed. As he headed down the passage, his only thought was that he was going to have to toss her over his knee and teach her a lesson. His pace quickened.

Chapter 12

Tess made her way down the long candlelit passage, thankful for the carpets that silenced her
footfalls. Dance slippers were wonderful for moving
about quietly, and the fact that the servants were busy
with the festivities downstairs made this the perfect opportunity to investigate Countess di Notari's
chambers. If only her muslin skirts wouldn't whisper
so loudly.

From her discussions with the footman, Tess knew
that she was headed in the right direction, and once
she made the next left, she would be at the door to the
countess's rooms. People tended to keep those things
most precious to them near, so the bedroom was the
ideal place for potentially sensitive items. What exactly, Tess had no idea, but if there was anything to
uncover, she would soon find out.

Peering over her shoulder, she checked the hallway,
and upon seeing no one, prepared to enter.

Nonchalantly, but with a bit of a widening of her
eyes and drooping of her mouth, she opened the bed-

room door, ready to pretend that she was more than a bit foxed and had gotten lost in the corridors.

Upon seeing the empty chamber, she swiftly entered the room and closed the door behind her.

Grand ivory and gilded Egyptian-inspired Thomas Hope furniture graced the chamber's sitting room. The fire burned low in the hearth, indicating that the countess wasn't expected here anytime soon. Good. She should have at least a half hour if she'd timed the festivities right.

Distantly she wondered if Heath missed her at the ball. She doubted it; he was too busy with his fiancée-to-be and her mother. Anger simmered within her, but she pushed it away. Why should she care how he wasted his time? What did it matter to her that he was courting a high-minded, toffee-nosed chit?

Oh, she'd done a little digging on Miss Penelope Whilom tonight, and Tess wasn't impressed. And it wasn't only the fact that the girl was related to George Belington, the toad.

A bump resounded. Tess jumped, but forced herself to calm. Someone had dropped something upstairs; she had not been discovered.

Blast, she couldn't afford to be distracted.

Clear-eyed, cool, steady. Get results. Trounce Napoleon. King and country. She felt her body relax and her senses sharpen as she honed in on the task at hand.

Silently Tess moved into the chamber's inner sanctum. The bed was large enough to swallow the countess whole. The frieze-adorned tester was supported by a headboard at the back and by fluted columns at the front. The bedclothes, pillows, bolsters, and feathered quilt would be handled by servants, so Tess doubted they held many secrets. Still, she removed her evening gloves and set down her reticule. Then she felt every pillow and bolster until she was certain nothing lay hidden within.

Straightening, Tess leaned over to examine the decorative needlework bedcover, curious about the odd design. The needlework depicted sloping cliffs overlooking the ocean, with waves foaming as they came up upon the sand. It reminded Tess of a beach she'd visited once along the English coast. The needlework was a bit sloppy, and it was an unusual choice given the Egyptian-inspired furnishings. She made a mental note of the depiction and filed it away in her head for later consideration.

Her hands grazed the fluted columns and along the wooden bedframe, finding nothing of note. Squatting down on her hands and knees she peered beneath the bed. Chamber pot, slippers—

"What the blazes are you doing?" a male voice cried.

Tess jumped, her heart in her throat.

Heath stood in the doorway dressed in his black and white formal attire, nauseatingly handsome and well turned out down to his shiny black shoes.

"You!" The breath rushed out of her in a heady swell of relief.

"What the hell are you doing here?" Heath's handsome face was darkened with anger.

Gritting her teeth, Tess hissed, "Lower your voice!"

"Why? Is your paramour hiding beneath the covers?" His tone was scathing.

"Paramour?" She blinked. "Oh, botheration! You think I have an assignation?"

"Why the hell else would you be off in a bedchamber during a ball?"

"Can we please discuss this another time?" She had no idea what she would tell him, but would figure that one out later. Moving forward, she grabbed his arm, trying to propel him toward the outer sitting room. His muscles beneath her hands were knotted with tension, and she felt as if she were trying to push hardened cement. "You have to get out of here."

"Why? So you can meet your lover uninterrupted?"

"Don't be a dolt. I'm not meeting anyone."

"I don't believe you."

"Hush!" Tess froze. Female voices could be heard nearing the chamber. The countess! "We've got to move, now!"

His fists curled. "I'm not going anywhere until I—"

"Don't say another word!" Her eyes scanned the room searching for an escape.

The voices drew closer.

"I should have that Lady Mares tossed out on her bottom for ruining my new gown!" The countess's tone was incensed.

"Calm yourself, we'll go to the dressing room and I'll help you change." It was Miss Gammon's voice, rock steady.

Grabbing Heath's chin and pulling his face down to

hers, Tess met his gaze. "If you have any care for me whatsoever, pray keep quiet and follow my lead!"

His brow furrowed as the realization dawned that there might be more to this than he'd considered. At last there was some sense in his thick head!

Hooking her arm through Heath's, Tess dragged him in the direction opposite the entry door, deeper into the chamber.

His cocoa brown eyes flashed with anger and inquiry, but blessedly he held his tongue.

They moved into a room bursting with colorful gowns, lace, petticoats, and shoes. The heavy scent of eau de carnation perfume filled the air. The dressing room to which the countess was headed! Tess's grip on Heath's arm tightened. Could this fix get any worse?

Tess spied another door, veiled behind the armoire. She threw it open and shoved Heath inside, falling in on top of him and closing the door just as a voice called from within the dressing room, "Which would you prefer—the white or the green?"

"The one I'm wearing!" the countess cried, entering the chamber. "This is all your fault, telling me to butter up that buffoon Mares and his bitch of a wife!"

Tess held her breath; her heart was racing. She was a puddle of fear on the floor of a dark tiny closet. A stream of light came in from around the casing, and the door was thin enough for her to hear Miss Gammon command, "Lower your voice."

"There's no one here, not even the stupid maid! Why are you always so suspicious? It doesn't become you."

Tess relaxed, barely releasing a tiny breath. They had no idea that she and Heath were here.

Heath.

Tess suddenly realized that she sat flanked by Heath's muscular legs with her buttocks pressing deeply into the juncture between his thighs! She was glad for the darkness and for the fact that she was facing the door, as her face had to be as red as a tomato!

She swallowed, suddenly finding it hard to breathe.

If she'd had any doubt that he was sensitive to her shocking position, she only had to feel the evidence of his awareness pressing like a tipstaff into her lower back!

Her shoulders pressed against his hard, broad chest, his arms encasing her in a cocoon. She was overly warm, burning up from the intimate contact, achingly aware of every inch of his virile form. With his every heavy breath skating across her ear, she felt the desire rising up in her like a torrent. Her own breath felt locked in her throat as she tried to suppress her passion.

But she was overwhelmed.

She closed her eyes, suddenly unable to concentrate on the words being spoken outside the thin door. In the darkness, there was only Heath's body pressing enticingly against hers, the air heady with the earthy scent of him. Every hair on her body rose up with excruciating awareness of his maleness and his heat, igniting a desire in her she hadn't felt in years. It was a mind-scrambling honing of the senses that left her pulsing with need.

Oh God. She didn't know whether to be mortified or delighted that he was aroused, too. Or perhaps it was an involuntary reaction on his part? It was simply the situation, being pressed so close in a small space . . .

His hand slowly crept to encircle her waist, hugging her possessively. Her eyes flew open as her heart skipped a beat, and then thundered to a gallop.

Could he . . .?

Listening to his heavy breathing, and feeling the heat he emanated, she knew that he desired her. Perhaps as much as she wanted him!

His warm hand slid up her gown and cupped her breast. She bit her lip to quiet the cry aching to escape. Part of her was shocked. Part of her prayed that he would be bolder.

His hand kneaded the soft flesh of her breast. Her head fell back against his shoulder. She shifted against him, licking her lips and tasting desire.

His other hand moved to her thigh, singeing her with the contact. Of their own volition, her hips rocked, barely an inch, but his body tensed to iron and his member jolted with urgency.

His lips nibbled her ear, igniting a wave of yearning rushing through her. She sucked in a breath, the scent of desire thick in the air.

His fingers curled, clawing her gown upward, exposing her foot. Then her calf. Then her thigh. She swallowed, desperate for air. Her heart was pounding, her body aroused to a fevered pitch.

If that door opened, she would be discovered exposed on the floor of a darkened closet with a man she'd sworn would never touch her. But she couldn't think of that now. She closed her eyes and her mind to all thought.

With his fingers clawing the gown up, he was rewarded by the touch of silken stocking. She felt his breath seize in his chest. All her senses were focused on those roving hands.

His fingers skimmed up her calf, then over her thigh to the private place between her legs. Her heart was hammering, her body flushed with desire, the crevice between her thighs wet with wanting. He stopped, his hand big and warm, cupping her with urgent persuasion. She knew that he could feel her desire and know how desperately she wanted him.

Please don't stop. Please don't stop.

Gently his fingers slipped past her undergarments and between the folds of her womanhood. Her back arched and she bit back a groan as her body flamed like tinder.

His fingers delved into her sensitive flesh, stroking, gliding, playing, driving her mad . . .

She was on fire. She couldn't think, couldn't move, couldn't breathe. Her world coalesced into a swirl of colors, a plethora of sensations centered in her core.

Lost, she gripped his arms, holding on for dear life. Then she let go, falling, falling, falling . . .

"Did you hear something?" a voice called from very far away.

Heath tensed, halting his fingers.

Dazed, Tess opened her eyes in the darkness.

"You're so suspicious. There's no one here." It was the countess.

Tess's heart skipped a beat as realization dawned. Instinctively she closed her thighs, intimately wedging his hand between them. Her head swam and she bit her lip, trying to leash the desire surging through her.

"But I thought I heard something. From over there." A movement drawing closer. "What's in this closet?"

"My gardening gowns, the ones I won't be seen in. Why?"

"I thought—"

"You were the one insisting we make it back to the party posthaste, what are you going on about now?"

"Mistress!" a young woman's voice cried.

"Where have you been, Jane?" the countess demanded.

"I was helping downstairs like you'd instruct—"

"Oh, enough of this. I have a ball to host. See if you can repair this gown immediately."

"Yes, mistress."

"Come along, Miss Gammon. You're going to make nice with Lord Mares while I work on Lord Huntington. We've lost enough time as it is!"

Sounds of movement, then silence.

Tess exhaled, sagging against him.

"What now?" he whispered in her ear, his breath hinting of champagne.

Unable to speak, she didn't answer. Her body was still flaming, and she wanted him so badly, she ached.

"We . . . we should probably see if the coast is clear," he whispered.

She nodded, forcing her ardor to cool. At least he was keeping a clear head; there was still the possibility of being discovered.

Carefully Tess reached up and turned the knob, easing the door open a crack. Cool air rushed into the hot closet.

"They're gone," she murmured.

Heath's hands lifted her waist, helping her rise to her feet and dropping her skirts.

He stood, adjusting his breeches. "I think there's a lady's shoe up my arse."

"Was that what I was feeling?" She raised a brow.

"Much better—and bigger—than any lady's shoe . . ." His smile was wicked and his eyes blazed with passionate intent.

Hugging her waist, Tess withheld the wild laugh bubbling up inside her. She felt so good, so sinful, and the desire in his gaze was more intoxicating than any libation.

"The mistress wants the gown repaired posthaste!" a young feminine voice declared from the adjacent bedroom.

Footsteps neared.

"She wants everything posthaste. It's the only way she knows!"

Tess moved back toward the closet, but Heath had other ideas in mind.

Quickly Heath grabbed a voluminous shawl hanging on a peg and tossed it over their heads, covering them both. "Come on!" He pulled her out the dressing room door.

"What the—!" a female shrieked as they charged into the bedroom.

Tess spied something white flash as they ran. *My gloves! My reticule! Partway under the bed!*

Tess grabbed Heath's arm, making him stop and move back as she snatched up her gloves and reticule. All the while he kept them covered.

Had the countess seen her possessions? Probably not, or she would have searched the room.

"I'll give 'em credit for nerve, whoever those two are," the servant commented, seemingly unconcerned. "Having at it in the hostess's bedroom."

The rest of her words vanished as Tess and Heath raced out the door and down the corridor.

Tess giggled. Heath chuckled. Together they laughed, carefree and giddy, running as if the devil himself was at their heels.

Chapter 13

Heath was laughing and out of breath as he and Tess approached the ballroom once more. The sounds of the orchestra and the buzz of the crowd grew louder with each footstep.

As Heath dropped the shawl on a nearby table, he realized that joining the throng was the last thing in the world he wanted to do. Tess's nearness was a heady reminder of the intensity of her passion and the desire she inspired. And his member still throbbed with unrequited need. So instead of heading back into the very public ballroom, Heath steered Tess down a carpeted hallway away from the crowds.

Tess's blue gaze was questioning, but she silently followed his lead.

Heath opened the first door they came to. Upon seeing that the drawing room was empty, he gently propelled her inside. He closed the door, instantly muting the sounds of the orchestra and the hum of the crowd.

In the quiet room he turned to her.

Tess's skin was flushed, her blue eyes sparkling. Her hair was a wild mess of crimson curls and haphazard white pearls. Her peach-colored lips were parted, and her luscious breasts rose and fell with each breathless pant. She couldn't have looked more delectable.

He wanted her. Badly. More than any other woman, ever. He wanted to take Tess and make her his. The need was so great, he had little thought for anything else. He knew that he should be demanding answers about what she was doing in the countess's bedroom, knew that he shouldn't be allowing his passion to rule him. But she was so achingly close and the honeyed scent of her was so overwhelming.

He needed to touch her, taste her, feel her . . .

Tess stared up at him, wonder in her eyes, soon replaced by a hint of apprehension in the tense silence. Blinking, she turned away, scanning the room. "I must look a fright."

She moved to stand before the window and using the reflection, raised her arms to fix her hair.

Striding up behind her, Heath gently grasped her hands. "Don't."

Her hands stilled, coiled in his.

He could feel her confusion in her every intake of breath.

"Heath." She swallowed. "What happened back there . . . I think—"

"Don't." Spinning her to face him, he grabbed her

waist and drew her body to him. She was soft in all the right places. The scents of lavender and desire beckoned.

His lips curled into a smile. She was incredible. And she was about to be his.

His mouth lowered, but he hovered a mere inch from her lips, savoring the moment. The anticipation was almost as heady as touching her. Their breaths mixed and he inhaled her sweet scent.

Slowly his head lowered and he savored the taste of her. She was like wine: heady, sweet, and intoxicating. His tongue delved deeper, making love to her mouth as he'd so desperately wanted to do in that little closet moments before.

She clung to him, groaning slightly as her body melted into his.

Triumph surged through him. *She's mine!*

His hands roved, relishing the strength of her back, the lushness of her bottom. He kneaded the soft flesh, desire spiking through him, its urgency overpowering him. He had to have her. *Now.*

"Mr. Bartlett!" a distant voice called.

"Mr. Bartlett!" There it was again, nagging.

"Heath!"

Blinking, Heath opened his eyes. He tore his lips from Tess's, gasping for breath.

Solicitor-General Dagwood stood in the threshold, his face a dark mask of fury. "Finally! I was starting to wonder if I was going to have to call for the fire brigade!" Dagwood was incensed. His brows were lowered, his square jaw locked into a disapproving line, but it was his eyes that were most unsettling—they blazed like black coals of rage.

"Sir!" Heath's voice was a rasp.

"Remove yourself from that woman, at once!"

Heath was torn over what to do, but his respect for Dagwood and concern for Tess's reputation won out.

He slowly disengaged, unwrapping his arms from her but grasping her silky shoulders. She was a bit wobbly on her feet, but the sight of Dagwood glaring at her stiffened her spine. She went from supple softness to rigid iron in mere seconds. She was no longer the fiery woman he'd been kissing; her face closed and her lids hooded and she became as icy as her diamonds. If he weren't so shocked he would have been fascinated.

She moved away from Heath. His hand on her shoulders slid off with obvious reluctance. She gave Dagwood a long, hard stare, as if to say, *I'm not the least bit afraid of you*, then turned and stepped over to a side door. Not speaking a word, she opened the entry and slipped out without a second glance. The exit closed with a resounding thud behind her.

"Have you gone mad?" Dagwood stepped deeper into the room and jabbed his cane like a sword.

Straightening his clothing, Heath swallowed.

"Have you lost sight of everything we've worked for?" Spinning on his heel, Dagwood began to pace. "I thought more of you, man!"

Mortification washed through Heath; Dagwood's good opinion meant the world to him. And how could he explain? He knew better, but when Tess was near, it seemed hard to care.

Mayhap she was an enchantress.

Dagwood paced, his heels clicking on the hard wooden floors. "Granted, with a face like that and a shape like hers, she could charm the devil . . . but lust is not love, and it is no foundation for a marriage. For it *will* fail."

"Sir, I—"

"You've got a respectable, good girl to court, a chance at a real marriage with a strong future."

"I know. But—"

Shaking his head, Dagwood opened his hands. "Have you no thought for what that chit could cost you? She wears scandal like a second skin! She's trouble, through and through!"

From the other side of the doorway, Tess listened, and tears burned her eyes and spilled down her cheeks. But she wiped away the tears with the backs of her hands, impatient with her agony. She deserved it. She'd opened up to Heath, oh God, she'd been his for the taking. She was a stupid little fool. Scandal clung to her like rotten leaves in mud. She would forever be tarnished by her husband and all that society painted her to be.

"Start thinking with your other head, man!" Dagwood charged. "She'll only soil you and your reputation. Word is she caused Lord Berber's death and then her husband's."

Tess seethed with impotent anger at the terrible lie that wouldn't die.

"But even if the gossip isn't to be believed, the reality is that her husband was a double-dealing, cheating knave, and she had to know what kind of character he was when she married him."

Tess felt the mortification burn in its usual spot between her breasts. It lived there like a viper, ready to strike her at any moment. Yet at times like these the acuteness of its bite stole the breath from her throat. Dagwood was right: Tess should have known better. She should have been more discerning in choosing her mate. She's been so swept up in passion, so blind to Quentin's true character, so passively accepting of all that was happening to her . . .

She swallowed, angry with herself and Dagwood and . . .

Why wasn't Heath defending her? Or at least saying *something* useful? His silence was beginning to feel like condemnation.

Dagwood went on relentlessly, "Obviously she and her husband deserved each other. But for you to get trapped in her web like a greenhorn! Where's your sense, man? You're begging for a scandal! And at a time when you must preserve your reputation most assiduously!"

Leaning back against the hard wooden door, Tess tried to fathom what Heath might be thinking. He hadn't intended it to happen, any more than she. They were innocent really, if one considered good intentions. And they hadn't really gone that far . . .

Oh, whom was she trying to fool? It had been hot, salacious, and definitely scandalous! She just prayed that the solicitor-general would keep his mouth sealed. At the very least Heath should try to convince the man to keep quiet. Why wasn't he saying anything?

Moving closer to the crack in the door, Tess pressed her ear to the wood and listened.

"What were you thinking, man?" Dagwood cried.

"I wasn't," Heath finally spoke. "I lost my head."

"That's obvious! But you're supposed to be investigating the chit, not plowing her!"

Plowing me? She withheld a snort.

Investigating? She stiffened. Her heart began to race as the words sank in.

Swallowing her fear, she pressed her ear harder to the door.

"Nothing's changed," Heath assured.

"Except that you've lost sight of your goals."

"I haven't lost sight of anything, sir. The investigation is progressing. I am accepted at the Society for the Enrichment and Learning of Females. It's going well."

Heath's spying on me?

Her heart was beating so fast, her head swam. Her mind scrambled to keep up with the implications. She was being investigated. By officers of the Crown. The solicitor-general was in charge of an inquiry against her and it was being executed by Heath Bartlett, scheming betrayer.

The ramifications knocked the breath from her throat.

Could Heath know about her work for the Foreign Office? Why would the solicitor-general be scrutinizing the Foreign Office? Was it intergovernmental politics or something more sinister afoot? Or was it simply something personal to her? What in heaven's name had she done wrong to invite this examination?

Her heart raced. Her hands shook. Swallowing, she forced a quiet breath. Then another. She needed more information. Only with that could she understand how serious this truly was.

She pressed her ear so tightly against the door that it pained her.

Heath continued, "I'm looking into her business affairs . . ."

"And other affairs." Dagwood snorted.

Tess's anxiety spiked. *He's looking into my business affairs? What the blazes is going on here?*

She needed to talk to Wheaton.

But he was out of town! Away in the north, Reynolds had said. That left Reynolds as her only contact! The idea of confiding in him repulsed her; she couldn't trust him. Not with this. Reynolds was a muscle man, no tactician. Tess needed a strategist, someone who could think through the twists and knots of the legal implications and intergovernmental politics. Moreover, she was unsure of what Reynolds would do if she told him, especially what he might do to Heath.

But why should she care? Heath obviously had little concern for her welfare. The man was investigating her! For Lord only knew what purpose! The lying snake! He didn't deserve her concern!

She wanted to die for having tolerated his touch! And for allowing him to stoke the fires of her passion after it had long thinned to embers! Why, oh why, did it have to be *him* to finally resurrect her desire?

Tess gritted her teeth. She needed to put aside her feelings and understand the implications. More was at stake than her ruptured pride. An inquiry meant there could be a trial, a very *public* affair that would impact her activities for the Foreign Office. And, since now Tess was a woman who considered the worst possibilities, if she was found guilty . . .

There could be a *hanging*.

Tess ignored the chills of fear slithering up her spine and focused on her options. Wheaton was gone. She couldn't trust Reynolds. It was up to her to take matters into her own hands. To do what, she did not know, but she had faith that it would come to her. She just prayed that it did so quickly.

"I expect results, Bartlett," Dagwood chided. "I've staked my reputation on you! We cannot afford another scandal! We cannot afford anything less than success."

"Upon my honor, sir, your trust is not misplaced. I will see this matter to the end, and ensure that the guilty party is punished."

"See that you do."

Pushing away from the door, Tess strode across the book-lined library, intent on getting away as fast as she could. Apollo's horses couldn't get her home fast enough. She needed to think, needed to plan. She needed to prevent this investigation from harming her. That meant crafting a strategy to protect herself that would also safeguard her work at the Foreign Office, take care of her book business, and insulate the society.

And perhaps while she was at it she might find the time to plan a bit of revenge . . .

Chapter 14

It took all night for Tess to decide that Heath Bartlett was the link to all the answers. Oh, she'd come to it quite quickly, but then had talked herself out of it a thousand times before realizing that she wasn't *just* motivated by a thirst for revenge. She didn't *simply* hunger to use him as he'd used her. She didn't *only* want to hurt him as he'd injured her. Nay, since he was investigating her, he would know the underlying reasons for it, who had ordered it, if anyone beyond Dagwood was instigating the nasty business. He would also know who else might be under the scope of the investigation.

She should've known that there was more to Heath's attempts to join the society than a stupid little bet! He was spying on her. No wonder he'd followed her into the countess's bedroom! That whole business about worrying that she was meeting a lover had been a ruse! Oh, the actor! He should be on Drury Lane!

So this was why Heath had suddenly showed up

in her life again after ten long years! Had the meeting at Andersen Hall Orphanage been a charade? Was he supposed to play on their childhood relationship? Or perhaps on her guilt for having had his father sacked? Had any word that had dripped out of his forked tongue been remotely true? She wanted to scream for the indignity of having cried her heart out to the knave! Wanted to die for having allowed him to touch her as no man had done in years!

For the thousandth time she tried to shove away the mortification eating at her like a parasite. She forced her mind to focus. Heath Bartlett was the link to all the information she needed. She just had to break him.

But how to find out everything without him knowing he was disclosing the facts? How to uncover his information without him appreciating that she knew what he was about?

The first golden rays of dawn had speared through her chamber's curtains before the truth struck her with an intensity that had her popping straight up in the bed.

Passion. It was his weakness. It caused him to lose his head. He'd admitted so himself.

When it came to desire, he wasn't able to keep his eyes on his goals. When it came to matters of the flesh he was as weak and malleable as a newborn pup.

She would use this against him. Twist and bind him until he knew not which way he was headed.

And as a bonus, at the end of the matter, she would ensure that everyone knew of their affair. It would be the scandal of the season. It would destroy everything he'd worked for. His precious reputation would be in tatters. The priggish Miss Penelope Whilom would reject him. Hell, if Tess did a really bang-up job, his boss might actually sack him. His prized political career would be in the jakes.

The possibilities left her positively giddy!

Wheaton would be pleased.

The thought gave her a moment's pause. Wheaton was a cold-hearted bastard. Could she be the same? He was in a tough business. He'd been through countless challenges that she knew little about, except for his vague allusions. She supposed that it was the situations that had forced him to harden his heart, to stiffen his spine.

Well, she had no choice but to do the same.

An investigation by officers of the Crown was a serious matter. And it was personal. Heath had said that he was looking into her business affairs. Hers. And the fact that the Society for the Enrichment and Learning of Females was involved raised the stakes. Aunt Sophie, Janelle, Ginny, Edwina, Lucy . . . Too many people could get hurt.

It was up to Tess. Was she up to the challenge?

She had to be.

She had to be willing to do anything . . .

Anything . . .

Tess inhaled a shaky breath. Intellectually she understood that this meant seducing or allowing herself to be seduced by Heath. But in her belly, anxiety coiled like a viper. She was attracted to him. Annoyingly so. He was a good kisser . . . all right, a great kisser. Better than Quentin had ever been. And Quentin had been pretty darned good.

And those magical fingers . . .

Her insides stirred just thinking about them and what they'd done to her.

But still, could she pull it off? Now that she knew that he was a lying knave, could she suffer his touch without trying to scratch his eyes out?

Tilting her head, she considered the options.

Perhaps she should get foxed? That might ease her inhibitions. Shaking her head, she pushed aside the idea; she needed to keep her head clear. She could get *him* drunk. That was a nice possibility. Or better yet, what if Heath thought she was in her cups, but she actually wasn't? He would ask her questions and she would know what he wished to know.

Still, it all felt so . . . lewd and Delilah-like. It went against the grain, and she really didn't know if she was up to it. But she had to do something!

Rising, she called for her maid and prepared to dress. She would check on Fiona today at Andersen Hall Orphanage and see if anyone had been asking questions, and if so, about what. And while there, she would look into why Heath had been named as a trustee. An excellent start.

Was Andersen Hall involved? At this point, Tess wasn't willing to dismiss any possibility, no matter how remote.

Being there would also give her some time to think. Knowing Heath, he would likely try to speak with her this morning. Well, she would be conveniently absent.

Even though it was infantile, the idea pleased her just the same. Heath Bartlett definitely brought out the devil in her. Oh, how she'd love to stab him with a trident right in the rear!

She couldn't imagine how she would act, what she would say when she finally faced him. All she knew was that she was mad as hops and Heath Bartlett was going to pay.

At Andersen Hall Orphanage Tess was relieved to discover that no one had been asking Fiona about her business. The young assistant had been so shocked by the notion that she would ever discuss Tess's affairs with anyone that it had taken well over thirty minutes to soothe her injured feelings.

Tess felt exhausted by the exercise. But she'd still called on Catherine Dunn, Headmaster Dunn's daughter-in-law and now the mistress of the orphanage. Tess was motivated by more than her admiration for Mrs. Dunn, which was quite genuine. She wanted to know how Heath had been named to the orphanage's board of trustees.

The visit had been positively excruciating for Tess. She realized that her emotions were raw, like the frayed edge of a rope. Catherine Dunn was so madly, passionately in love with her husband, Major Marcus Dunn, that she positively glowed. It was utterly disgusting.

Tess knew that it was all an illusion set to burst at some point or another. But Major Dunn was a good sort, Tess had to admit. And so was his wife. Tess couldn't quite believe the sacrifices she'd made for Andersen Hall. In fact, Catherine Dunn's example gave Tess a nice idea for a small way to help out Andersen Hall Orphanage . . .

A feeling of goodness lifted her sprits a bit. Maybe charity was the way to help diminish her anger? But Andersen Hall was run by the *all male* board of trustees, *Heath Bartlett among them*! The conniving, manipulative bastard!

Catherine Dunn had known nothing about Heath's appointment to the board, leaving trustee matters to her husband.

Men. Why did they always have to be so blasted territorial? Often they acted more akin to wild dogs than civilized adults.

Her father shouldn't have taken out his rage on his innocent daughter. Quentin shouldn't have been a lying, cheating knave who stole her inheritance and left her penniless! He was beyond worthless—he was destructive! And that shamefully opportunistic Heath Bartlett! Grasping for more, using her to elevate his standing at the solicitor-general's office.

Tess made her way down the path toward the stables to take her leave.

Wears scandal like a second skin! She harrumphed, then tripped on the edge of her skirts.

Righting herself, Tess recognized that she was boiling mad, and as such, a bit unstable. Catherine Dunn had seen it and had asked what was wrong. Even the not very astute Fiona had noticed and asked if Tess was having difficulty with her "monthlies."

My monthlies! As if I don't have any other issues to challenge me! Nay, I couldn't possibly be dealing with a lying betrayer who rouses my passions and makes my insides melt like hot butter!

As the stables neared, Tess's heart began to race and her palms to sweat. She wasn't ready to face Heath, or anyone else for that matter. She needed to cool her emotions, find a way to steady her nerves. She needed to be alone, and find that inner calm that had always rescued her in times of need. For at the end of the day, she was the only one she could truly depend upon.

As if of their own volition, Tess's footsteps turned to the left and headed into the woods. There would be no reminders of Heath or her past or her father or Quentin in the quiet forest. There would be only Mother Nature welcoming Tess into her bosom and giving her the haven that she so desperately required.

Her boots made no sound on the blanket of moss and Tess listened to the birds chirping in the trees. A raven squawked. The air was crisp, but clearly spring was trying to gain a toehold on these woods. The trees were flush with buds and a hint of pine filled the air, along with the unmistakable scent of earth.

Tess scowled. Why couldn't Heath use one of those fancy scents like otto of roses or Hungary Water that smelled anything but natural? The man vexed, even out here in the copse!

Stepping onto the gnarled roots of an old oak tree,

Tess leaned back against the rough bark and inhaled a deep breath.

I need to be calm. There will always be someone to knock me down or put me out. The key is to be impervious. Not to allow anyone or anything to unsettle me. To accept and forgive myself for how I am and for whatever I've done, and ignore the lot of them. No one shall bother me. I am calm personified.

Slowly she sank onto the thick limb and stretched her legs out before her. Crossing her ankles, she inhaled a deep breath, then another. She closed her eyes.

Her heart slowed and her muscles relaxed. Her mind drifted, then cleared, like clouds splitting to reveal the glorious blue sky. A small smile teased her lips. She felt good. Calm. Powerful. In control once more. She wasn't going to let anything or anyone trouble her.

"There you are!" a familiar voice called.

Tess's eyes flew open.

Heath came storming down the path, his muscular legs eating up the distance between them like an invading army. His presence was authoritative, a commanding general leading the charge. His gray cape fluttered behind him like a standard, and his dark hair flew like ribbons.

As his black Hessians stomped up the path, he chatted idiotically, "Your butler informed me of where you'd gone and Mrs. Dunn saw you walking this way. It's a lovely day for a stroll, don't you think?"

Anger crashed over Tess like an avalanche. All

thought of calm and steadiness evaporated like mist after a summer rain.

At the look on her face, the smile fell away from his lips. "I can see that you're upset. And understandably so. Dagwood's interruption was a bit . . . inopportune . . ." His smile was self-effacing, and wholly insincere.

Tess jumped to her feet, her hands clenched, her anger at full boil.

He stopped mere inches from her. Too close for propriety.

The presumptuous bastard.

"Look, I know it was . . . dreadfully embarrassing. And, well, Dagwood wasn't very politic about it." He grinned as if he'd said something funny. "Dagwood not being politic. Who'd have ever thought?"

Fury consumed her. His face swam before her in a crimson haze, and she had no thought in her head save for how much she hated him. She actually quivered from the force of the fury pounding through her. Her teeth hurt from gritting so hard and her palms stung where her nails bit into them.

His made a face. "I know it's not amusing. I'm sorry about that. Dagwood coming in on us was dreadful actually. But it wasn't really so terrible, now was it?" His hands grasped her arms and he smiled down at her, his eyes questioning.

Her gaze fell to the hands gripping her upper arms. She looked up and snarled.

She felt the stinging burn as her palm met his face. His head jerked back but he didn't let her go.

Her hand lifted for another blow, but he grabbed her wrist. "Don't!"

Struggling against his viselike grip, she raised her other hand for another shot. He grabbed that one, too. Clenching her wrists like iron cuffs, he shook her. "Stop it!"

She growled.

Pulling her close, he hugged her, enveloping her in a prison of his arms. "Come on, Tess! Don't!"

She was panting, hard. His words and his hard body pressed against hers reminded her of the passion they'd shared. White-hot fury flashed, and she struggled against him.

But his grip was too strong. He hugged her close, his hard muscles encasing her in a cocoon of iron.

"Tess, please!"

She looked up at him then. "I hate you."

"Really?" he gritted out. "I'm not feeling so well disposed to you at the moment, either!"

"Release me!"

"Have you calmed down?"

"Enough."

After a long moment, he let her go. She stepped back and punched him in the chest so hard that her fist stung.

"What the blazes is wrong with you?" he cried, his hand pressed to his chest.

"You! I can't stand you. Or your touch!"

Reaching for her, he pulled her close. "Really?" He raised a brow.

His lips pressed down, crushing hers. It was like igniting a rocket inside her. The violence of her passion exploded, shocking her with its intensity. She quaked, overcome by the force of a primal need that only he seemed able to inspire.

Her mouth opened to his with a groan. Her body flamed. Her head swam. The red haze of her anger was gone, transformed into a scorching flame of desire that enveloped her in its fire.

His tongue delved into her mouth and she welcomed it, demanding more. Growling with the ferocity of her hunger for him, she bit his lip, tasting blood.

He jerked back, staring down at her.

She was panting, glaring at him, daring him to finish what he'd started.

His mouth claimed hers once more. There was no tenderness in his kiss, instead a stirring demand that she submit to their passion.

She clawed at the buttons of his coat, yanking them open and exposing the slit at the opening of his shirt. Closing her eyes, she licked the silky flesh, tasting salt and male.

He gasped. His body hardened to marble.

Suddenly his hands were everywhere, making haste with her coat and tossing aside her bonnet. His fingers raked her hair.

She groaned, wanting more. Much, much more.

Shoving her back up against the tree, he pushed his muscular thigh between her legs. The press of that hard muscle against her core caused a hunger to rise up from deep within her.

Her hands gripped his waist, tugging up his shirt

and finding the soft skin underneath. He sucked in his breath. Her hands roamed the silky flesh, teasing, gripping, caressing, and reaching down.

She touched him. He was thick and ready.

The rocket inside her burst once more, and she was overcome by the need to have him take her.

As if he was reading her thoughts, his hands wrenched at her skirts and made short work of her underclothes. She heard rips and tears but couldn't care. Nothing mattered but removing whatever lay between them.

His hands gripped the tender flesh of her buttocks, lifting her. Her legs spread, wrapping around his waist. Pulling her arms out from under his shirt, she coiled them around his shoulders, hanging on with her thighs and arms.

Somehow he managed to undo his breeches, for suddenly his hot, throbbing member was pressed along her inner thigh.

Eagerly she shifted, opening her innermost flesh to him.

He entered her with a deep thrust.

She hissed at the size of him, feeling stretched and full and so good, her head swam.

Closing her eyes, she was lost to the ferocity of his lovemaking. He plunged more deeply inside her, again and again, carrying her back to that place . . .

Her cry broke through her lips, shattering the silence.

His body shuddered. She felt his release deep inside her womb.

Spent, she clung to him, knowing that she could not stand, could not move, could not think. She was overcome, shaken to the core by their passion. And by the fact that she'd just made love to a man she despised . . . and it had never felt so good.

Chapter 15

Heath's heart was racing, his breath struggling, and his body quaking with the force of their lovemaking. He thanked heaven his legs were locked, or else he might have dropped right to the ground. When he inhaled a shaky breath, the scent of passion and lavender overwhelmed him.

She was relaxed in his arms, her head lying on his shoulder, her legs still wrapped around his waist. Her body was limp as a doll's, and she was as soft and light as one as well. With each inhalation of breath her lush breasts pressed into his chest and he could feel her heat and how gloriously tightly she cocooned him. Even now, as spent as he was, he felt himself stirring, and knew that it wouldn't be long before he'd be ready for her again.

She was incredible, and making love to her was even more amazing than he'd imagined. And he'd imagined a lot. He'd dismissed his fantasies as innocent, but now he knew there was nothing innocent whatsoever in how he felt about Tess.

She was enchanting. Like a mesmerizing spell that made him forget all else . . . The thought was unsettling . . . but he felt too blazingly good to care.

Swallowing, Tess lifted her head. With her lids still lowered, her lush, peachy mouth slightly puckered, and her flaming hair wild around her flushed face, she was breathtaking.

When she opened her eyes, her gaze was unfocused, as if she'd been roused from a long sleep. He knew the second her mind wakened to the reality of their situation; her crystal blue gaze sharpened, then skated away from him. Gently but firmly, she laid her palms to his chest and pushed.

Silently he helped her extricate herself from his body, immediately missing her extraordinary heat.

After adjusting her clothing, she moved to sit on a thick root, not once meeting his eye.

He repaired his clothing as best as possible and moved to stand by a nearby tree. The silence between them was deafening.

The implications of his actions crashed into him with a force that left him reeling. He ran his hand through his hair, disconcerted by her effect on him. To break the silence, he attempted a jest. "You're a witch. That has to be it. You've bewitched me like a wood nymph."

He looked up, hoping she'd laugh or scoff or anything to dispel the notion that she had such power over him.

Her already flushed cheeks tinged to a deeper shade of cherry. "I didn't ask for your touch. I didn't ask for . . . any of this."

He stiffened. "Are you saying that I forced myself upon you?"

She scowled. "Of course not. It's just, well, I didn't intend for this. I didn't . . . I don't want your attentions."

He fumed. He didn't like the effect she had on him, but to say that despite everything between them, she didn't want him! A woman couldn't feign *that* response. Not the heat, the wetness, the pulsing desire . . . He gritted his teeth, feeling his manhood stir.

"I just don't want you," she continued, almost as if to convince herself.

"Sorry to disappoint," he growled, feeling angry and nettled.

"Don't be daft. You didn't . . . disappoint." She licked her lips as if remembering the taste of him.

He resisted the impulse to pound his chest and crow. But just barely. Tess had a way of jabbing at his most basic apprehensions, like a hot poker to tender flesh. "I'm so glad I could be of service," he scoffed, reminded once more of the divisions between them during childhood.

"Stop taking this so personally—"

"You can't be any more personal than we just were!" Raking his hand through his hair, he wondered why he was bellowing.

"Calm down. I'm simply trying to tell you that we . . ." Her hand waved back and forth between them. "We are not meant to be."

"What? Can't have a man who doesn't have a title?"

Her eyes narrowed. "Don't be a dolt."

Gritting his teeth, he clenched and unclenched his hands, trying to get a rein on his anger. "You're right. We have no future. I didn't intend for this any more than you did."

"If you would only stop following me—"

"Following you?" he scoffed, looking away.

"At the society, around town, at the ball, and now here in the woods. Why do you keep pursuing me?"

Reaching for his fallen hat, he ignored the lure; he wasn't about to disclose the investigation. Not now, not ever. It was bad enough that his relationship with her was so . . . unusual. She was the target of his inquiry. He needed to get back on the trail. "This all started when I saw you go into the countess's bedroom. What were you doing there, anyway?"

"Actually, this all started when you came to the society making your application. And I'm not quite convinced that you didn't attempt to join simply to get near me." Was it a jest or was she digging? Her face was closed and he couldn't read her.

Scowling, he rubbed his eyes. "Don't be funny."

"I'm simply trying to decipher your motives. First there's the society. You trail me about. You seem very intent on being near me. And no matter what you tell yourself, I am not doing anything to entice you. The very opposite, in fact."

"You haven't answered the question: What were you doing in the countess's bedroom? You said that you weren't meeting a lover . . ."

"Maybe I lied. Since I'm such a seductress . . ."

"So I'm one in a line of how many?"

Her cheeks reddened. "It's been years since I've been with any man!"

Years. The fact made him feel like a conquering hero, but he didn't want to dwell on it. "And your husband died, what was it?"

She looked away. "Three years ago."

"So you think it'll be another few years . . .?"

She harrumphed, but gave no answer.

He had no idea what that was supposed to mean. He didn't want to think about what he wanted it to mean. But the idea of being with her again heated his blood and clouded his judgment, making him want to take her again. The mossy ground didn't look that hard . . .

"Aren't you engaged?" she asked, chilling his scintillating thoughts to wintry frost.

"We're not engaged. Yet. But you're right. I shouldn't be out here doing . . ." He swallowed, feeling his arousal like a beacon on a foggy night, beckoning him once more. "What we did."

"I daresay Miss Whilom is too well chaperoned for you to take such liberties . . ."

"I don't wish to discuss her with you." He dusted off his hat. "Unless you have another point?"

"I was just wondering what kind of woman you're seeking in a wife."

"Why? Are you applying for the position?"

"Heaven forbid. I'd rather cut off my own foot than marry again."

The silence stretched uncomfortably long. There

were undercurrents here that Heath didn't understand.

"Does Mr. Smith work with you at the solicitor-general's office?" she asked.

The change in topic took him by surprise. He looked up. "No. Why do you ask?"

"You two seem as thick as thieves. I wonder if it's because you conspire on projects together."

Was it he or were her word choices unusual? "We're always up for lending each other a hand. But no, we do not formally work together. Speaking of which, I don't know much about your business. It's the book trade isn't it?"

"Yes."

"Is there much money to be made in it?"

She raised a brow. "Do I ask you how much you earn in a year?"

"I'm a government employee; you can guess I don't earn much."

"Well I'm a private citizen and my business is just that, private." Her eyes glittered with challenge. "And please note that I do not appreciate anyone nosing about in my affairs."

Did she know about his inquiries? He'd been very subtle. Still . . . "Do you think I'm nosing about?"

"Are you?"

"No." The lie came easily. Self-preservation, he supposed. He didn't want to face Tess's wrath if she knew about his role in the investigation. Then again, she was livid right before they'd just . . . Again, desire wrapped itself around him like a noose he'd welcome.

"And just what do you do for the solicitor-general?"

He blinked, pulling himself back to the conversation. "Whatever he wishes me to do. I give counsel on matters affecting the Crown, such as debts to the Crown or thefts from the Crown. Answer questions involving public welfare. Pursue litigation in the interests of the Crown."

"So how is it that the solicitor-general got involved in the whole Beaumont affair?"

Heath made sure his face was impassive. "The solicitor-general can pursue certain prosecutions."

"What kind?"

"Exceptional prosecutions. Where the matter involves a grave miscarriage of justice."

"Or political ambition. Isn't that what happened with the Beaumont affair?"

"What's your point?" he ground out, suspecting that the little lady was a bit too sharp for his liking.

She shrugged. "I was just asking. It seems like you spend an inordinate amount of time *not* working these days, and I was wondering how your superior felt about this."

A small swell of relief washed through him; she was concerned about how he spent his time. It could be about the investigation, but possibly not. They'd just made love, and she was bound to think about future dalliances, wasn't she? He certainly couldn't wait to find the next opportunity.

He opened his hand. "The whole Beaumont thing left us feeling a little . . . burned. So I'm taking a bit of a respite, and do have some free time on my hands."

"So you like Solicitor-General Dagwood."

She didn't take the lure about the free time. He hid his frown. "I like Mr. Dagwood very much. Why the litany of questions?"

Those lovely shoulders lifted in a shrug once more. "I'm simply trying to understand."

"Understand what?"

"You."

"Why? Do you intend to further our relationship?" Although he made it sound like a jest, hope floated within reach.

That crystal blue gaze fixed on him, and for a moment he felt as if he were under a magnifying glass. "Perhaps." Pushing an errant crimson curl from her face, she looked away.

He knew he shouldn't allow this affair to go one step further, but he couldn't help the spark of excitement within him. "So what now?" *When can we next meet?*

"Perhaps we should simply pretend it never happened?"

His mouth dropped open; he was so appalled that she could disregard the greatest sex of his life. "You can do that?"

She grimaced. "No, I suppose not."

"I'm being serious."

She looked to the left, her brow furrowed. "Did you hear that?"

"Hear what?"

"It sounded like a twig breaking. Over there." She pointed to a thick oak tree.

"You don't have to pretend to hear something to avoid the issue," he grumbled, irritated with her, but more so with himself for caring.

"I'm not pretending. I really thought I heard something."

"Well, I didn't hear a thing."

"I swear I thought . . ." Tess muttered. "Well, just so you know, I don't need to feign an excuse to avoid a question . . ."

From behind a nearby tree, Fiona drove her back against the scaly bark, her heart racing, her breath locked in her throat. She shouldn't have pressed her luck and moved so close. But she'd been so fascinated, and more than a bit shocked by the whole scene.

Letting out a little breath, Fiona carefully pushed herself away from the tree and deeper into the next shadow.

As she slinked through the woods, the rest of the words were lost to Fiona, but she didn't care. She'd seen and heard more than enough.

Fiona was thankful for the thick moss that hid her footfalls as she scurried back toward the orphanage. The cries of the birds masked her departure as well.

As she skirted the path and headed back to the main building, her mind was filled with the images of Tess and Mr. Bartlett and what they'd done. She couldn't quite believe that her employer could be so . . . depraved. Or the seeming gentleman Mr. Bartlett so . . . barbaric. Her cheeks heated as she recalled their bawdy act in intimate detail.

She consoled herself with the fact that it was so enthralling because it was so wicked. Her fascination was a natural reaction to such an unnatural act. And there was the fact that she needed to memorize every detail. Every action. Every utterance.

For her contact would accept nothing less.

Chapter 16

"What the devil's the matter with you?" Bills exclaimed the next day as the two men walked to the society for the Enrichment and Learning of Females. "You've got your head so high in the clouds I couldn't even reach you with a kite! What's on your mind?"

"Nothing," Heath lied, his thoughts filled with the memories of Tess's head thrown back, her cries of passion, and the feel of her body wrapped around his. Though he'd bathed, her scent still lingered in his nostrils like a heady perfume, and her sweet taste made his lips feel branded by her kiss. His body thrummed with the need to have her again, to mark her as she'd marked him.

He'd never experienced anything like this, where the coupling haunted him like a dream from which he couldn't wake. And Lord, how he didn't want to wake from this luscious fantasy! This morning life had kept encroaching on Heath in the form of his manservant, his messages, his breakfast, when all he'd wanted to do was lie in his bed reliving the fantasy of Tess. But to the rest of world, this morning was the same as every other morning when Heath had risen at dawn ready to attack the day.

What was happening to him?

And was she similarly affected?

"I beg to differ." Bills intruded on his thoughts once more. "You're acting like a lovesick pup."

Glaring at a reckless hackney driver, Heath scowled. "I am not! I haven't mentioned Tess the entire afternoon!"

Satisfaction flashed in Bills's perceptive gaze. "So you admit it. Lady Golding has caught your eye."

"She hasn't caught anything of mine." Heath kicked at a stone in the walkway. Had she caught him? Ensnared him like a fly in a web?

"I've been known as a bit of an observant fellow a time or two, and what I'm seeing is quite fascinating."

Heath licked his lips, trying not to be distracted by the memories. "What are you observing?"

"You're preoccupied, short-tempered. The only time you perked up was when I suggested we go to the society for females. And I wonder who it is you wish to see?"

Heath's cheeks warmed as he veered his eyes from Bills's shrewd gaze. "It's very simple, I didn't sleep well last night." Oh, the dreams he'd had . . .

"But yesterday were closing arguments in the Blumenthal trial and not only did you not attend, but you didn't even ask about it!"

Heath blinked, shocked that he'd missed it. He

wasn't required to be at the trial, but he'd made a point of being present at every notable case. To see what was happening and to be seen. It was politically prudent and kept him in the forefront of any news. How had he missed that?

"I think Lady Golding has gotten under your skin," Bills surmised.

Evading a mangy dog, Heath increased his pace. "Bollocks."

"You've no better answer than that?" Bills inquired, stepping up quickly alongside him. "The great orator finding no words?"

"Shut your trap, Bills."

Waving his cane, Bill flashed a gratified smile. "I'm just glad you're finally realizing that Miss Whilom isn't the lady for you."

Heath barely slowed his pace as he crossed the street, dodging carriages and horses. "I never said that."

"But you've slept with Lady Golding."

Heath's boot toe jammed the curb and he almost fell but righted himself. Making a business of adjusting his coat, he muttered, "I never said that, either."

"You didn't have to."

Heath looked up.

Bills pulled Heath out of the way of a passing horse and rider. "Look, I'm the last man to berate you about it. I'm simply trying to point out that you're better off with Tess."

"With a woman who wears scandal like a second skin?" Heath quoted Dagwood, but the words felt ugly on his tongue and he regretted them immediately. "I don't mean that. She's just . . ."

Infuriating? Breathtaking? A seductress?

His hand traced his cheek where she'd struck him. Had it all been a ruse? Nay, she'd been livid. But about what? About Dagwood finding them, probably. She hadn't overheard anything, had she? He'd checked the door she'd gone through right after Dagwood had left. The room had been blessedly empty. Still, what had set her off like that? And could he do it to her again . . .?

"What is she?" Bills asked, pulling Heath's thoughts back to the present. Bills was right; he was astoundingly distracted today.

Meeting his friend's gaze, Heath shook his head. "I hardly know."

"Do you think she wishes to marry you?"

Heath snorted. "She's sworn off it."

"Ladies are wont to change their minds. More importantly, do you wish to marry her?"

"Tess is not the kind of lady one marries."

"Then she's the perfect kind of lady to bed."

Scratching his chin, Heath tried to unscramble his thoughts. "She's not for me. I want to settle down. Have a family."

"Are you trying to convince me or yourself?"

Gritting his teeth, Heath growled, "I know what I want. I want a family. A secure future. A good life."

"No scandal to sully your name . . ."

"Definitely no scandal. My father tainted our family enough with his exploits."

"Exploits? You usually call them misjudgments."

Anger filled him. "Whatever you call them, he did us a disservice, one I will not visit upon my own children."

"So his affairs reflected poorly on you."

"At least my mother wasn't alive to see it. But I was always the lad whose father had taken liberties with his betters." Heath snorted. "His betters. As if they weren't jumping into the bed with him."

"Speaking of beds, I'm curious, was Lady Golding as good as she looks?"

Glaring, Heath didn't bother to answer.

Bills didn't even look chagrined. "Very well, then, don't tell me. But do you still think she stole Belington's blunt?"

Scratching his ear, Heath brought his mind back to the investigation. "I don't know. I know she's up to something. Her husband squandered her dowry and her entire inheritance, the bugger. He left her barely outpacing the constable. Then her father cut her off when she refused to marry his nephew."

"So she's without resources."

"She's got her book business. But it's hard to imagine it supporting her in the life she lives."

"Perhaps it's all a sham? I mean, it's been know to happen where the upper classes serve champagne in the front room while the back rooms go without two sticks to make a fire."

"I need to get inside her house to know for sure."

"Oh, so now you need an excuse?"

Heath grimaced. "It would probably be better if

she wasn't there so I could get a good look around."

"I disagree. Exhaust her. Make love to her until her knees are too weak to stand. Then go about your duties. It's the way to do it."

Heath smiled, imagining the pleasure of executing such a plan. Seducing her was a delightful idea, but for ulterior motives? He wasn't so sure he could do it. Still, he could go with the first half of the plan and figure out the rest later. His body hardened at the thought.

"But she may not be very cooperative. She wasn't exactly happy about the whole thing."

Bills frowned. "I'm disappointed in you, man. You should be more disciplined; please her, then yourself."

Disciplined was not exactly how he would describe himself when he was with Tess. Still, recalling her passionate cries and the feel of her wrapped around him, Heath rubbed his chin. "She was well satisfied. No doubt about it."

"Then what's the problem?"

Heath shook his head. "She didn't seem to want it . . . I mean me, any more than I'd thought I'd wanted her."

"That makes no sense. Either you want her or you don't."

"I don't want to want her. I want to want Penelope."

"Really?" Bills's gaze was disbelieving. "Who wants cod when you can have *filet de bœuf*?"

"Please don't compare Penelope to a fish."

"A bland, white fish, no less."

"And I can't marry a steak, no matter how tender."

"As you said yourself, she's not interested, so wedding bells don't enter into the matter."

"How many times do I have to tell you? I want to settle down. That means marriage."

"Then I posit to you that you *need* this little affair to be able to sustain yourself for the long famine to come." Raising a hand, Bills asserted, "I know you, once you give your word, you won't stray, heaven help you. So you need this, my friend. Badly. Then off you go to marry your Miss Whilom. You have your cake or cod or whatever, and eat it, too."

Heath liked Bills's logic. Thanks to Lady Bright's machinations, Heath hadn't given Penelope his word yet. So technically he was free to do as he wished. But for all his justifications, Heath somehow doubted he'd be able to stay away from Tess, regardless. It would be like swimming against a powerful tide when all he wanted to do was float along with it.

"A last fling, huh?"

"Exactly. But I'm not clear on why you think she won't be interested in another swing."

"There's more to her than meets the eye. She's hiding something. There's no doubt about that."

"So what better way to loosen her tongue than to butter her up with a little pleasure?"

Patting his friend on the back, Heath nodded. "There's a reason I seek your advice, my friend."

"Seek?" Bills snorted.

"Well, there's a reason I take it."

"Because I tell you what you wish to hear?"

Heath smiled. "That, too."

Chapter 17

"**S**o how do I ascertain Heath's true purpose?" Tess asked Janelle over tea as they sat in the society's front drawing room. Tess knew she was really at her wits' end if she was asking Janelle for advice. But to give the matron credit, she had a mind almost as Machiavellian as Wheaton's. She wasn't mean or wicked, just wily. And Tess desperately needed help right now, and wily would do.

The incident at the orphanage had proved that Tess couldn't use passion against Heath any more than she could jump the English Channel. Desire was a double-edged sword that cut her deeply. When he touched her she couldn't think, couldn't scheme. Heavens! She could hardly remember to breathe.

"I'd use Lucy to soften him up and then drink to loosen his tongue," Janelle advised with a sniff, pouring herself another cup of tea.

Tess blinked, bringing her mind back to the point. "Mr. Bartlett?"

"No, his friend Bills. He's the loose boulder."

"Loose boulder?"

Janelle rolled her eyes. "Easily toppled. The other one, Bartlett, is too quick and too guarded."

Tess leaned forward, excited about an option she hadn't considered. "You think he'll talk?"

"Bills likes to please. And he's got a *tendre* for Lucy."

From across the room, Lucy looked up from her writing table and made a quizzical face.

"You can stop pretending that you're not listening and join us." Janelle sniffed.

Shrugging, Lucy stood, strolled over to the table, and selected a fruit tart from the platter. As she nibbled on it, a bit of crumb stuck to the corner of her lip.

"You have . . ." Tess motioned to her mouth.

Lucy licked it and then nodded her thanks.

Seemingly irritated by the interruption, Janelle motioned to the young widow. "As I was saying, Bills follows you around like a lost pup. He's besotted and you know it."

Lucy smiled, seemingly not displeased by the situation.

"Are you willing to help me, Lucy?" Tess asked the doe-eyed widow.

Shoving the last bit of tart into her mouth, Lucy moved over to the secretary and scratched a note. After a moment, she handed it to Tess, who read aloud, "'Why don't you believe them about it being a wager?'"

"I'm not saying that I don't," Tess lied. "I simply

want to be sure. It's to protect the society." That much was true. "I don't want them making a mockery of us and the work that we do." *Nor do I want them upending my affairs or my life.*

She still hadn't figured out what they could be investigating, and Wheaton, blast him, was still out of town. It wasn't a bad idea to find out more before she involved him and Reynolds, anyway. Reynolds in the meantime had requested a meeting, but Tess had ignored the request and had sent a note instead, saying that she had nothing to report.

She needed more time. And more information.

Besides, no matter what Wheaton said about grooming Reynolds for bigger responsibilities, Tess didn't trust his judgment and felt better relying on her own, with a little help.

For now, at least, she had some measure of control of what was going on. Once she told Reynolds or Wheaton, she'd be expected to follow orders. And when it came to Heath Bartlett, Tess wasn't sure what orders she'd be willing to execute. He had her tied up in knots, not knowing which way was right.

In the earliest hours of the dawn, as she'd lain awake in bed, she'd forced herself to rake up every last memory of Heath from childhood, trying to decipher the enigma he'd become.

One astonishing memory had surfaced that she'd completely forgotten until now. It had been a Sunday morning, the first when she would be allowed to sit next to her father in church. She'd sworn to sit still, not to hum under her breath as she was wont to do, and to behave the perfect little miss. She'd felt like a princess in her new pink gown and matching bonnet with fancy frills and lace.

As she'd stood waiting outside by the front entry, something had splattered against the wall just inches from where she was standing. She'd been so shocked, it had taken her a few moments to grasp that her wretched older brother Timothy had launched a mud ball at her. It was only Heath knocking aside Timothy's arm at the last moment that had saved Tess's dress, and her vulnerable feelings. Timothy had tried to cuff Heath for ruining his aim, but Heath had been too quick, and a chase had ensued.

Father had come outside just then, and he'd blamed Heath for inciting the incident. Heath had been sent off to perform additional chores for his infraction. Timothy had been loaded up in the carriage and got to sit beside Father for the morning service. Tess sat on her father's other side.

And now that lad who'd so kindly saved a young girl's feelings was investigating her and could ruin her life. Moreover, he ignited a scorching passion within her she hardly recognized. She couldn't recall that coupling in the woods without her skin tingling and a primal heat warming her in very private places. It was exasperatingly disconcerting. She shifted uncomfortably.

Tess felt something in her hand and looked down. Lucy had written another note.

Collecting herself, Tess read aloud, "'I don't think Bills would do that. Why would he lie?'" She looked up. "I'm not saying he is lying. I just want to be sure. Will you help me?"

After a moment, Lucy shrugged and then nodded.

"Thank you." Tess turned to Janelle. "So what do you propose?"

"Lucy sends him a message asking for a quiet drink together to talk."

Lucy made a face.

Rolling her eyes, Janelle waved a dismissive hand. "You know what I mean."

"We set out a decanter of some of that fancy brandy to loosen his lips."

Lucy made a motion, then scratched a quick note.

"'He prefers port,'" Tess read, then smiled. "You really like him, don't you, Lucy?"

Looking away, Lucy lifted a shoulder, but her cheeks had turned pink. She wrote, "I like his stories."

"Well, then port should get them rolling," Janelle interjected.

Lucy scribbled another note that Tess read, "'He has a fine sense of humor, too. Does his friend?'"

Tess frowned. "He used to. Now, I'm not sure." They hadn't spent much time talking; they'd been too busy with . . . other matters. She knew a fair amount about his earthy scent, his hands, his mouth, how his hard—

"Are you all right, Tess?" Janelle's gaze was keen. "You seem flushed."

Coughing into her fist, Tess looked away. "I'm fine. You were saying that . . . what were you saying?"

"Bills is the means to obtaining the answer. He's an

easier target than Bartlett. Bartlett's polite. Kind, even. But you won't get him to talk. He's too stiff-lipped."

His lips were anything but stiff. Tess recalled their smooth feel and how they'd ignited her slumbering passions to a scorching fire that she couldn't seem to contain. Desire kept flaring up, reminding her of how good it could be. She hungered for another taste, longed for that passionate elixir . . . all the while knowing that it was poison. Knowing that it could only lead to trouble. Knowing that he was using her. That it was Miss Penelope Whilom he would marry. Miss Penelope Whilom to whom he would give his name.

Not that she wanted his name. But still, she wouldn't mind if he'd *wanted* to give it to her. But what he was willing to do was probably in pursuit of his investigation.

Oh, he desired her. There was little doubt of that. They had a natural attraction, one that she would recognize if they'd been strangers meeting in a desert. It was a potent thing, hard to come by and harder yet to ignore.

Tess forced herself to remember the grave mistakes she'd made with Quentin. How her passion and naiveté had blinded her to his true nature. On top of that there was that one big mistake. She couldn't think of the terrible blunder she'd made the year after Quentin's passing without her stomach clenching.

Lucy shoved a note into Tess's hand, bringing her back to the present. Tess read aloud, "'So what happens after Bills comes for the drink?'"

Janelle waved a hand. "Tess, you meet with him instead of Lucy. You tell him that Lucy likes him, but that she worries about his motivations. Then see what he says. Get him to talk. Then we'll know."

"Know what?" Aunt Sophie asked from the doorway. Her slate gray hair was tucked neatly into a pink bonnet with blue ribbons that perfectly matched her blue gown. The color complimented her pale skin and brightened her dove gray eyes.

"Aunt Sophie! What a treat. I haven't seen you in days. How's Aunt Matilda feeling?" Tess rose.

Aunt Sophie planted a dry kiss on Tess's cheek. "Better, thank the heavens. She sends her love." Turning to the others, she smiled. "Hello, Janelle, Lucy."

The ladies made appropriate sentiments of gladness and welcome. Tess was pleased that her aunt was so well liked; she knew how much the society meant to her. A fresh resolve filled Tess. She had to find out Heath's intentions and ensure that nothing tainted the society or its members.

Folding her hands before her, Aunt Sophie sighed. "So what has you three so engrossed? You look like a group of ministers attending a Privy Council meeting."

Tess's skin prickled as if touched and heat warmed her shoulders. She was being watched, and she knew, without doubt, by whom.

Once she turned, she would see those brawny shoulders that she'd clung to, those large hands that had performed wonders on her body, and those smooth lips that she'd tasted with hunger. Her belly fluttered with nerves and delicious anticipation.

Chiding herself for being the fool, she fixed her face to appear calm and turned.

The force of Heath's gaze scorched her from across the room. Heat and promises reflected in his eyes evoked an instant spark of recognition inside her.

The very air between them was charged with the current of their desire. He wanted her as badly as she wanted him. Her head swam, her insides warmed, and she braced herself on the arm of the chair to support her weakened knees.

Beaming, Janelle waved a hand. "Ah, Mr. Bartlett, Mr. Smith, just the men we've been waiting for."

Heath pulled his gaze from Tess's, and she felt shattered by the broken connection.

"It can't be . . ." Aunt Sophie whispered, raising her hand to her mouth. All color drained from her face.

Then she wilted to the floor.

Chapter 18

"Aunt Sophie!" Tess crouched down beside her aunt, her chest constricting with fear. Her aunt had never fainted and she'd hardly been sick a day in her life! She was one of the hardiest people Tess had ever known. In fact she used to secretly ridicule ladies who would fall into a faint at the slightest provocation, calling them "lilting willies" instead of wilting lilies.

"Get back!" Janelle brandished her hands at the hovering crowd.

"Who has smelling salts?" Heath stepped forward and crouched down beside Aunt Sophie.

"I do!" Janelle cried, but at the look on everyone's face, she frowned. "Not for me, you fools, but for occasions just like this."

Heath grabbed the salts and squatted down, opening the small vial and holding it under Aunt Sophie's nose.

Aunt Sophie's nostrils twitched and she blinked rapidly.

Tess pressed her hand to her chest as relief washed over her. "Are you all right?"

Aunt Sophie's eyes widened. "Oh my. Please tell me that I didn't faint."

"It happens sometimes," Heath replied calmly. "Don't sit up just yet. Wait a moment to get your senses back."

"My senses are just fine," Aunt Sophie murmured, adjusting her bonnet. "Please."

Heath held her arms and assisted her to stand on one side while Tess helped on the other.

Releasing Tess, Aunt Sophie patted her hair. Her cheeks were flushed. "I'm all right. Thank you. I simply . . ." Her eyes flitted to Heath and then away. "Well, I fainted. What can I say?"

Tess placed her hand on her aunt's back, unwilling to let her go just yet. "Can I get you something? The tea is likely cold by now, but you should drink something, I think. It's good to do that after a faint, isn't it?"

"You've never fainted a day in your life," Aunt Sophie chided, obviously embarrassed.

Tess lifted a shoulder, wanting to help in some way. "It can't be a bad idea, though."

"Must you always have a suggestion?" Aunt Sophie's tone was sharp. "Sometimes things just need to be left alone."

Hurt, Tess pursed her lips, not understanding the signals from her aunt.

Mr. Smith handed Aunt Sophie a cup of tea.

"Thank you. But I do wish that you would all stop

making such a fuss. I got a bit light-headed, that's all."
Aunt Sophie smiled at Mr. Smith. "And whom do I
have the pleasure of thanking?"

He bowed. "Mr. Smith at your service. But everyone calls me Bills."

Aunt Sophie nodded. "Lady Braxton. Pleased to
make your acquaintance."

Glad for the veneer of normalcy, Tess motioned to
Heath. "I don't know if you remember him, but this is
Heath Bartlett, Mr. Henry Bartlett's son—you remem-
ber, our former tutor."

Aunt Sophie's cheeks reddened. "Ah, yes, I *vaguely*
recall a Henry Bartlett."

Tess could tell that her aunt was lying and suddenly
suspected that her aunt knew more about the incident
with Mr. Bartlett and her mother than she'd let on.

"Your father was from Beverley, was he not?" Aunt
Sophie asked.

Heath inclined his head, since obviously it was
hard to bow while he was still holding Aunt Sophie's
arm. "Yes. I'm surprised you remember. It is a pleasure to see you again, Lady Braxton. I trust that you
are feeling better?"

Aunt Sophie's hand flapped around her flushed
face. "Uh, very much, thank you. It was a silly little
nothing. I'm usually quite resilient."

Tess's eyes narrowed. Her aunt's voice was high
and she was acting oddly. Had she hit her head? Her
normally pale skin was very pink. Was she ill? Maybe
a visit from Dr. Winner was in order.

Aunt Sophie beamed up at Heath, her eyelashes

fluttering. "I must say, there's a benefit to fainting if there's a handsome man around to catch you."

Heath smiled. "It'd be my pleasure to catch you any time you feel woozy, Lady Braxton."

"How gallant of you."

Tess realized that her aunt was leaning on Heath. "Do you feel dizzy, Aunt? Do you still feel light-headed?"

"I'm fine, really, dear." Aunt Sophie replied without looking Tess's way.

"I think we should call for Dr. Winner, just in case."

"Oh, nonsense, dear. I'm fine." Aunt Sophie's tone had taken on an edge. "I really am feeling quite recovered."

"Oh. Well, ah, did you receive my letter about the plans for Uncle Jack's party?"

Aunt Sophie's eyes veered away. "I did. Thank you, but I'd prefer to discuss it another time."

Looking to Aunt Sophie, Heath motioned to a nearby chair. "Shall we?"

"The chaise," Aunt Sophie directed. "The one by the window, if you please." Her lips quivered. "So tell me, Mr. Bartlett, how is it that you've come to grace our little society?"

Feeling useless and rejected, Tess did not follow as Heath led her aunt to a narrow chaise and sat down beside her.

Moving to stand alongside Tess, Mr. Smith murmured, "Oh, don't feel badly. It's a little flirtation, nothing more."

Tess blinked, confused. "What? You think . . .?"

"Even I can recognize that he's shockingly hand-some. She'll flutter her lashes a bit. Feel a bit of her youth. It's harmless."

"Flirt? My aunt Sophie? You must be mistaken." Involuntarily Tess's gaze shifted to her aunt and Heath. Aunt Sophie was *fluttering her eyelashes!* And to make matters worse, she was leaning forward, giggling, touching her hair . . . doing everything to prove Mr. Smith's words to be true!

"I can't believe it," Tess muttered. "Here I am terri-fied that there's something wrong with her and she's acting the coquette!" Tess tried to ignore the little pinch of jealousy in her heart. This was her dearest aunt, for heaven's sake!

Mr. Smith leaned forward conspiratorially. "Don't worry, if you still want him, he's yours."

Tess gasped aloud.

All eyes turned to Tess, and silence descended in the salon.

She offered a weak smile. "Uh, I . . . just . . . uh, had a tickle in my throat . . ."

After their attention had seemed to wane, Tess turned to Mr. Smith. "What the blazes are you talking about?" she whispered.

"You and Bartlett."

"There is no 'me and Mr. Bartlett.'"

"That's not what it looks like from my vantage point."

She crossed her arms. "Did he say something to you about me?"

"Nay. The man's a steel trap; he never lets on about anything. This is all from observation. The attraction between you two is quite palpable."

Opening and then closing her mouth, Tess had no response.

Mr. Smith shrugged. "He's a fine fellow, even if he does have an overblown sense of ambition. But who can blame him? I mean, look what happened to his father."

Uneasy, she uncrossed her arms. "What do you mean?"

"The man never had a care for his career. From what little Bartlett says, I get the impression that his father was brilliant and could have gone quite far in academics or any other avenue he chose, but . . ."

"But what?"

Mr. Smith's shoulders lifted in a shrug. "The man tends to have 'lapses in judgment,' as my friend likes to call them."

"What do you call them?"

"Indiscretions."

"Affaires?"

"Yes, and often with the wrong kind of ladies."

"His employers' wives?"

Mr. Smith's face was apologetic. "Yes. But I must add that the elder Mr. Bartlett seems a perfect gentleman, so I daresay his attentions only fix when he's duly invited."

"Duly invited." Tess snorted. *My mother was an idiot to have risked her family so.*

"As a result Heath's prospects were somewhat diminished and he had to scrape for every bit he's gotten. And I daresay he never traded on his good looks. I've never met the elder Mr. Bartlett; does Heath resemble him much?"

"I think so." As Tess's gaze shifted to Heath, she realized that the attributes that she'd never noticed in her tutor, Mr. Bartlett, were the very ones with which she was becoming obsessed in his son. Those strapping shoulders, large hands, and cocoa brown eyes were treacherous traps for the unwary. Having succumbed, Tess was finding it hard to regret it.

Had her mother been similarly affected? If she'd been discontented, lonely . . .

Tess shook her head, not wanting to understand.

Mr. Smith scratched his ear. "All I'm saying is that Heath has worked hard not to follow his father's model. He wants more for himself. More for his children. He wants a solid career and a respectable reputation that's not tainted by whispers."

"That counts me out," Tess muttered under her breath. *I wear scandal like a second skin.* Her cheeks heated with anger.

"Not necessarily."

Tess looked up. Her eyes narrowed. "What are you about, Mr. Smith?"

"He wants respectability, but I don't think he realizes that it's not all it's cracked up to be. It's certainly not worth all the fuss it requires."

"I don't understand. Don't you want your friend to get all he wishes for?"

"Of course I do. Just not necessarily in the way he wishes to procure it."

Tess's eyes widened. "You don't like Miss Whilom."

"I didn't say that."

She couldn't keep her lips from lifting into a smile. "You think he's making a mistake."

Mr. Smith raised a shoulder. "It's been known to happen."

A swell of relief interlaced with victory warmed her chest. But that made no sense. She didn't want to marry Heath Bartlett, any more than she could be the perfect respectable wife to him. They didn't suit. "Why are you trying to toss him my way, Mr. Smith?"

"To give him some perspective. A comparative scrutiny, so to speak."

Nay, the idea of marrying Heath was too incredible to be considered, so Tess rejected it outright. She straightened. "I am not a scientific experiment. Nor do I have any interest in your friend. We knew each other once; now we are adversaries." End of discussion.

"Adversaries? Don't you think that's a bit severe?"

Swallowing, Tess cursed her traitorous tongue. "In the bet, I mean. You will not make a mockery of this society. I won't let you. I will win that wager."

Tess noticed that her aunt had excused herself from Heath's company and had exited the salon. Wanting escape, Tess turned to Mr. Smith. "If you would excuse me."

He nodded. "Be kind. She's just being a female."

Tess stopped short. "What the devil does that mean?"

"She can't help but flirt; it's in her nature to be absorbed with men."

Shaking her head, Tess snorted and then followed her aunt out of the room.

Chapter 19

As her aunt headed down the hallway, Tess hurried to catch up. "Aunt Sophie!"

Her aunt's steps slowed and she turned with obvious reluctance. "Yes, dear?"

Stopping before her, Tess scrutinized her aunt's face. "Are you all right? Really?"

"I'm fine."

"Then were you flirting with Heath Bartlett?"

Aunt Sophie's cheeks flushed pink.

"You were!" Tess cried, appalled that Mr. Smith could see what she'd been blind to, and even more disgusted that he had ammunition that supported his pigheaded notions about women.

Aunt Sophie's eyes scanned the empty hallway, and then she led Tess into an empty reading room. After closing the door, she turned. "It was an innocent little nothing. Don't make much of it."

"But he's practically my age!"

"It wasn't about him. It had more to do with . . . me."

Tess was taken aback. "What's going on with you?

I've never known you to flirt a moment in your life. You and Uncle Jack had the most solid of marriages. And you never faint. Are you sure you're not sick? Dizzy? Shall I call for Dr. Winner just in case?"

Sighing, Aunt Sophie grasped Tess's hand. "I'm fine. I just . . . well, I'm finally beginning to accept the fact that Jack is dead."

"Oh." Tess swallowed. "Go on."

"And, well, I'm *not* dead."

Tess squeezed her aunt's hand. "Thank heavens."

"I'm forty-nine years old, Tess. I was married for twenty-seven years to the love of my life. I like . . . I like being with a man. I like . . . having a partner."

Tess ignored the uneasy twist in her belly pertaining to her aunt's choice. "What does this have to do with Heath Bartlett?"

Aunt Sophie wrung her hands. "You'd not believe me if I told you."

"Try me."

"Well, I was recently starting to . . . think about certain things . . ."

"Men," Tess supplied, irritated once more that Mr. Smith had been correct. In this instance, at least.

"Yes. And, well, I was starting to ponder this quite a bit. Imagining what kind of man I might like to . . . be with. I don't envision getting married, not at this point anyway, more like a dalliance."

Tess nodded, reminded of how good it felt to experience passion once more. Feeling that incredible heat, the desperate yearning for—

Aunt Sophie laid a hand on Tess's arm, drawing

Tess back to the conversation. "Please understand that I'd never considered such a thing before now. I mean, I never strayed from your uncle Jack."

"Ah, yes, I know, Aunt. You loved him well."

"I did. I still do. But as I said, I'm not dead, and, well, in considering such an affaire—for fun, of course—"

"Of course."

Aunt Sophie bit her bottom lip. "Well, Heath Bartlett bears a striking resemblance to the kind of man I was thinking about, and then . . ." Her smile was deprecating as her cheeks reddened and she gushed out, "Well, last night I had the most *shocking* dream, and I swear he was the leading man." Pressing her hand to her mouth, she watched Tess, her gray eyes animated but vulnerable.

Tess exhaled. "Oh."

"You must think me mad."

Scratching her cheek, Tess shook her head. "Certainly not. He's attractive."

"Attractive? That's like calling Wellington an 'acceptable soldier.' Heath Bartlett is a stallion. One of the first order."

Inhaling a deep breath, Tess blushed. "I . . . ah, hadn't noticed."

Aunt Sophie snapped open her fan and waved it about. "I know you have no interest in men these days, Tess, but you couldn't miss that muscular physique!"

Powerful, too. Strong enough to lift a woman in his arms so easily that she feels lighter than air.

Brandishing the fan, Aunt Sophie moaned. "And those shoulders!"

Strapping and firm in all the right places.

The fan quaked. "And that long raven hair!"

Like strands of silk through my fingers.

Pressing her hand to her breast, Aunt Sophie raised her brows. "The resemblance to the man I'd dreamed about was such a shock, well, it was all a bit much for me. Hence the faint."

"That must have been quite a dream," Tess muttered, feeling warm and slightly breathless.

"Decidedly." Shaking her head, Aunt Sophie inhaled. "Then to see him standing in our society, as real as day . . ."

Tess bit her lip, wondering why she was so distressed. "But Heath isn't the man in your dream. He only resembles that man. I mean, you're not *really* interested in Heath, are you?"

"Oh no, of course not. No matter how much of a stallion he is, he's far too young for me."

Although Tess felt guilty about it, she felt the need to reiterate, "Almost twenty years. A whole generation, actually."

But she loved her aunt so much and didn't want her to discount any possibility for her happiness—broadly speaking, of course. "But there are so many men who would be lucky for a chance to spend some time with you."

"Old men, you mean?" Aunt Sophie's dove gray eyes were amused.

"No, of course not. Just not a man *well* over twenty years your junior."

"I thought it was only *almost* twenty?"

Tess scowled. "You know what I mean."

Aunt Sophie smiled. "I do. So you don't hold it against me?"

Wrapping her arms around her aunt, Tess hugged her close. "I want you to be happy. I want you to have a companion. Other than a censorious and petulant niece, that is."

"You're not petulant."

"Very funny."

Releasing Tess, Aunt Sophie sighed. "I'm so relieved. I was worried that you would think ill of me. That I couldn't have loved Jack if I could be with another man. I know you've been quite the nun since Quentin . . ."

Shrugging a shoulder, Tess didn't meet her aunt's eyes. "Perhaps because you loved so well, you know how to love. I don't seem to have that talent. Mine seems to be in making mistakes."

Aunt Sophie squeezed Tess's hand. "Don't say that, Tess. There's a man out there waiting for you. Paul Rutherford is certainly interested."

Tess changed the topic to one she was much more interested in discussing. "I can't help but wonder if you picked a man who resembled Heath . . . because you knew his father."

Releasing Tess's hand, Aunt Sophie adjusted her sleeve. "I don't know what you mean."

"Heath looks nothing like Uncle Jack, but he surely resembles his father. You know, the one you 'vaguely' recall."

Aunt Sophie's eyes skirted away. "Oh, that's . . . a mere coincidence . . ."

"Is it? Or is it that when you considered a dalliance, you couldn't help but think of another affair?"

"What do you mean?" Aunt Sophie's voice was high-strung with tension and she would not meet Tess's eye.

Tess suddenly knew that every word Heath had said about Mr. Bartlett's abrupt departure was true. But had he told the entire story?

Releasing her aunt's hand, Tess crossed her arms. "I know about the painting of my mother. The one without clothing. Did my mother have an affaire with Mr. Bartlett?"

Aunt Sophie rubbed her eyes, her face troubled. "Why dredge up the past, Tess?"

"I want to know."

"How did you find out?"

"Heath told me."

Aunt Sophie nodded. "He was old enough to understand."

"So was I."

"No, you weren't. You were a smart child. But you were naive, and you deserved to stay that way as long as possible."

Tess didn't know if she agreed, but that was neither here nor there. "What happened? Did they have an affaire?"

"No, not really."

Tess sighed, relieved. There were so many troubling things about her mother bedding Heath's father, not the least of which was the fact that Tess had just been with Heath!

"But something went on between them, nonetheless," Aunt Sophie added. "It was more emotional than physical. Your father was a bit . . . absent. Off with his hunting and his clubs and his dogs. Your mother felt . . . ignored."

Aunt Sophie held up her hand. "I'm not justifying what she did, mind you. She should have spoken with your father, at least tried to improve things before . . . well . . . She wanted more but didn't want to work that hard. My sister, I hate to say it, is a bit lazy. And Mr. Bartlett was right there. A widower. Not a servant, but not quite an equal. Very handsome, like his son . . ."

Aunt Sophie's face looked pained. "The painting was her idea. And . . . I can't help but suspect that your mother made sure that your father found out about it. She arranged it so that she could get your father's attention, you see."

Tess scowled, disgusted by her mother's antics. "She used Mr. Bartlett horribly."

"I know. I'm not proud of her. She was always selfish, even as a girl. She wanted what she wanted when she wanted it."

"No matter who got hurt."

"But she's a wonderful mother to you, and I suppose she did what she thought she should for her marriage."

Tess gritted her teeth. "My parents deserve a real thrashing."

"You won't tell them that you know?"

"Good God, no! I'm just saying that they ought to

pay for what they've done. But I'm certainly not the one to mete out the punishment. Heath, on the other hand, has every right to feel upset."

"He doesn't seem ill disposed toward either one of us. In fact he was quite amiable. I suppose he's too much of a gentleman to carry grudges."

Glancing away, Tess shrugged. Her feelings about Heath Bartlett were so confused. She hated him for lying and for targeting her for an investigation. But her family had caused his father quite a bit of grief. Mr. Smith's words haunted her: *Heath had had to scrape for every bit he'd gotten*. His father's loss of employment without references couldn't have helped. Tess suddenly recalled how her father had offered to assist Heath's admission to a good university in Scotland. No doubt that promise was reneged after Heath's father was let go. Yet Heath had managed to come so far. Obviously it hadn't been easy.

Guilt wormed its way inside her heart, for her mother's selfishness, for her father's misplaced fury, for her own neglect in understanding why Heath had left.

"You're not interested in Heath Bartlett, are you?"

Tess looked up. "Why do you ask?"

"Because I think your father would have an apoplectic fit if he found out. Even if Heath Bartlett doesn't hold any resentment, your father's never gotten over the whole mess."

"Yes, well that makes two of us," Tess mumbled.

"What do you mean? How did this affect you?"

"Never mind." She scowled, thinking of her mother.

"Why do women do such stupid things sometimes?"

Aunt Sophie sighed. "It's in our nature, I suppose."

Score another for Mr. Smith. The man was too astute for comfort.

"I need to have a talk with Lucy," Tess muttered. Janelle's plan was sounding better and better. Mr. Smith was sharp, and he was Heath's best friend. If anyone knew about the investigation, he would.

The loose boulder, Janelle had said.

Well, Tess was about to rock it.

Chapter 20

Having dressed with care that evening, Tess stood outside the door of the society's small drawing room, preparing herself to face Mr. Smith and extract from him the information she needed.

Anxiously smoothing the hunter green silk of her gown and adjusting the fringe of her ivory merino shawl, she inhaled a deep breath. Then, pressing a hand to her coiffure, she checked the long, feminine curls to ensure that the pins were still in place. It never hurt to look her best when trying to appear confident and in control, even if she felt quite the opposite.

Her belly fluttered with nerves. It was one thing when people offered information and she quietly listened or asked a pointed question here and there. It was wholly another when, under false pretenses, she drew Mr. Smith here to be interrogated. The whole affair left a sour taste in her mouth. She wasn't an inquisitor, and she certainly wasn't anything like Reynolds. She hoped.

Pressing her lips together in a firm line, Tess warred

with the uncertainties that tempted her feet to turn and silently tread down the stairs. But she couldn't afford to slink away like a sluggard. Mr. Smith knew about the investigation, was likely a part of it, and the inquiry by the solicitor-general could possibly, no matter how remote, end with her neck stuck in a noose!

Shuddering, she lowered her hand and hardened her resolve. She needed information. Badly. And Mr. Smith was the best means of obtaining it.

Who was instigating the inquiry? Aside from her, who was the target? Was the society at risk? Were the society members at risk? What was the purpose of the investigation?

Why Heath? That thought troubled her. Did he volunteer or had he simply taken orders? Were his intentions predicated on revenge or was he simply doing his job as he saw it? Was he selected because he could play on their childhood friendship? Or did some prophetic person have some notion of how hungrily she'd desire him?

Oh, dear Lord in heaven! She would go mad if she kept this up! Once she had the facts in hand, she'd be better able to face them.

Inhaling a deep breath, she pressed a hand against her belly and stepped forward into the drawing room.

Mr. Smith was sitting in one of the tall-back chairs by the blazing hearth, sipping a glass of port. Tess was glad to see that almost one third of the port sitting on the table beside him was gone.

Mr. Smith was dressed quite conservatively for him; gone were his usual bright colors and dandified ruffles. Still, there was a fashionable flair to his burgundy coat, and his neck cloth was the usual intricately tied knot seemingly locking his head in place.

She smiled. "Hello, Mr. Smith."

He jumped up, his face reflecting his astonishment. "What? Lady Golding?" His blond hair was a bit mussed and his eyes slightly glazed, evidence that he was well on his way to tipsy. Good, anything to make this easier.

With her hands clasped by her waist, she moved to stand before him. "I hope that you haven't been waiting long."

He blinked. "Ah, no. Not at all . . ." His gaze roved about the room as if he expected some surprise.

He seemed nervous, and she hoped to put him at ease. "Ginny says that you have a preference for first names, so please, call me Tess."

"And call me Bills; everyone does."

"May I?" She motioned to the chair opposite him.

Looking about the room as if still expecting someone, he nodded. "Of course."

"Thank you." Adjusting her skirts, she sat.

"Ah, would you like a drink?"

"No, thank you."

Obviously taking this as permission, he took a long swig of his own drink and sat across from her in his recently vacated chair. His foot tapped silently on the carpet and his eyes seemed to have a life of their own as they roved about the chamber. The poor man was truly disappointed that Lucy wasn't there. Guilt swelled in her middle, but she pushed it aside. He and Lucy would have their time together. For now Tess needed to safeguard her friends and her life.

"I know you must be wondering why I'm here," she began.

"It's your society, of course you should be here . . ." His voice was loud, evidencing his unease.

"I mean, me and not Lucy."

His mouth opened and then closed. "Well, yes."

"I am here on Lucy's behalf." Tess bit her lower lip, unable to contain a genuine smile. "Lucy's quite taken with you."

His face brightened. "Is she, now?"

"She has expressed a certain interest in you . . ." Her smile waned.

"I sense a *but* coming."

"She wonders about your intentions."

"You mean . . ." He swallowed. "Marriage?"

"She never mentioned matrimony to me."

His face showed a mixture of relief and disappointment. Interesting.

Biting her lip, Tess leaned forward. "She does not believe your story about a wager and wonders why you and Heath are pursuing the society so vigorously."

He opened his mouth to speak, but Tess held up her hand. "Don't bother protesting, I know about the investigation."

His gaze shifted about nervously and he gulped the remains of his glass. "Investigation?" he asked too loudly.

"I know all about it, but am not at liberty to discuss it with Lucy. Not without your permission."

Setting his empty glass on the side table, he stood, moving over to the grate by the windows. "You want my permission to tell Lucy about an investigation about which I know nothing?"

His nervousness was palpable, and she hoped he confided in her soon. After sharing a secret people usually calmed down, as if it eased their burden.

Rising and moving to stand beside him, Tess opened her hands. "Please save your pretenses. I know about the investigation and must warn you that you will earn no credit with Lucy until she knows the truth of it. The whole truth of it. She is no fool."

"That she is not."

Silence descended in the room.

Pursing his lips, he sighed. "I confess I'm delighted to learn of Lucy's interest . . ." His voice lowered to a mumble. "And especially that she has no interest in pursuing my name."

Exhaling noisily, he continued in a louder tone, "But I am most troubled by your notion of an investigation—"

"It is not my notion, but yours and Heath's and Solicitor-General Dagwood's."

Bills straightened, his hands curling into fists at his sides. After a moment, he seemed to come to a decision, and his fist unfurled. "Why didn't you just tell Lucy?"

Tess released the breath she'd been holding. She was so close she could almost taste the answers she needed, but his response wasn't the unequivocal confirmation she wanted. "What should I tell her? That you've lied to her, that you're making a mockery of an institution that she loves—"

"I'm not making a mockery of anything."

"Pretending to have a wager—"

"There is a wager—"

"Pretending that there's nothing more to it than that."

He ran his hand over his hair, looking away.

"She needs to understand the truth of it, or else any possibility for a future with Lucy will bear no fruit."

He chuckled. "Fruit. Is that what you call it?"

She willed her cheeks not to redden. "What can I tell Lucy?"

Silence descended as Tess counted her breaths. Twelve dreadfully long breaths passed before Bills spoke, "You can tell her about the investigation."

Tess was surprised by the shaft of disappointment in her gut. She hadn't realized that she'd been holding out a last glimmer of hope that Heath hadn't been manipulating her.

Licking her lips, Tess lifted a shoulder. "May I also inform her that it does not pertain to the Society for the Enrichment and Learning of Females?"

"Yes, of course. We have no interest in the society as a community."

Thank God. "May I also assure her that there is no danger to any member at the society?" She watched him closely. "Aside from myself, of course."

His gaze was speculative. "I must confess, I'm quite astounded by your ability to be so selfless. Most people wouldn't worry over the other members; they'd be more concerned about their own hide."

She looked away, powerful emotion threatening her poise. She swallowed. "The members of the society are my friends and family . . . I would not want any of them to be harmed in any way. Especially not because of me."

"But to be so cavalier about an investigation instigated by the solicitor-general's office?"

Instigated by the solicitor-general's office.

Bills shook his head. "You're either the pluckiest woman I've ever met, or the most dim-witted, and I daresay you're not stupid."

Her smile was bittersweet. "Or innocent. You seem to have left that off as a possibility."

"Innocent or not, most people would be shuddering in their shoes just knowing that the solicitor-general was inquiring about a theft and viewed her as the only suspect."

It's only me. It has nothing to do with the society or the Foreign Office. And she'd never stolen a thing in her life. Tess pressed her hand to her heart, and her shoulders drooped with relief.

"I daresay that's why the solicitor-general ordered that you not be approached or questioned directly," Bills added, tapping his finger to his lips. "That, and the fact that he feared that you might try to cover up your crimes."

"So the thought that I might sue him for harassment and cause another scandal never entered his concerns?"

Bills's face was sheepish. "That, too."

Straightening, she inhaled a deep breath, feeling calmer than she ought. This was the solicitor-general they were talking about, and something had to have prompted it. "So tell me, when the solicitor-general completes his investigation and learns that I have stolen no such . . . ah, what is the claim again?"

Although his gaze was quizzical, he answered, "Jewelry, rare books."

A guffaw burst from her mouth before she could contain it with her hand. This was getting better and better. Her relief was overwhelming. Smiling, she held out her bare wrists. "As you can see, I'm a true jewelry aficionado. This is so glaringly absurd as to be comical."

Tilting his head, he held open his hands. "I make no judgments."

"Pray, remind me who made these ludicrous claims."

"You didn't really know about the investigation, did you?"

"I did."

"But not the who, the what, or the why."

"No. I confess I brought you here in the hopes of learning those very things. And you have been most informative. Thank you."

He scowled. "I don't like being manipulated."

"I didn't lie about Lucy's feelings, and she gave me permission to question you as I did."

"And the part about being forthright with her about the investigation?"

Tess sighed. "I'm hardly the person to give advice

about relationships." Or honesty. "I think I'll have that drink now. Care to join me?"

He nodded, as if deciding to forgive her. "I believe I will, Tess. If I may still call you that."

Stepping over to the side table, she poured them each a generous serving of port. "Of course. And I apologize for manipulating you like I did. I just had to know what was going on, and you seemed the perfect man to ask."

"Not Bartlett."

Sipping the sweet, smooth liquid, Tess rolled it around her tongue. Heath. Joy, anger, guilt, excitement, and desire swirled inside her in a tempest of feelings. She peered down into her glass. When it came to Heath she couldn't keep her head on straight. She doubted that she would have been able to carry out the interview. Likely they would have ended up tearing off their clothes and rolling around on the floor . . .

She swallowed, then hastily took another sip of the port, hoping that Bills would believe that it was the drink, not her thoughts, that colored her cheeks.

"I'm an easier nut to crack, I suppose," Bills supplied.

She looked up. "Please don't feel badly. I simply needed to know what was going on, and you did no harm in telling me, I assure you." Biting her lip, she cringed. "If you don't mind, can you please enlighten me as to who the mystery claimant is? Whose jewels did I supposedly filch?"

"George Belington's."

The drink sprayed from her mouth before she could cover it.

Jumping up, Bills tried patting her gown with a handkerchief, but upon realizing that it meant being a bit too personal, gave up and simply handed Tess the linen.

"Ah, thank you." She tidied herself as best she could, trying not to worry over the stains.

"You seem surprised," Bills commented.

"Shocked, actually." She frowned. "I suppose I gave Belington more credit than he was due."

"So you're acquainted with him."

Anger made her fist curl. "I can't believe he'd actually set the solicitor-general on me!"

"Why does he hold a grudge against you? What did you do to him?"

"So you blame me for his wretched actions?"

"Nay, but it only makes sense that he had to have been incited in one way or another to have gone to such lengths. Anyone with sense would understand that at some point everyone would find out that his allegations were unfounded. So he has to be a few cards shy of a full deck. What happened between you two?"

Staring at the liquid swirling in her glass, she pondered the question a long moment.

Bills shifted in his seat. "If it makes you feel any better, I will not repeat what you tell me."

Bills's assurance along with Tess's anger loosened her tongue. "I would not say that George is addled, but he is more desperate, and more conniving than I would have supposed."

"Why is he so desperate?"

"George's aunt died a few months ago, and in her will she provided for him, but only if he marries. He needs the funds and is of the opinion that I am the only woman for him."

"So he's in love with you."

She shook her head. "Hardly."

"Then why is he so set on marrying you?"

Exhaling, Tess looked down at her lap. "I suppose since he was willing to brand me a thief and set the solicitor-general on me, I shouldn't worry overmuch about protecting his reputation."

"I know I wouldn't. Still, as I said, I will not repeat what you share with me."

Nodding, she came to a decision. "George wants to marry me so badly because he felt that I am the only woman with whom he might . . . be able to have relations and bear children."

Bills leaned back and pursed his lips. "He has difficulty . . . performing? Is that it?"

Looking away, Tess shrugged. "Apparently so."

"But why would he believe that even though he couldn't perform with other women, he would be able to do so with you."

Tess grimaced. "Because he had."

"What?" the draperies bellowed, followed by a horrific tearing sound. The far curtains flew open and Heath strode out. "You slept with George Belington?" His hair was mussed, his clothing unkempt, and his face darkened with anger.

Tess jumped up from her seat. "What—?" She

blinked. "Why are you—?" Her eyes narrowed. "Why, you lying, eavesdropping—"

"Lying? You're the liar! You failed to mention your affaire with George Belington!!"

"It wasn't an affaire! It was only once and when I realized what a mistake—"

Bills stepped toward Heath. "I think you're missing the point, old chap—"

Stabbing his finger at Tess, Heath charged, "You said that you hadn't been with a man in years!"

She gritted her teeth. "If you would allow me to explain—"

"Either you lied or you didn't! Did you sleep with George Belington?"

Loaded silence engulfed the chamber, broken only by Heath's heavy breathing. It had probably been quite suffocating hiding out in a drapery. Tess blinked hard, suddenly seeing Bills's loud voice and his wayward eyes as what they'd been: a ruse to ensure that she didn't discover Heath eavesdropping behind the hangings. *I will not* repeat *what you tell me*, Bills had said. He wouldn't have to since Heath was listening the whole time!

Shaking her head, she was filled with disgust. She'd congratulated herself for working the loose boulder to extract information when all the while she was the one being worked upon. Some spy she was.

"Well," Heath demanded. "Answer me!"

At his tone, she stiffened. *Answer me? Like I'm some child to jump at your command?* She glared at Heath a long moment, hating how handsome he was, how much her body wanted him, even now, after he'd wronged her so terribly.

"I'm a fool," she muttered, then turned and strode from the room.

"Leave her," she heard Bills say. "She needs some time to cool off. And so do you."

Heath didn't follow her.

Fine. He could have all of blasted eternity to cool off. She never wanted to see that scheming, lying knave again.

Chapter 21

Heath swallowed, anger and some unknown emotion racing through him like a scourge, burning him. He pushed aside the unsettling emotions and forced his intellect to the fore. Nothing was explained. Not her money, her secrecy, what happened with George Belington. She'd slept with the bugger! Jealousy speared his gut so piercingly that his vision blurred.

"No wonder George Belington's so obsessed with her; he believes that she's his cure." Bills released Heath's arm. "Still, to charge her with a crime goes beyond the pale."

Forcing the green-eyed monster away, Heath bit out, "We don't know the full story."

Bills stepped over and refreshed his glass, then poured another for his friend. "She's furious. You won't get anything out of her at this point. Once she calms down, you can speak with her and get the facts."

Heath gulped down his drink in one swig, then made a face. Too damned sweet. Not enough burn.

Bills shook his head, amazed. "When speaking of the investigation she truly seemed more concerned about her friends than herself. Astonishing faithfulness there."

"But why doesn't she worry more over herself?" Heath demanded, angry with her for a thousand things, one of them being that she wasn't more careful. "Innocent or no, she should have been more blasted concerned." Unless she had some kind of protection . . .

Recalling her camaraderie with Warden Pitts and how she'd admitted to sleeping with George Belington, Heath was overcome by the terrible notion that she had a benefactor somewhere, someone rich, someone powerful, someone that she relied upon to protect her. And what did she have to give him in return . . . The thought made him ill.

"Don't go down that road, my friend," Bills warned. "You looked into her business dealings, investigated her household, her servants, and even where she slept. There was no indication of a secret lover. No male visitors, no fancy gifts, no secret trips, no late night excursions. None of the trappings that indicate a male presence making demands on her life in that manner."

Heath nodded, desperate to believe his friend. He reminded himself how she'd felt in his arms; there had been no manipulation when she'd been with him. No quid pro quo, no sense that this was currency for bartering favor. No, she'd been on fire, as if kindled from deep inside, and no woman, no matter how talented, could fake a response like that. She'd been hot, vibrant, and tight as hell. He swallowed as desire flashed through him, quick and demanding.

But he pushed it away, needing to *think*!

He'd known Tess for years; why was he having so much trouble getting a sense of her? Maybe because she'd changed so much. She wasn't that sweet, teasing girl who'd stolen pastries from the kitchens for him when he'd been sent off to bed without dinner. She wasn't that biddable chit any longer. She was a grown woman, strong, demure, yet passionate, making his body thunder with longing.

Sipping from his drink, Bills sniffed. "I don't care what happened with George Belington; she doesn't seem the kind to trade her favors to any man."

"You're right. She's not that type of woman." Heath stared longingly at the empty doorway, wondering if he'd made a mistake in not going after her.

"I confess, I didn't realize it before, but she's really quite genuine underneath that reserved exterior."

"Tess is not one for false pretenses." As he knew full well. Stepping over to the window, Heath looked out, hoping for a look at her carriage. Blast, it was a side alley view!

"And once she cares for someone, he obviously becomes a priority for her," Bills added.

Heath nodded. She'd always been loyal, but never had she shown her faithfulness so much as when she'd worried that her friends might be under investigation. Between her friends, her society, her book business, Tess had a very full life. One into which he didn't seem to fit.

An uncomfortable sense of insignificance overcame him. Whereas she'd crashed into his life turning everything askew and becoming central, she had no trouble simply walking out that door.

His stomach dipped with disappointment. She didn't need him. And he was finding it hard to get through a day without her!

Upset and frustrated, Heath ran his hand through his hair. "She has too many damned secrets."

"But does that paint her a thief? Does that make her a liar? Or is Belington the liar?"

Pushing aside his hurt, Heath considered all he had learned. Could his unbidden passion for Tess and his jealousy have been clouding his judgment?

Bills went on, "And I don't care what she says about Belington, the man has to have a screw loose to think that he can corner her into marriage with an arrest warrant. I would posit that every claim he's made is suspect."

Jealousy pierced his chest; she'd been with George Belington! But he could finally see what he'd been blind to: He'd wronged Tess. Heath covered his eyes. "I should have asked her about the thefts straight away."

"Dagwood—"

"I shouldn't have listened to him. A true friend would have worked to clear her name, not hound her like a criminal." He looked up. "Devil take it, I've been a fool!"

A faint smile shadowed Bills's lips. "Don't tell me, tell her."

Hope ignited in Heath. "It would have taken time for her carriage to be brought around. I can still catch her." Setting down his glass, Heath sprinted toward the door.

Heath loped down the long carpeted staircase, two stairs at a time. The marigold and purple uniformed butler looked up and then quickly opened the door just as Heath darted through.

Tess's carriage was just rolling away from the curb.

"Tess, wait!" he cried, sprinting forward.

Not that he'd expected it, but the coach didn't stop.

Heath raced after it, jumped up, and thrust his arm through the open window. He hung on to the moving coach, his boots scrambling for purchase on the thin lip of the carriage door.

"Stop, Tess!" He bore himself up and stuck his head through the carriage window. "I must speak to you!"

With her eyes narrow and angry and her lips pinched tight, she reached beneath the seat, picked up an umbrella, and smashed it on his head.

"Ow! Stop it!"

"Go away!" She smacked him again, harder this time.

"Not until you listen to me!"

"My lady!" the driver cried as the carriage jerked to a halt, tossing Tess against the cushion.

Heath used the moment to unlatch the door and swing inside the cabin, slamming the exit behind him.

Tess raised the umbrella but Heath wrenched it out of her hands and thrust it through the door handles, locking them inside the small cabin.

"Lady Golding!" the driver called as he scurried from his post.

Heath slammed the window closed and dropped the shades. "I'm not leaving until you hear me out!"

The door handle shuddered. "Madame!"

Crossing her arms Tess glared at the wall, but at least she wasn't trying to do him violence anymore.

Heath held up his hands. "I'm sorry about upstairs, but I had to find out the truth and I wasn't allowed to ask you."

"A poor excuse," she scoffed.

"You're right, I should have just asked you about it, no matter what my superior ordered."

"Ma'am!" The door quaked and banging rang out.

Heath ran his hand through his hair, praying she'd understand. "You must believe me that I didn't know the investigation was about you when I accepted the task!"

"Oh, must I?" She unwound her arms, hands fisted in her lap.

A carrot-topped head appeared in the opposite window. "Ma'am!"

Reaching across the small cabin, Heath closed the other shade. "I swear I didn't! But once I knew that you were a suspect, if you were innocent—"

"I am innocent!"

"I didn't know that at the time."

"You should have presumed it!"

"You're right. I should have known that you wouldn't steal anything. But I was prepared to see justice done—"

The banging ceased.

"Smash the window!" someone ordered.

"Tess, let's discuss this like civilized human beings!" Heath pleaded.

"How can we when you're a snake?"

"One! Two!"

Tess cried, "I'm all right, Carter! There's no need to break the window!"

"Are you certain, ma'am?" a male voice bellowed.

Looking at Heath, she directed, "Release the latch. They won't be satisfied until they see me whole. Some people are loyal that way."

Ignoring the well-deserved dig, Heath removed the umbrella, and the door swung open. A carrot-topped man peered inside, his freckled face flushed red and contorted with anger. "Are you all right, ma'am?"

Tess smiled reassuringly. "I am fine, Carter. Thank you for being so diligent."

A brown-haired, sallow-skinned man pressed forward. "Are ye quite certain, ma'am?"

"Yes, Paulson, I am." She held open her hands. "As you can see, I am quite unharmed. But I thank you for your concern for my safety."

"Your safety is my only concern!" the fellow named Paulson cried.

Tess looked to Heath. "I believe you have something to say to my men."

Heath inclined his head. "I apologize for frightening you. I had no intention of harming your mistress, and please accept my word that I never will."

Paulson shook his fist at Heath. "Ye shouldn't've done that!"

Heath nodded. "You're right. My behavior was completely wrong and I apologize."

Smiling overly sweetly, Tess motioned to Heath. "As you can see, my good men, Mr. Bartlett appreciates how horribly and totally he is in the wrong. He was a fool to have acted so thoughtlessly and with such utter disregard for basic human respect."

"Playing it up a bit, aren't you?" Heath muttered.

Her gaze was sharp blue crystal. "Am I?"

Inclining his head, he grimaced. "I suppose not." Heath raised his voice for the benefit of the men. "I apologize." His gaze met Tess's, and he hoped that she could see how truly repentant he was. "I am so very, very sorry."

Carter glared at Heath as if not quite satisfied, and although the men seemed relieved that their mistress was well, they quite obviously still did not trust him.

"Are ye certain ye don't want me to toss him out on his nervy bottom, ma'am?" Paulson asked, clearly still itching to do so.

Pursing her lips, Tess stared at Heath a long moment, those crystal blue eyes considering. "I suppose not today, Paulson."

Heath bowed, pressing his hand over his heart. "I swear to you good men that not only will I never harm your mistress, but from this moment forth, I will do my utmost to protect Lady Golding in any way that I can."

Paulson glared. "I'll hold ye to that promise."

"Please do."

Carter looked to Tess. "We're in the middle of the street, ma'am . . ."

"Then I suppose we must move."

Paulson jerked his thumb toward Heath. "Will 'e be coming with us?"

Silence fell, and Heath tried not to hold his breath. With one word these men would be on him like an army of ants.

Biting her lip as if unsure, Tess nodded. "For the moment, at least."

Relief washed over Heath. "Thank you."

"Where to, ma'am?"

"Home, Carter."

Carter's head disappeared, and after some scuffling of feet the carriage began to move once more.

Chapter 22

Tess stared out the window of the moving coach, palpably aware of the tall, attractive man sitting across from her. Heath Bartlett was far too appealing for his own good. Mayhap that was why she was finding it so hard to be angry with him.

Oh, slamming him over the head with the umbrella had been pure instinct; the man brought out the fiercest feelings in her. Whenever he was around she wanted either to do him violence or to make passionate love to him. For a lady who had been without real male intimacy for so long, it was maddeningly delicious. Tess had to withhold a quiver just thinking about it. But she kept her face impassive, allowing him to stew for a few moments longer.

Yes, she'd been angry about being duped, but when she'd had a moment to consider the matter, she'd had to admire Heath for taking advantage of a ripe situation. Obviously he and Bills had suspected a trap, and had turned the tables on her quite admirably. She'd always appreciated a sharp mind, and Heath had a fine one, in even finer packaging.

He sat across from her now, raking his fingers through his dark ribbons of hair, obviously not knowing how to make things right. In actuality, things weren't so terribly wrong. She hadn't exposed anything about her business or her work for the Foreign Office, and now she knew everything she needed to about the investigation.

Tess sighed, still overwhelmed by the relief that it was so inconsequential. Yes, she understood that dealing with an Officer of the Crown was serious business, but compared to the dangers of spying, the legal system seemed straightforward.

"Can you . . . would you mind telling me what happened with George Belington?" Heath finally broke the silence.

After a long moment, Tess nodded.

Heath ran his hand through his hair, not meeting her eye. "When did . . . it happen?"

She raised a brow. "The big 'it' or all of it?"

Shifting in the seat, he nodded. "All, if you please."

"About nine months after my husband's inopportune death, I ran into George at a bookshop. He was nice. And, I confess, it was a relief to speak with someone who didn't seem obsessed with the whole scandal business."

His nod was almost imperceptible. "Go on."

"I began running into him quite frequently. Then, after a few more encounters, he called on me. He began to stop by for tea. Then he asked me for my assistance in selling his library collection. He never asked me about my dead husband or Lord Berber or about finances or even about what I was going to do with my mess of a life. It was nice having someone to talk to about the trivial things."

"I understand."

She looked up. "Do you? Do you have any idea what it's like to find out that the man you thought you knew better than all others was a lying, cheating scoundrel who didn't have enough good sense in his thick head to take care of himself?"

"I may not know exactly what you experienced, no. But I do understand being disappointed in someone you love. I know how one person's transgressions taint his whole family. I understand that disappointment . . . that terrible sense of betrayal."

Betrayal. Heath was right; that was exactly how Tess felt it. Like a spear through her heart every time she considered what her husband's depravity had done to her life. Quentin may have had a weakness for cards, but that didn't mean that he could toss away her future without so much as an "I'm sorry." The losses had accumulated over years and there could have been plenty of time for Tess to try to repair the damage before all was lost. If she'd only known. So much lost: her innocence, her safety, her trust. All for being ignorant of the danger.

Feeling as if they had a sort of scarred kinship, she sighed. "I'm just so glad we never had children. The scandal would have tainted their lives."

He nodded. "You wouldn't have wanted them to have had to suffer like you did."

"Or as you did."

From the look in his eyes she could tell that she'd touched a nerve.

She licked her lips. "The Mr. Bartlett I knew was a wonderful tutor, a charming man who always had a joke on his lips or a sweet in his pocket for the young ones."

Heath's handsome face darkened. "My father is a bit too charming for his own good."

Tess shook her head. "I can't imagine your father being anything but a complete gentleman."

"*True* gentlemen don't sleep with another man's wife."

The silence grew thick, and Tess wished there was a way she could ease his pain. "We suffer under the sins of our parents, I suppose . . . Which, again, makes me thankful that I never had children."

"I find it hard to believe that you feel that way. If I recall correctly, Elizabeth was your favorite name if you had a girl."

Tess swallowed, surprised by the fact that he remembered her dreams and by how deeply it moved her. "Not having children left me with more choices."

"What kind?"

Pursing her lips closed, she forced herself to remember that she needed to be more careful with Heath. He was a skilled inquirer and she tended to let her guard down when he spoke of their childhood. She made mental note not to allow that to happen again. No one could know about Wheaton and her work for the Foreign Office.

Pasting a smile on her face, she met his gaze. "My book business, of course. I am independent. If I'd had children, I would have had to do as my father told me."

"Could you have done that? You'd always sworn you would only marry for love."

"And my parents castigated me for being so naive. 'People marry for convenience,' they told me. I suppose that I would have done what I needed to do."

"And now?"

"Now I wouldn't take anyone. Marriage, being locked with someone for eternity . . ." She shook her head.

"Eternity?"

"Even though my husband is three years gone, his family members are still mine. They spend so much time trying to paint me the devil that they almost make it a sport."

"They're only doing it to curry favor with Lord Berber's family."

Her mouth dropped open; she was shocked that he could be so astute. "I'd always thought so, but how . . .?"

His burly shoulder lifted in a shrug. "If they side with you, then it's almost the equivalent of saying that Lord Berber was a bloody idiot for attempting to sail a dangerous channel drunk. It's much more politically advantageous to vilify you."

Tess exhaled, feeling an amazing sense of relief that *someone* understood. "Well . . . ah, what was I saying?"

"You were speaking of marriage being for eternity."

"Oh yes." Considering her own mistakes and Bills's opinion of Miss Whilom, Tess felt that she had a duty to warn Heath. She didn't want to dwell on the fact that every time she thought about Heath and the golden-haired chit she wanted to kick something. "Marriage is a serious commitment. It should never be entered into lightly."

"Why did you marry your husband, Tess?"

Frowning, Tess looked away. "I was so giddy with the idea of being in love that I was blind to Quentin's true nature."

"So you don't blame your parents who guided you?"

"I shouldn't have followed along so blindly."

"What about his parents? His family purposely hid his gambling addiction."

She blinked. "How did you know about that?"

"I've asked around. His father was quite fastidious about keeping the problem hidden, but he was one of the men pulling his son out of the holes that he dug for himself. No matter how much they might try to deny it, they knew."

Tess exhaled, feeling an odd sense of wonder. Heath Bartlett was the first man of her acquaintance who actually sifted through the lies and unearthed the truth of it all. Lightness expanded in her chest, and she felt liberated by his understanding. Amazed, she shook her head. "I wish I'd have known sooner."

Heath felt his fist curl in impotent anger for all Tess

had been through. And she took too much responsibility upon her small shoulders. "And done what? You were married; everything you owned belonged to him."

Her lovely face was determined. "I would have found a way."

"I believe that you would." A smile teased his lips as he realized that Tess was a lioness when it came to protecting those she loved. It made perfect sense that she would try to stop her husband from joining his friend on a dangerous sailing excursion that was more akin to suicide than a race. Heath couldn't fathom how anyone could fault her for that. If it were Heath, he would treasure such concern.

What must it be like to be loved by such a woman?

"Never again will I trust my future to any man," she murmured.

Heath straightened, surprised by how upset her pronouncement made him. "So because of your deceitful husband you can't trust any man?"

"I couldn't trust you, could I? While pretending to have a wager to join my society, instead you were investigating me for a crime."

"I had honorable intentions."

"Yes, like putting me in prison. Tell me, when we were at Marks-Cross Street Prison, did you imagine it was me begging behind the bars?"

Heath shifted uncomfortably, reminded that he'd had that very thought. "I was actually upset by the notion that you might someday be in such a position if the theft charges were true."

"Why did you take this case? Especially if at the time you didn't know that it pertained to me?"

"Belington is Lady Bright's cousin."

"Ah. I see. You saw this as a mean of gaining an advantage with your new mother."

"In-law, you mean."

"Yes, of course, although, to her credit, my mother-in-law always treated me as one of her own, and had me call her 'Mother' like her other children. Until after the accident, that is."

No matter how welcoming, Heath couldn't quite imagine Lady Bright treating him as one of her own, but rather as a superior servant. But he would win her over, eventually.

The notion snaked into his mind that the end result suddenly didn't seem quite worth the effort. Heath pushed it aside; of course he wanted to be accepted by Lady Bright and all her kin.

Tess bit her lip. "I never knew what happened to your mother."

Heath blinked as, unbidden, images of his mother surfaced from his memory. Long raven tresses tied back in a bun so big he could barely grasp it in two little hands. Sympathetic eyes, golden brown like honey. Slender fingers that had lovingly caressed his cheeks when he'd fallen to sleep at night. Her palms had been rough from her labors, but her hugs had been wonderfully soft and she'd smelled endearingly of leather and parchment. "She was a librarian. Second generation, actually. Her parents had run a lending library in Bath."

He chuckled, the memories wrapping around him like a blanket warmed by a fire. "She used to call me her 'little solicitor' since I negotiated for everything. Reading another page in a book before dinner, when I would go to bed, whether I could go out and play . . ."

"So she planted the idea in your head of entering the legal profession?"

"Yes."

"What happened to her?"

That warm imaginary blanket slipped away as the darker memories crept in. She'd been so resourceful, so resilient, that everyone had been surprised when she hadn't stood back up. "Struck by a carriage."

"I'm so sorry." Tess's eyes were tinged with sadness and her brow was furrowed with concern for him. He was touched. "How old were you?"

"Ten."

"So young . . ."

"It was a long time ago . . ." He shrugged, looking away. "I don't talk of it much."

Heath realized that his family had broken then, irreparably. His father had accepted the first post he could find away from Bath, removing Heath from the only home he'd ever known.

Heath stared out the window, finding it hard to imagine that living with the Whilom clan was going to feel like being "home." Still, he wouldn't feel the interloper the way he'd had when he'd been going from family to family with his father. Or would he? Would he always be the son-in-law whose presence had to be explained? "Picked himself up from humble beginnings . . ." "Has promise . . ." "Works with the solicitor-general, you know . . ."

But what if his potential came to naught? What if the political winds changed and he was left out in the cold? Would his new family stand by him then? He hoped . . . but it was a hollow feeling tinged with doubt.

He didn't want to think about the future, and instead shifted back to what he could control. He straightened. "The investigation, yes. Lady Bright drafted Solicitor-General Dagwood to her cause. Or else we probably never would have gotten involved."

Tess nodded, accepting his change in topic. "And you took the assignment without knowing it was about me."

"Yes." His hands fisted, but he forced them to relax. "Would you please tell me what happened with Belington?"

Looking out the carriage window, Tess exhaled as if upset. Heath wondered with whom. "I was lonely, he was an ardent pursuer . . . it was a stupid mistake. I knew it even before . . ." She looked down at her fingers knitted in her lap. "It was a stupid mistake I never should've made."

"*A* mistake?"

A rueful smile played on her lips. "Yes, only once. I ended it immediately."

"You said earlier that you didn't believe he was in love with you. How can you be so sure?" Heath could easily see how it might happen. Tess was exactly the kind of woman a man could fall head over heels in love with.

Heath gulped, shock and some unknown emotion surging through him that was tinged with fear. Head over heels in love? With Tess?

"So . . ." His voice cracked, and he coughed into his fist, clearing his throat. "So . . . what were we talking about?"

Her gaze was speculative. "George Belington."

"Yes. Belington. So he lied in his affidavit," Heath stated, feeling stupid.

"I'm surprised that when you interviewed him the truth didn't come out. He's not very sly."

"I didn't interview him. If I had . . ." Then Heath would never have pursued the investigation and wouldn't have followed Tess. He wouldn't be with her right now, feeling these chaotic, scorching emotions that made his head spin. Or the thundering desire that made him burn to be with her.

No matter that he didn't believe in such things, it was destiny that had brought them together, destiny that had foreseen this from the moment he'd bumped into her at Andersen Hall.

Furrowing her brow as if deep in thought, she bit her lower lip, something he longed to do. She was too tempting for either of their good. "So how could he make the charges against me?"

He pulled his mind back to the conversation. "It was all laid out in an affidavit, with Lady Bright pursuing the claims."

"Neat and cowardly. Just like Belington. He probably expected that I would go haring off to the country begging him to drop the charges."

"The man obviously has no idea with whom he's dealing."

Tess looked up. "Why do you say that?"

"I think you'd sooner take up arms than go begging to someone who'd wronged you."

Her peach-colored lips lifted at the corners. "Methinks you may finally be taking my measure, Mr. Bartlett."

His insides stirred. Tess couldn't be flirting with him, not after he'd deceived her. Could she? Her dark as coal lashes lowered across the top of those petal-soft cheeks.

She licked her lips, spearing him with longing to taste her. "So what would your advice be to me, if, perchance, you would deign to grant me the favor of your . . . legal attentions."

"I . . . ah." He coughed into his fist, his mind scrambling to interpret the signals she was sending. He ached with desire for her, but didn't want to presume. "I . . . ah, would return anything he'd given you, as a sign of your good faith, and provide any receipts for the books."

"And it would end there?" Her voice was like a caress.

Tugging at his cravat, Heath swallowed. "I believe so."

She looked up, her crystal blue gaze swirling with heat and desire, piercing his soul. "And so your reason for being at the society . . . your reason for being near me . . . would be gone."

He was across the space between them and had her in his arms in a breath. "You're not going to get rid of me that easily."

As his mouth claimed hers, his body thrummed with aching need. He needed her as he needed air and water and sustenance. He could no more stop kissing her than fly to the moon.

A delighted sigh escaped her lips, and he *knew* that she accepted their fate.

Chapter 23

Tess surrendered to Heath's kisses and to the desire pulsing between them, feeling safer and freer than she had in years. There was nothing false in her kisses, no part of herself that she held back. She wanted him, hungrily, and wasn't afraid to show it.

With his arms wrapped around her, Heath made love to her with his mouth, his tongue caressing hers so enticingly that her head swam.

"You're incredible," he moaned into her mouth. His words caused a quiver deep in her middle, warming her in places she yearned to be touched.

Tess sucked his bottom lip, savoring the taste of him. Her hands roamed his broad shoulders, hugging him closer, pulling his hard chest more tightly against hers.

His fingers threaded her hair and cradled the base of her head, leaning her back against the cushions. Of their own accord, her legs spread, welcoming him. His hard hip pressed through her skirts deep into the juncture between her thighs. She shifted against him, needy and demanding.

His hand cupped her breast, and desire spiked through her. Her back arched and her head fell back as she gasped for breath.

His lips claimed her neck, sucking gently as his hand slipped beneath the folds of her coat. He kneaded the soft flesh of her breast as his mouth trailed up the column of her neck, raising the hairs of her skin.

His warm breath caressed her ear as he licked her earlobe. Her hips rocked and her mind scrambled. Her only awareness was of the need to have him deep inside her. Now.

Shouts permeated Tess's fog as the carriage rolled to a halt.

Heath grabbed the door handle before it could open. "Give us a minute!" His voice was thick.

As she collected herself, Tess's only thought was how to make it to her bedroom as quickly as possible. She'd never wanted anything or anyone more in her life.

Heath helped her to sit and adjust her clothing.

"I must look a fright," she whispered, her voice husky, her thoughts jumbled.

Kissing her swollen lips, he growled. "Frightfully tempting. I can't keep my hands off you."

The walk inside was a blur. Thank heavens it was the servants' half day off and no one was in the front of the house except for trusty Anna. The young maid accepted Tess's outer garments with a wink and a smile, clearly not censorious of her employer's activities. Tess recalled that Anna had always liked Heath and distantly wondered if it was that fondness or the fact that Tess was finally engaging in some wicked fun.

But Tess couldn't dwell on that now; she just had to move in the direction of her bedchamber.

With Heath.

His presence beside her was like a powerful wind pressing against her, silently urging.

Anna departed, closing the door behind her mere seconds before Tess was in Heath's arms once more.

They tore frantically at their clothes, kissing each inch of skin as soon as it was exposed. They explored, touched, savored, each movement heightening her desire until she could take it no longer.

"Heath, please," she groaned.

He lifted her in his arms.

"Burgundy, not crimson," he murmured, eyeing the bed.

"What . . .?"

"Nothing. I like the coverlet." He carried her to the bed and deposited her onto the soft mattress.

Covering her naked body with his, he lay on top of her, comfortably positioning himself between her open thighs.

His kisses were hot and wanting, his skin burning as if with a fever.

He entered her with a deep thrust, and her body wrapped around him with pleasure.

Sighing, Tess closed her eyes.

Every sensation was a color surging through her.

Reds, oranges, and golds swirled behind her closed lids, like the sunlight of a new dawn. She felt free; she felt whole.

Heath rode her, carried her . . .

His pace quickened; his body went taut.

Her heartbeat sped up. Her breath seized. Her body tensed. She clung to Heath, waiting, anticipating, needing, wanting . . .

Stars exploded behind her closed lids as her world shattered.

Together they were lost.

Chapter 24

Tess rolled over and sighed, unable to believe how deliciously wonderful she felt at this moment. It was as if her worries had been twisting her in knots, and over the course of many hours of Heath's extraordinary attentions, she was suddenly free from all burdens. Either that or she simply no longer cared.

With her eyes still closed, she inhaled the heady scent of lovemaking that perfumed the tangled sheets and relished the feel of him pressed along her side as he slept. His skin was softer than she ever would have imagined, and smooth, nearly hairless. His limbs were sinewy and strong, yet he was astoundingly flexible when it counted. She, on the other hand, felt stretched and deliciously achy as a reminder of their love play. She had forgotten how vigorous making love could be, and how incredible she could feel afterward . . . or had it ever been this good?

Thinking back, she couldn't help but recall the astonishing delight she'd felt at those first forays into desire with Quentin. She'd been heady with the thrill of it all, the rush of newfound sensations that she was suddenly free to explore.

Still, it mostly had been about Quentin and his pleasure, the assumption being that she'd get hers in the meantime. As a result, she did not feel comfortable taking her pleasure or making her preferences known. She'd always held something of herself back with Quentin, never really letting go. Then his late nights and foul moods had soured their relationship, making the bedchamber experiences disappointing and hollow.

In contrast, last night with Heath she'd practically lived among the stars. She'd felt free to be herself and take her pleasure. And it had been the most liberating experience of her life.

Wanting to see him, she opened her eyes and blinked at the morning sun soaking through the draperies of her bedroom.

On the bed beside her, Heath lay on his stomach with his muscular arms cushioning his head, the sheets negligently tossed aside as if he was too hot for such cosseting. His broad back sloped downward into those glorious mounds of muscle that she'd kneaded and explored with astonishing pleasure. Heat roused inside her, making her want to kick off the sheet covering her legs and reach for him once more.

Heath stirred, turning his head to face her and shoving the dark, tousled hair from his face, his eyes still closed in slumber. His cheekbone was pink from where he'd slept, and fuzz shadowed his cheeks and chin. His lips were lush and red and looked delicious enough to taste . . .

But she hesitated. To wake him meant they must face the day, a reckoning she loathed. For no matter how much they wanted to pretend otherwise, their normal lives would breach the intimacy that had co-cooned them in the darkness of the night.

Tess sighed, suddenly sympathizing with Shake-speare's Romeo and Juliet pretending that the dawn had not yet come.

"'It was the nightingale, and not the lark that pierced the fearful hollow of thine ear,'" Tess whispered.

Heath's smooth lips lifted in a sleepy smile.

"You weren't supposed to hear that," Tess com-plained, smiling.

"If 'I must be gone and live, or stay and die,'" Heath quoted Romeo, "'Let me be ta'en, let me be put to death.' I'd certainly die a happy man."

"I don't recall that last line being in the play."

"It's all mine." Reaching over, he wrapped his arms around her and held her close, nestling her body against his like pages in a book.

Closing her eyes, Tess pressed her nose into his arm and inhaled his rich, earthy scent. The hairs of his skin tickled her nose and a small hum emerged from deep in her throat that sounded astoundingly like a purr.

"Don't you sound satisfied," he murmured, setting his lips to her shoulder and taking a nip.

Muted sounds of disruption resonated from down-stairs, followed by raised voices. The words couldn't be heard, but there was no doubt of their belligerent tone.

Tess felt the interruption like a peal of doom.

Slowly she unwound his arm and scooted off the bed.

He leaned up on his elbow, his handsome face still smooth with repose. "Where are you going? I'm not done with you, yet." He must have finally heard the commotion, too, for suddenly he sat up. "What's that about?"

Tess walked over to the wardrobe, quickly removed her pale blue dressing gown, and put it on. "I don't know." She tied her sash tightly. "But it can't be good."

He was up in a flash, quickly donning his shirt. "I'll go with you."

Surprisingly, his offer comforted her. Still, she turned. "I don't think you should—"

A loud bang crashed at the door and an exchange of words could be heard outside.

"My mistress is abed, I tell you! You'll not go in there!" It was Ferguson, her butler.

"An' I'll not 'ave you giving 'er warning so she can make escape!" a man bellowed.

Heath shoved his legs into his breeches and jumped in front of Tess. "I'll get it."

"You can stand outside the door—" Ferguson asserted.

"You'll not be tellin' me what to do!"

Heath reached over and squeezed Tess's hand, a reassuring look in his eyes. "I'm here with you. Whatever this is, we'll deal with it together."

Gratitude swept through her, but also an odd sense of disquiet. She was unused to a man taking charge in her life. "Thank you."

"Of course. Ready?"

"As I'll ever be."

Heath turned and swung open the door.

Ferguson's back was to the entry, obviously barring the unwanted guests. Two burly men stood before the loyal butler, one wheat-haired, the other carrot-topped, both dressed in street clothes. By the requisite tipstaff gripped in the blond one's hand, Tess surmised that they were Bow Street Runners. No, this was definitely not good.

"What's going on here?" Heath's commanding voice instantly halted the bickering.

Tilting his head, Ferguson quickly stepped aside. Smart man; she'd be sure to reward his efforts on her behalf.

The carrot-topped Runner peered around his comrade, his pudgy nose lifted in the air. "I'd ask the same of you."

"Officer Kelly, isn't it?" Heath asked the blond-haired Runner.

The man straightened. "Do I know you, sir?"

"Heath Bartlett. I work for Solicitor-General Dagwood."

Kelly blinked. "Ah, sorry, sir. I didn't recognize you without . . ." His voice trailed off.

"No matter, Officer. Why don't you and your friend wait downstairs and we will join you shortly?"

Kelly shook his head. "Can't do that, sir, I'm sorry ta

say. I've an arrest warrant for Lady Golding here, and I'll not be having her make escape on my watch."

An arrest warrant? Had Lady Bright tried to circumvent Heath's investigation and pursued an alternative route? Still, what judge would issue a warrant on such skimpy evidence? Tess seethed. George Belington had a lot to answer for.

"I'm certain there's a mistake here." Heath's voice was confident enough to be reassuring.

"No mistake, sir," Kelly replied. "Magistrate Brown made sure everythin' was done to the T, since we're dealing with the upper class."

Heath scratched his chin. "Magistrate Brown, eh? He is a good sort. But I assure you that there was no theft."

The two officers exchanged a glance. "Theft?"

"The charges were fabricated based upon a grudge. The items in question were never actually stolen."

Tess hadn't realized how important Heath's confidence in her was until that very moment, and she wanted to kiss him for believing in her. And for being so chivalrous. And she might as well kiss him for being so terribly kissable. Hmm. She blinked, forcing herself to focus on the exchange before her. No matter how baseless the charges, she was still going to have to deal with them.

Officer Kelly scratched his head. "Items in question? I think, sir, that we're talkin' the King's English an yer talkin' Chinese."

"Which is why you men need to go downstairs and

await Lady Golding, so we can discuss this in a civilized manner."

"There's nothin' ta discuss," the carrot-topped Runner countered. "We're takin' her ta Newgate and that's that."

"Newgate Prison?" Ferguson gasped, his face draining of color.

Tess stepped forward. "Don't worry, Ferguson, I'm not going to Newgate Prison. This is a misunderstanding that will be resolved in a trice."

Again the Bow Street Runners exchanged an uneasy glance. "Ye seem to be takin' this quite lightly, m'lady. This is serious business."

Tess smiled. "I know all about it, Officer Kelly, and I'm not worried. The truth will win out, and you will see that this is all a terrible mistake."

The red-topped officer stepped forward menacingly. "Why you hard-hearted wench! A woman's dead, for lawd's sake!"

Tess froze, fearing that she'd heard wrong, but terrified that she'd heard right. "Dead?"

"What woman?" Heath demanded, reaching for Tess's hand.

She clung to him, sudden fear clogging her throat.

"Miss Fiona Reed."

The room suddenly washed white and assumed an odd tilt as Tess's legs gave out from under her and she was brought down to her knees.

Chapter 25

Fear constricted Heath's chest as Tess fell to her knees. "Tess!"

With her hands clutched in his, she looked up at him, her gaze lost and searching, as if he could somehow supply the answer. "Fiona?" her voice cracked.

"Get her on the bed!" Ferguson cried, pushing past the Bow Street Runners.

"I've got her." Heath gently lifted her into his arms. She was limp as a doll, terrifying him even more. She burrowed her head in the cradle of his neck, her pain palpable.

"Not Fiona," she whispered. "Poor, sweet Fiona."

Heath gently deposited her on the sagging mattress, trying to ignore the fact that they'd been blissfully happy in that very spot only moments before. He adjusted the pillow behind her so she could easily sit.

"She was a child," Tess muttered, covering her face with her hands. "Barely eighteen . . ."

Heath's heart was pounding like a race horse's.

He willed his panic to recede; he needed to think! He needed to help Tess!

"When did it happen?" Heath demanded, knowing that Tess needed an alibi.

"Hold on there, sir." The red-haired Runner raised his hand. "It's none of yer business, if I'd say so—"

"The body was found last night," Kelly interrupted as he gave his partner a hard glare. The man, it seemed, would give information while trying to glean it. Dagwood had said that the man was one of the better Bow Street Runners. Heath didn't know if he was glad for it or terrified.

"Last night?" Heath swallowed his relief, knowing it couldn't be that easy to overcome an arrest warrant. "Lady Golding was with me all night long. Ask her maid. And I'll swear to it in any court of law."

Kelly slipped the tipstaff into his pocket. "I said the body *was found* last night. She was pretty ripe."

"Ripe?" Tess's eyes widened and filled with unshed tears. "Oh, dear Lord in heaven." Wiping her hands over her eyes, she shook.

Heath sat down beside her and wrapped his arm around her quaking shoulders. "It'll be all right."

Removing her hands from her eyes, she cried, "Not for Fiona! It'll never be all right for Fiona!" She straightened. "Oh my God! Her mother! Mrs. Reed must be heartbroken!"

"She's beside herself with it." Officer Kelly agreed with a nod. "She went looking for her daughter when she didn't come home and found the body in an alley near the house."

The red-haired Runner's lip curled. "And it was an ugly thing. The smell alone—"

"That's enough, Kim," Kelly interjected with a look of warning. "I think they get an idea."

Somber silence descended in the chamber as the horrible images rose in each person's mind.

With her hands balled into fists in her lap, Tess inhaled a shuddering breath and then moved to stand.

"Sit down, Tess." Heath gently squeezed her shoulders. "You're upset."

"No. This is too important. I need . . ." Her gaze appeared lost for a moment, then it filled with determination. "I need to understand."

She rose from the bed, straightened her shoulders, and faced the two Runners like a war-weary soldier—sorrowful yet resolute.

Heath stood beside her, moved by her bravery.

"Please tell me . . ." She swallowed, obviously at a loss for words.

"How did Miss Reed die?" Heath supplied.

"Beaten to death." Kelly's tone was cold as steel.

Reaching for him, Tess grasped Heath's hand.

He moved closer, supporting her around the waist. "You can hardly believe that Lady Golding beat another woman to death."

Kelly shrugged. "It's not my job ta believe. I'm just here ta serve the warrant and see her ta Newgate."

Tess licked her lips. "Why . . .? Why do you . . .?"

When no more words came, Heath finished her question, "Why do you believe that Lady Golding is responsible for this terrible deed?"

"Certain items were in Miss Reed's possession . . ." Officer Kelly tilted his head. "Such items were recently sworn out in an affidavit as having been stolen by Lady Golding."

Tess opened her mouth, but Heath squeezed her waist, advising, "Don't say anything. It'll be misconstrued, and we can work this out."

The Runners glared.

Shaking his head, Heath said to the men, "There's more to this than you know, and she won't help herself or us to find the true culprit by saying anything here and now."

"You can't be her lawyer." Kelly glowered. "You represent the king."

"True. But I can be her friend."

"Oh, so that's what yer callin' it now," the redhead jeered.

Ignoring him, Heath turned to Kelly. "Take a look around the room; there are no other exits. Lady Golding needs to dress."

The red-haired officer jerked his head toward the draperies. "What about the window?"

"We're two stories up." Kelly motioned for his comrade to proceed to the hall. "We'll be outside the door. Have her ready in twenty minutes."

"Thank you."

After they'd gone, Heath looked down at Tess. Her face was wan and her eyes glazed with sorrow. He had a million questions, but only one was important now. "How are you holding up?"

"Not well." Still, she turned to her butler with stoic

grace. "Ferguson, if you would please ask Anna to assist me?"

"Of course, ma'am."

"And thank you, by the way, for . . . for being so loyal."

Ferguson's eyes watered but he held himself stiffly in check. "Think nothing of it, ma'am. And I will have Cook prepare duck for dinner, your favorite, for surely you must be home by then. Surely you must."

Biting her lip, Tess nodded. "Pray it be so."

Heath squeezed her waist, trying to give her some support through this terrible ordeal. "I need writing instruments, please, Ferguson. David Bernard is a contentious prig, but he's the best criminal barrister in town. I'm sure he'll take the case if I ask."

"Criminal . . ." Tess shuddered.

Nodding, Ferguson quickly left the room.

Her crystal blue gaze was so filled with pain, it almost broke his heart. "Thank you, Heath. I'm so sorry that you had to go through this—"

"Don't be ridiculous!"

"But I'm so glad you were here."

He squeezed her tight, realizing how precious she was to him. "Me as well. And don't worry. I'll see you through this."

"It's a mistake, Heath."

"Of course it is; you didn't kill anyone!"

"I mean it's a mistake for you to associate with me. The scandal—"

"Don't even say it," he growled. His hands gripped

her closer. "I don't abandon ship at the first sign of clouds."

"Clouds? More like a gale." Still, she stepped closer and leaned against him as if accepting his aid. He was filled with gladness and no small sense of responsibility for this courageous woman. "I hope you don't come to regret this, Heath. I lead a complicated life—"

The door opened and the maid, Anna, peeked inside, her face pale. "The man says we have fifteen more minutes."

Pushing back from Heath, Tess directed, "Pack five of my work gowns."

"Five." Anna's eyes were wide with fright. "You'll be there that long?"

"I don't know. Besides, there might be others in need of clothing at Newgate. You know what to do otherwise, Anna. And pray, be quick."

After Anna had moved into the dressing room, Tess looked up. "Heath, I need you to do something for me."

"Anything."

"I need you to go to the Bank of Newcastle and speak with Mr. Lowery. Tell him what happened. He'll know what to do."

Heath frowned. "It sounds like you expected something like this?"

She shook her head, muttering, "Never like this." She bit her lip, suddenly anxious. "Please go, quickly; I haven't much time and those funds had better be ready by the time I get to Newgate. Warden Newman is not an unreasonable man, but he is no philanthropist."

Chapter 26

The prison room was small and the furnishings sparse and shabby. It contained a little bed, a side table with a chipped porcelain pitcher and stained china basin, a scratched-up secretary set, a rickety wooden table and chairs, and, thank heavens, a hearth.

Tess exhaled with relief; no matter if it smelled musty and had a slight layer of dust, it was far better accommodations than she had feared. The warden, Mr. John Newman, continued the ancient practice of letting out a room in his residence and treating it as a part of the state side of the prison. The rental was costing Tess thirty guineas per week, a fee she considered well worth paying in view of the unspeakably overcrowded, pest-ridden accommodations she would have otherwise had.

Thank you, Mr. Lowery, and Heath, for coming through. The funds had arrived by breathless courier just as Tess had been brought into the warden's office. Even though she knew that the warden probably would have accepted her word regarding future payment, for at least a day or two, a bird in the hand spoke volumes in this environment.

"There's not much to it, sorry to say." Warden Newman scratched his craggy cheek. "But for the moment, it's the best I have to offer."

"I'm glad for it, and I thank you, Warden Newman, for welcoming me into your home."

Anna entered the room, a portmanteau in her hand and a fearful look in her eyes. She'd very rightfully never counted on this kind of service when she'd signed on as Tess's maid.

Warden Newman tilted his head. "Yer maid won't be able to stay, unless of course she pays her room and board as well."

"She won't be staying."

Anna straightened. "I am, too!"

Tess sighed. "This is no place for you, Anna. You can come during the day to assist me, but can return home at night. I assure you, I'm fine."

Anna's face was horrified. "Begging yer pardon, ma'am, but my mother would kill me if she found out that I'd abandoned my post!"

"Not if I dismissed you for the night."

Snorting, Anna pushed into the room, opened the portmanteau and began unpacking it.

Tess didn't like putting her maid through this, but she was inordinately relieved that Anna didn't want to go. She wasn't looking forward to being alone in this frightening place.

"I got here as soon as I could." Heath strode into

the room, his face flushed, his dark hair whipping behind him. He was such a welcome sight, it brought tears to Tess's eyes.

I won't break down. Not now. Not ever.

She looked down, pretending that she was smoothing her skirts while she collected herself. This was going to be a difficult morning and she needed to be strong to get through it. Her biggest fear was that Heath would abandon her. She knew that he cared for her, but she was going to test that fondness, and the threat of losing him was more than she could bear at the moment.

Looking up, she gave him a wobbly smile, and the look he shot her warmed her down to her soul. He was the best of men, mayhap he'd understand . . .

"Warden." Reaching out, Heath shook John Newman's hand.

"Mr. Bartlett. Are you prosecuting Lady Golding?"

"No, sir. I am here to lend my support."

"Support. I didn't know that Officers of the Crown did such things."

"My role here is to see justice done."

The warden's gaze was knowing. "I see."

Bills entered the small room, huffing and pressing his hand to his chest. "It's a blasted maze getting through this place."

"What are you doing here?" Heath asked.

Bills's gaze was confused. "The letter was signed Lady Golding, but I thought you were behind it."

"Not I."

Both men's gazes moved to Tess. She clasped her

hands before her to keep her nervousness from showing. She felt like a juggler in a carnival with too many plates in the air. She just prayed that nothing broke. Especially not her relationship with Heath . . . "Thank you for coming, Bills."

Warden Newman bowed. "Since you have so many visitors, I will take my leave, Lady Golding. If your maid will come with me, I will show her where she can find certain necessities."

Tess licked her lips, fearing to insult the man, yet unwilling to take any chance with Anna's well-being. "Thank you, Warden. I feel I must ask . . . Anna's safety . . . I would not want—"

The warden held up a hand. "Have no fear, Lady Golding. You maid will be extended every courtesy and will be perfectly secure within these walls." His gaze sharpened. "No one shall molest her or you."

Tess exhaled. "Thank you, sir. Very much."

After Anna and the warden had left, Heath pulled Tess into his arms. "Are you all right?"

She sighed. "I'm better now. Thank you for coming, and for taking care of the funds."

"Of course I'd come. I won't leave you."

His words were so sweet, she smiled. Inhaling his rich, earthy scent, she leaned her head on his shoulder, relishing the shelter of his embrace. It was amazing how much his touch inspired confidence. It was as if she were a well running dry and he a welcome spot of rain. She prayed that it would not end, not anytime soon, anyway. Even though all good things inescapably ended . . . just not today, please not today . . . *I need him.*

The thought was more than a bit unsettling. She hadn't relied on a man since her husband . . .

His hug tightened, and then he pulled away, looking down at her. "I believe we have much to discuss."

Silently she nodded, sad for the intimacy to end, but sensible that this discussion was inevitable just the same.

Holding open his hands, Bills asked, "Do you want me to step outside?"

"No, Bills, I asked you here because I wish to retain your services." Tess motioned for them to sit at the table. "If you would?"

Moving away from Heath, Tess sat. She needed to be strong and not depend too heavily on anyone. She had to resist the desire to crawl into Heath's arms and ignore the world. She understood from past mistakes that only she could navigate her future.

Bills lowered himself into the chair opposite her. "As I told you at Marks-Cross Street Prison, I'm not a criminal lawyer."

"I know. But what I need is counsel and I trust your opinion."

"You don't have to retain me for that." Bills chuckled. "I'm quite free with the stuff."

"Yes. But I want all communications between us to be privileged."

Bills nodded. "I see. Very shrewd of you. Then yes,

I will take you on as a client. But I set my fee at one guinea."

Tess smiled, touched by his gallantry. "You hardly know the nature of the services."

"I'll take my chances."

Reaching across the table, Tess squeezed his hand. "Thank you."

Heath sat down beside Tess, his nearness reassuring. "We're both here for you. You can count on us."

Bills jerked his head toward his friend. "You do realize, Tess, that any communication with Heath is not privileged. Heath can only represent the Crown."

Heath stiffened. "Don't be ridiculous! I'd never share a word!"

Looking up at his dear face, she understood that she needed to give him one last chance. "Heath, I don't want to put you in a situation where you have divided loyalties."

Heath held her hand in a cocoon of warmth and reassurance. "My only concern is protecting you, nothing else."

Bills shifted in his chair. "I feel I must speak up on this issue, Heath. I know that you are the most loyal, best friend anyone could have. But let's be realistic, you do prosecute cases. What if helping Tess conflicts with your work for the solicitor-general?"

Shaking his head, Heath looked determined. "It's impossible to have a conflict when seeing justice served is my primary goal."

Tess smiled, touched. "You believe I'm innocent."

He leaned back as if utterly confident in his knowledge. "Of course. You are incapable of harming anyone, and certainly not someone you love."

"I can't help but agree," Bills intoned.

For a moment, Tess couldn't speak, emotion constricted her throat. She busied herself with taking a linen from her pocket and wiping her eyes.

She exhaled. Maybe this wouldn't be quite as terrible as she'd feared. "I am innocent of . . ." The words wouldn't come as sorrow lashed through her once more.

Wrapping his arm around her shoulder, Heath hugged her, giving her his strength. "Do you know of anyone who would want to harm Miss Reed? Do you know anyone who might want to blame you for this terrible crime?"

"Whoever did it needs someone to blame," Bills interjected. "It may be directed at Tess, but it may be simply a way to deflect a murder charge. Kill Miss Reed and then cover it up by implicating Tess. If the murderer has a gripe with Tess, all the more reason to point the evidence her way."

"Well, he's doing a bang-up job of it," a lilting voice intoned.

A short man with wild gray hair framing his ghostly pale face stood in the threshold, a rectangular satchel in his arms. With his untamed mane, bushy brows, and large gold spectacles bordering dark eyes, he reminded Tess of a barn owl staring down at her.

Heath jumped from his seat, his hand extended. "Mr. Bernard, thank you for coming. May I introduce

Lady Golding. Mr. David Bernard, Esquire, the barrister I told you about."

Bills rose, a look of distaste on his face. "Mr. Bernard."

Bowing to Tess, the little man shoved his spectacles up the bridge of his pointy nose. "Lady Golding. I wish I had the pleasure under better circumstances." He lifted his nose in the air. "Mr. Smith."

The little man made a drama of taking a seat and adjusting his papers while Bills stood behind Tess, with Heath sitting beside her.

Mr. Bernard began, "I will get right to the crux of the matter, if I may, Lady Golding. The charges against you are quite serious and the evidence against you compelling."

"What evidence?" Heath asked. "What could possibly tie Tess to this crime, since she had nothing to do with it?"

From the pile on the table before him, Mr. Bernard pulled a sheet of foolscap with chicken scratch on it. "The victim in question was found with a satchel of jewelry in her possession, that very same jewelry having been sworn out in an affidavit claiming that Lady Golding had stolen such property."

The muscle in Heath's jaw worked. "George Belington lied. Tess never stole those jewels."

"If you would allow the lady to speak," Mr. Bernard chided, his eyes boring into Tess.

Tess licked her lips. "The jewelry was a gift, given to me by Mr. Belington. I tried to return it on two occasions, but he refused to accept it. A third time I even left it at his residence, and later that afternoon it was delivered to my door."

"You see!" Heath pounded his fist on the table.

Shoving his spectacles up his nose, Mr. Bernard asked, "Why, then, do you believe that Miss Reed had them in her possession?"

"I asked Miss Reed to deliver them to Mrs. Catherine Dunn, Headmaster Dunn's daughter-in-law and the current mistress at Andersen Hall Orphanage. The institution is struggling financially since Headmaster Dunn's death, and I thought . . . well, I don't like the jewelry, I will not wear it, so it might as well go to some good use."

"The jewelry is hardly indicative of a murder," Heath insisted.

Mr. Bernard nodded, his face impassive. "Perhaps. But I have a friend at the magistrate's office who tells me that the case is hardly insubstantial."

Heath shouldn't have been surprised that Bernard had a "friend" at the magistrate's office; he'd always suspected as much. The man was too clever by half, but for the first time Heath was glad for it.

"Hardly insubstantial?" Bills straightened. "What the blazes does that mean?"

Heath nodded. "Yes. What could possibly tie Tess to this terrible crime? The jewelry can be explained. Belington lied, and once we interview him, I'm sure he'll recant. So what else could they possibly have?"

Pulling the sheet of foolscap closer to his nose, Bernard pursed his lips. "I concur that the jewelry, although not a favorable bit of evidence, can be dealt with. Especially if Belington's servants can testify that what you say is true. The other evidence is more troubling and much more difficult to refute."

Heath smacked his hand on the table. "How can it be difficult to refute? Tess is innocent! So whatever the evidence is, it's faulty!"

"They have someone claiming that Lady Golding is not who she appears to be. That she is wicked and has engaged in some kind of terrible act." Bernard rubbed his nose. "The words are quite damning."

"Well, he's lying, and once we get him on the stand, the truth will win out!"

Removing his spectacles and cleaning them with a monogrammed handkerchief, Bernard sniffed. "That might be hard to do. Since the person making the claims is dead."

Chapter 27

Tess turned to Heath, her face filled with consternation. "Dead? The person accusing me of such things is dead? How can there be someone speaking against me who's no longer living?"

Heath could hardly imagine how she was able to maintain such calm in the face of such obvious injustice. Furious, he turned to Bernard. "This is bloody rubbish! You can't be serious."

The barrister shook his head. "I wish I weren't. The victim, Miss Reed, left behind a letter that marks Lady Golding as the prime suspect."

Tess stood. "What? That makes no sense."

The men rose to their feet.

Bernard handed a piece of foolscap to Tess as Heath and Bills leaned over her shoulder for a better view.

Sir,

You know that I only did what you asked of me out of concern for Lady Golding's safety. So your

*warnings that she was not who she appeared to be
rang false in my ears. I didn't believe it, I couldn't
believe it.*

*But now . . . oh, the shocking things I have seen!
The immoral way she has behaved! I cannot explain
in this letter, but must meet with you. Even then,
I don't know how I will find the strength to impart
the terrible details. Pray, you will tell me how I can
face her after seeing what I have seen, after knowing
what kind of wicked woman she is. She must never
know that I know! I fear how she will react! You
must guide me!*

*Your faithful servant,
Fiona Reed*

*P.S. Per your directions to share any and all mat-
ters pertaining to my employer, I have some jewelry
of Lady Golding's in my possession that she has
asked me to dispose of. I will bring them to you when
we meet.*

Tess's hand shook as she read the letter. Her face
was filled with shock and disbelief as she looked up.
"Fiona didn't write this, it's not her handwriting."

Bernard nodded. "This is not the original, Lady
Golding. This version was copied by my man at the
magistrate's office."

Tess looked pained as she shook her head and
dropped into the chair. "I can't believe that Fiona
would write such things about me."

"Are they sure the original note was written in Miss Reed's hand?" Heath sat, troubled. A victim's own words laying guilt upon someone could be potent evidence indeed where a jury was concerned. Even though Heath knew that everything in the note had to be false, it was going to cause them trouble.

Mr. Bernard removed the note from Tess's hand and sat down. "The victim's mother identified it as Miss Reed's writing, quite convincingly, I might add. She also spoke against Lady Golding, saying that her daughter was always honest. If she was upset by things that Lady Golding had done, then they had to be terrible indeed. It was her testimony that swayed the magistrate to issue the warrant."

Sitting, Bills whistled. "It's hard to call a victim a scheming liar."

Loaded silence descended in the small room, only broken by the *tap-tap* of the barrister's fingernails drumming on the table.

"Where was the note found?" Heath asked.

"Not far from the body."

Heath straightened. "So it wasn't actually in Miss Reed's possession."

"No."

"Was it sealed?"

The barrister shook his head. "The seal was broken and the letter crumpled, but very readable. I know what you're thinking. That the person to whom Miss Reed sent the letter could be the killer. It's a good supposition that we will bring up at trial, of course. But the prosecutor will likely argue that Miss Reed never had the chance to post the letter, implying that Lady Golding somehow knew of it. Regardless, the more difficult issue is why Miss Reed would write such things and what, exactly, they mean."

Bernard turned to Tess. "Does Mrs. Reed bear any ill will toward you?"

"We've always gotten on favorably well. Yet . . ." Tess bit her lip, her brow furrowed, obviously distressed.

Heath reached for her. "What is it, Tess?"

She looked up, those crystal blue eyes pleading. "I don't want you to hate me."

"I could never hate you." Heath squeezed her hand.

"Thank you, but you might not be so sympathetic once I tell you the truth about me. I've done some things . . . some things that many people would abhor . . ."

Bernard's fingers froze mid-tap.

Bills leaned forward.

Although Heath's chest constricted with anxiety, he said calmly, "Whatever it is, it cannot change how I feel about you." He realized it was true; his regard for her went well beyond anything he'd ever felt for any woman before. He couldn't imagine anything altering his powerful feelings.

Still gnawing that lower lip, Tess nodded. "I hope so. What I'd really hoped was for you never to find out. But I realize that such reticence will do me no good. And it certainly won't serve justice for Fiona."

The silence grew thick with anticipation.

Tess exhaled. "After my husband died, I was destitute. We'd lost the house, the bank accounts were empty, and the creditors were pounding at my door." Astoundingly, her tone contained no bitterness; she was simply laying forth the facts, facts that would have flattened most of the ladies he knew.

She continued, "My parents took me in. But they were appalled by the scandal and Quentin's behavior and suffering under pressure from my in-laws and Lord Berber's family, too. As a means of trying to distance themselves from all of it and show disdain for Quentin, my father pressed me to marry again, and quickly."

Bills made a reproving clicking sound with his tongue. "Heaping scandal on top of scandal."

"Very much so. But they were desperate and upset and irate with me." Tess exhaled. "I refused. They cut me off. My father thought I'd come running back, begging for the chance to do his bidding." She looked up at Heath, admiration in her gaze. "But as someone once told me, I'd 'sooner take up arms than go begging to someone I felt had wronged me.'"

"Bully for you!" Bills shook his fist.

Tess's smile was bittersweet. "Thank you, Bills, but I didn't necessarily have the most level head at the time. And choices made when you're tangled up in knots may not serve you so well when clear thought enters the picture once more."

She rubbed her head as if pained, obviously getting

to the more difficult part. "I was hurt, angry, and had a reckless disregard for the society that had spurned me based on the rumors surrounding my husband's demise. I couldn't believe the nonsensical things people would believe."

"People can be utter fools," Heath agreed, realizing that his hands were gripping the table so tightly, they ached. He knew from courtroom experience that she was leading toward a confession, and he feared it, just as one in a nightmare fears whatever is behind that ominous closed door.

Tess nodded. "The injustice of it all . . . well, I decided to show them. To take a scandal and sift through the truth, and show them what poppycock they'd believed and how far it ventured from the true facts."

The barrister's brow furrowed. "I'm not following."

Opening her hands, Tess explained, "I wrote an article in the *Girard Street Crier*. Under a pseudonym, of course, because if anyone knew that I'd written it, it would undermine the credibility of the article and would visit yet more scandal upon my family. I'd brought them enough grief already, no matter how unintentionally done."

Bills scratched his ear. "The exposé on the Brinkley affair. You wrote that?"

"Yes."

"But what does this have to do with Miss Reed's murder?" Bernard asked, his voice clipped with impatience.

Sighing, Tess turned to him. "A man came to me

threatening to expose me as the author of the article unless I did as he asked."

"The opportunistic bastard!" Heath gritted his teeth, forcing his face to calm when distress, jealousy, and fury swirled inside him like a maelstrom.

Her lips lifted slightly. "Oh, there's no doubt of that. It's his calling."

"Did he . . . take advantage of you?" The words were hard to get out.

"Yes and no. In one respect, he was the answer to my prayers. You see, in addition to his threats, he offered me a way to escape the creditors, a means of being independent. I had to admire how his mind worked; he made me an offer I couldn't refuse. And an understanding was established between us."

"Did Miss Reed find out about your arrangement with this gentleman?" Bernard asked.

Shrugging, Tess scratched her head. "I don't know. I can't imagine how she could have; I was so careful about when and where we met."

Heath tried to rein in his anger, recognizing that it was mostly for the bastard who'd taken advantage of Tess, but also for her. If she'd lied about being with another man, what else had she lied about?

But she was a victim, and obviously had her reasons.

And he could hardly blame her for trying to secure a better future.

But at what cost?

A loud crack resounded, and Heath was surprised

to see a piece of the table in his hand. Embarrassed, he slipped it under his chair. "Uh, sorry."

"No, I'm the one who's sorry." Tess's eyes were sad. "I never wanted to lie to you."

"So this is what you believe Miss Reed was speaking of in her missive?" Bernard asked.

Grief flashed across Tess's features. "It pains me that she thought so ill of me. I know what I've done isn't exactly right, but it's not really so terrible, and it is for the greater good."

"It's over now, right?" Heath bit out, his fists curling. "You don't still . . ."

Shooting Heath a look to try to be calm, Bills interrupted, "First things first. Who was the man?"

"Tristram Wheaton. He works at the Foreign Office."

The opportunistic bastard!

Lowering her head, Tess continued, "And for two years now, I've been supplying him with information."

Heath blinked, wondering if he'd heard right. "Information?"

Bills glared at his friend meaningfully. "Of course, information. What else would Tess trade?"

"Information?" Heath asked again, feeling like an idiot, but wanting to grab the ray of hope peeking through the storm clouds.

"You're an informant for His Majesty's government?" Bernard interjected, sitting up, his brown eyes alight with interest.

"Yes. The book business provides me with entrée to many homes and businesses in England. It was

Wheaton's idea, and although I'd had my doubts, it has worked out quite well."

"You like the business, don't you?" Bills asked.

Turning her head, Tess met Bills's gaze. "More that I'd ever have imagined. And I confess, being independent, earning my keep, well, it's been vastly rewarding."

Bernard nodded, scratching his chin. "So it's a real business, but they set you up in the book trade and helped you financially?"

"Yes."

"So you work for the Foreign Office?" Heath repeated dumbly, unable to grasp it.

Tess's gaze was apprehensive. "Yes."

Tess wasn't bedding anyone. Except for him. And she hadn't lied about sleeping with other men. Heath's blinding jealousy transformed into a relief so profound, he felt almost giddy.

Bernard's fingers began their dance on the tabletop once more, much faster now. "And in return for assisting your business, you provide what type of information and on whom?"

"Whomever Wheaton is interested in. Usually people in dire straits who may be receptive to influence. Those with family in France or known sympathizers. A combination of aspects that make keeping an eye on them a good idea."

"You work for the Foreign Office," Heath repeated as it finally sank in.

"Yes."

He nodded as the puzzle pieces fell into place. The

hidden source of funds, her secrecy . . . "Is that why you were in the countess's bedroom?"

Tess nodded. "Wheaton is very interested in her."

"The countess . . ." Bills face was troubled. "And what of the other members of the Society for the Enrichment and Learning of Females?"

Tess shook her head. "I've put off Wheaton for months because I cannot believe that any of the members are a threat."

"But?"

"But once the countess made application, and so quickly upon arriving in London, I had no choice but to do as my superior asked."

"You're a patriot," Heath declared, slamming his fist on the table. At the looks on Bills's and Bernard's faces, he removed his hand. "Well, she is."

Tess shook her head. "I don't know that the people I've reported on will agree. I was very circumspect about what information I passed along, but I was still informing on people. I know I would be upset if it were me."

"This is excellent." Bernard wagged his finger to the paint-peeled ceiling. "I can work with this story. If we can get Wheaton to cooperate, reasonable doubt shouldn't be too hard to secure. You're a patriot, working for His Majesty in fighting Napoleon. This could be very good, indeed."

"But it won't prove my innocence," Tess countered. "Nor will it unmask Fiona's killer."

Bernard tsked. "First things, first, Lady Golding. We must clear you of the charges, and the best way to do that is to show what kind of character you truly are. It will undermine Miss Reed's letter and lay the groundwork for other theories of the murder. There's a foreign conspiracy perhaps? Your employee is mayhap tangled up in the plot and murdered for her interference?"

Heath straightened as realization dawned. "This is treacherous business, this spying."

Tess's brow furrowed. "It can be, but—"

"You have to stop," Heath interrupted with utter conviction.

"You only just learned about it this moment, Heath. Once I explain—"

"You cannot do it any longer, Tess. It's too dangerous."

Tess's mouth worked and she exhaled as if put out. "Wheaton has assured me that with what I do, the risk is minimal."

"It's spying, Tess."

"I know what I do." She crossed her arms, looking away.

"Against foreign agents in our country while we are at war. At war! By definition it's dangerous!"

Gritting her teeth, Tess lifted her chin. "How about I tell you that you have to quit working for the solicitor-general?"

"It's hardly the same. Mine is a respected profession—"

"So public perception is the deciding factor?" Her tone was incredulous.

"Don't be absurd."

"Don't think you can tell me what I can and cannot do!"

Bills raised his hands in entreaty. "Can we discuss this *after* we see Tess cleared of murder charges?"

The silence was loaded with tension as Heath glared at Tess, willing her to see reason. But she lifted her chin, refusing to meet his gaze.

Obstinate girl. Couldn't she see that he was only trying to protect her?

Bernard sniffed. "Mr. Smith is right. First things first. Lady Golding will have no opportunity to spy if she is swinging from the gallows."

The image of Tess hanging from a noose materialized in Heath's mind, and his chest constricted with horror.

Tess's hand lifted to her neck, and fear flashed in her eyes. Her gaze sought Heath's.

Swallowing, Heath squeezed her shoulder. "We have enough battles at the moment, we needn't fight each other." For now. He wasn't about to let her keep up with this dangerous spying business.

Tess nodded, clearly unconvinced, but concerned with more pressing matters as well.

"The critical thing, as I see it," Bernard said, "is if this Mr. Wheaton will make himself and your connection known. Will he?"

Exhaling a shaky breath, Tess bit her lip. "Wheaton is . . . well, he's quite Machiavellian. But I think he will. He's out of town at the moment, though. Mr. Reynolds is filling in."

Bridging his hands before him, Bernard nodded.

"Two men who know about your work with the Foreign Office. This is getting better and better. I confess, at first I wondered if it was a domestic squabble or a quarrel over pay. But this is far better."

"Not for Fiona," Tess interjected, her features a mask of grief. "I want to know who killed my friend and I want to see him pay. We have a murderer running about scot-free, and that, I cannot allow."

"Hear, hear," Heath murmured, filled with admiration for Tess and her desire for justice.

She shot him a grateful glance. "Will you help me?"

"I'll be the first in the hunting party."

Reaching over, she grasped his hand, and he was filled with a sense of affinity. No matter the conflicts between them, when things got bad, they would stand by each other.

Bernard scratched his chin. "So how do we find these Foreign Office fellows?"

Tess's gaze moved to Bernard. "Downing Street. I have no idea where Wheaton went, but Reynolds will know. Still, he can confirm everything I told you is true."

"Excellent. I will speak with this Reynolds chap," Bernard said, rising. "Get him to step forward."

Heath stood. "I'm going with you to the Foreign Office." Tess's fate was too important for him to sit idly by.

"Count me in, too," Bills added.

Looking up at the men, Tess's eyes shone with unshed tears. "I'm a very lucky lady."

Scratching his cheek, Bills shook his head. "I don't know many other women sitting in Newgate Prison who'd say the same."

Pride and a possessive feeling that Heath couldn't identify surged through him. "Tess is no ordinary woman."

Chapter 28

"You lying bastard!" Furious, Heath grabbed Reynolds by the lapels. But the wiry man was much stronger than he appeared and shoved Heath off and moved behind the desk in mere seconds.

Reaching into a drawer, Reynolds pulled out a short sword and pointed it directly at Heath's chest. "You'll take your leave now and not bother me with your imaginary theories."

"If you're a secretary, I'm a proper seamstress," Bills growled, stepping to Heath's side.

Bernard held up his hands. "There's no call for violence, now, my good man. All we need is to speak with your superior."

"Mr. Wheaton's not here," scoffed the secretary, who no doubt had never seen this side of a quill. Reynolds was a reedy thing with a pointy face and a high, nasally voice. When the man had first called for them to enter his office, Heath had thought that the man seemed harmless enough, with his short stature and slender frame. But with the blade unwavering in his hands, matched only by his pitiless gaze, Heath suddenly knew that the bloke would kill without hesitation. How could Tess have worked with such a man? Well, it had to stop.

"Where is Mr. Wheaton?" Bernard inquired.

Like that of any vermin with a predator nearby, Reynolds's dull brown gaze did not leave Heath. "Out of town. But don't bother trying to reach him; he'll be even less patient with your wild accusations about us working with some trollop than me."

"Trollop!" Heath raised a fist.

"We're not accusing anyone of anything," Bernard countered, shooting Heath a quelling glance. "We're simply here at Lady Golding's behest."

Reynolds's eyes narrowed. "Don't know her, except by *reputation*, of course," he sneered. "I hear she's quite free with her favors."

"You son of a bitch!" Heath stepped forward.

The short sword jerked, aiming for his chest.

Bills laid a hand on Heath's arm, pulling him back. "You'll do Tess no good if you're in a grave or a prison."

Reynolds smirked. "You're mighty heroic when you know you can't do a thing. Feeling a bit *impotent*, are you?"

"The man's cracked," Bills whispered in Heath's ear. "And there's more than one way to bake a cake, my friend. Tess needs your help and this is not the way to do it."

Torn, Heath didn't budge. Reynolds was a double-dealing snake. And his insults went beyond the pale.

He knew that Tess wasn't lying. It simply wasn't her style. She might not tell the whole truth but she was not an out-and-out fabricator. Moreover, the facts were incriminating enough to be wholly against her interests. And she knew that they would be checked.

Why was Reynolds being such an ass? Afraid of scandal? Afraid of the *ton* taking up arms about being investigated? Concern over society putting pressure on the Foreign Office to cease some of its operations? Governmental rivalries?

No matter what possibility came to mind, Heath sensed that Reynolds's actions were directed against Tess. They had to be, to desert a woman when she faced hanging.

Bills tugged on Heath's arm. "We're getting nowhere here. And when you hit a wall . . ."

Dig a tunnel, was what they'd always said when they'd run into difficulty at the Inns of Court.

"You're a bug in need of squashing," Heath bit out, turning his back on the son of a bitch and heading toward the door. The hairs on the back of his neck rose. "Try it," he dared over his shoulder. "And you'll swing before the end of the week."

Bernard put his hat on his head. "Obviously we were mistaken, Mr. Reynolds. We're sorry to have disturbed you."

The three men silently filed out of the room.

Once on the pavement, Bills spoke, "Don't those fellows have some sort of code about not leaving a man behind on the field?"

Bernard adjusted his sleeves. "Apparently not, if what Lady Golding says is true."

"She's not lying." Heath's glare was matched only by Bills's.

"The Cat and Bagpipes is around the corner," Bernard offered. "I suggest we repair there to consider our tactics."

The men silently traversed the narrow streets and alleys, passing muck-scented livery stables and dilapidated lodging houses. The sounds of carriage wheels, horses' hooves, and hawkers plying their wares filled the air.

The Cat and Bagpipes was half empty as the men took a table near the front entrance by the door. They each ordered ale, but when it arrived, Bernard was the only one to drink.

Bernard leaned forward, his tone affable. "I heard that some of the public houses around here were hostels of old for pilgrims seeking the shrine of Edward the Confessor at Westminster Abbey."

Heath shrugged, his mind filled with Tess and her troubles.

"Still reading history, are you?" Bills made a face. "Well we have a lady's future to consider, if you don't mind."

Bernard sniffed.

Running his hand through his hair, Heath swallowed his frustration. "We need to find Wheaton."

Bernard snorted. "Why? So we can hit another dead end? I'm not a Bow Street Runner and neither are you."

"Mayhap Wheaton has a bit more honor than that nasty Reynolds bugger," Bills countered.

Shaking his head, Bernard sipped from his drink. "If you do find this Wheaton fellow, which will be difficult enough to do, you'll likely get the same response as Reynolds. I say we find another course. One more suitable to keeping our eyes on the real target—getting Lady Golding out of Newgate."

Heath had never admired the snippity barrister more than he did at that moment. Leaving Tess at Newgate that afternoon had been one of the hardest things Heath had ever done.

Heath peered out the window, wondering what she was doing. It was growing late, and his last hopes of clearing Tess so she wouldn't have to spend the night at Newgate were fading with the darkening sky. A night in such a place . . .

Curling his fists, Heath pushed aside the anxiety, refusing to give in to the phantoms. She'd be fine. She was inside the warden's residence. Warden Newman had given his word that she'd be perfectly safe. Anna was there, too.

Instead of allowing his fears to strangle him, Heath would use the anxiety to propel him forward to chase down whatever avenue would see her free and safe and in his arms once more. "So what do you propose we do, Bernard? I am open to any suggestions."

Belching, Bernard waved a hand. "First we bring up the fact that Lady Golding works for the Foreign Office, then we substantiate that claim by showing that she received funds from the Foreign Office. Then we float a few possible theories of what could have happened to Miss Reed and create reasonable doubt."

"Not bad." Heath nodded.

"But if we can't make the link ring true, then we may be able to use the Foreign Office claim as part of an insanity plea."

Heath wondered if he'd heard correctly. "Tess will not assume any responsibility for a crime she didn't commit. Besides, no jury would rule Tess insane."

Bernard shrugged. "I'm simply considering all of the possibilities. I do what it takes to get the job done."

"But a woman is dead, and there's a murderer running free!"

"Not my problem at the moment." Bernard coughed into his fist. "I keep my focus fixed and leave the investigative work to the Bow Street Runners. I suggest you do the same."

Heath banged the table with his fist, drawing stares from the other customers. He lowered his voice. "I can't. I cannot sit by while Tess is being blamed for some else's crime. It goes against the very code I've sworn to uphold." Not to mention that Tess was in danger as long as the murderer was roaming free. "You trace the money, and don't you dare go for the insanity plea without checking with Tess first. I'll find Wheaton."

Tapping his finger on the table, Heath had a sudden idea. "I want you to do something for me, Bernard."

"Yes?"

"Can you have your lackeys set up a watch at Downing Street?"

Bernard nodded. "We'll know if Wheaton shows up. And when he does?"

"Send word to me. I don't care where I am or what I'm doing, track me down and let me know."

"I'll take care of it."

Narrowing his eyes, Bills pursed his lips. "I may have an idea for how to find Wheaton, and it could be a lot faster than waiting for him to surface."

Hope rose in Heath's chest, and now more than ever he was grateful for Bills's friendship. "How?"

"We need to go to the society. I must speak with Lady Blankett."

Heath frowned. "Lady Blankett? Why?"

Bills's eyes twinkled. "She has a friend she told me about, an old chap named Sir Lee Devane."

"How can he help?"

"It seems he used to work at the Foreign Office. She claims he used to be pretty high up, a knight with connections, she says."

"Capital! He can give us a lead on where we can go or who we can ask to find Wheaton." But as quickly as his elation came, it suddenly died, and Heath frowned.

"What is it?"

"I don't think Tess wants anyone in the society to know about her work with the Foreign Office."

Bills scratched his cheek. "I don't know that we have much choice."

"I'll dash to Newgate and see what she says and meet you back at the society."

"You're worried about her." It wasn't a question. Bills understood.

Heath was already setting his hat on his head and heading for the door, intent on hailing a hackney. "Wouldn't you be?"

Chapter 29

"It's too damned cold in here," Tess muttered to herself, pulling her shabby work shawl tighter around her and leaning closer to the low-burning hearth. Removing her useless gloves, she rubbed her hands together, trying to get the blood flowing in the frozen sticks that used to be her fingers. Her feet were so cold they were almost numb, no matter than she wore three pairs of wool stockings.

It was almost as if the very air was too thin, and laced with a cold that nipped at your bones. Tess had visited prisons many times, but she'd always gone back to her nice cozy house; never had she had a taste of real confinement. Never had she felt so dreadfully alone.

While Anna was there, Tess had put on a brave face. But now, alone with the shadows, real and imagined, Tess couldn't decide which was worse, the sorrow or the terror. She vacillated between wanting to lie down and cry, and jumping at every noise, a fireside poker raised in her hand.

Tess once more checked the small glass clock she'd brought from her bedroom. Only three minutes had passed since she'd last checked? It couldn't be. Mayhap it was broken? Holding the clock to her ear, she listened for the clicks. Deliberate and steady. Closing her eyes, she sighed. The clock was perfectly fine; it was she who felt as if time had sputtered to a stop.

The wind howled outside, and she shuddered, anxiety interlacing her every shortened breath.

I'm a prisoner in Newgate!

Setting aside the clock, she stood and paced, trying to dampen the fear splintering her flesh and twisting her insides into knots. Once more she checked the open doorway, even though it was too soon for Anna to be back.

She was glad she'd sent Anna to the house to get some more clothing. Anna shouldn't have to suffer through this internment a moment longer than she needed to. The girl was too young to face this kind of environment, too sweet to be exposed to this other world.

Tess understood that she was far better off than any of the other prisoners, and counted herself blessed. Still, the fear gnawed at her composure and quickened her heartbeat to a racing canter. She was alone, a prisoner, surrounded by convicts and rapists and murderers . . .

"And guards," she reminded herself, taking another turn. Still, fear ate at her like a parasite, shooing all positive thought from her mind and leaving her with only hulking shadows. Her heels echoed loudly in the empty chamber as she crossed the small space before the hearth once more. How many other prisoners had trod this path with worry? How many of those prisoners had swung from the courtyard gallows below?

She ran her hand through her hair, loosening the coil and allowing it to fall around her shoulders.

"Could I be any more pitiful?" she muttered to the flickering candles. "Arrested for murder . . ."

Her steps slowed as grief overwhelmed. "Fiona . . ." A tear rolled down her cheek, one of the many that had fallen since she'd heard the news.

A crash erupted down the hallway. Tess started, holding her breath and eyeing the distance to the poker. Warden Newman had promised that she'd be safe, but her nerves found little comfort in those words.

When no other sound came and disaster did not fall, Tess exhaled. "Dear God, I have to stop doing this or I'll go mad." Either that or turn gray.

"Would Heath still like me if I'm a gray-haired Nervous Nelly?" She attempted a lame jest to the empty room.

Heath.

A small swell of joy trickled through the knot in her middle, loosening some of her fear.

Heath was out there, working for her release, fighting on her behalf . . .

If anyone could see her freed, it was Heath.

He believed in her, accepting that she was innocent. He took her word as truth, without doubt. He was the only man she'd ever met who'd really understood the truth of all she'd faced. The thought comforted her deeply.

And he wasn't upset about her work with the Foreign Office. A tiny thrill shot through her. She'd never shown that side of herself to anyone. And astonishingly, he accepted her. All of her.

He had grasped what happened with Lord Berber and Quentin with amazing shrewdness. He acknowledged her mistake with George Belington, and now her work with the Foreign Office. He knew it all and cared for her still.

A sense of awe and well-being blanketed her. She hadn't thought that a man existed who could accept her and the mistakes and the choices she'd made. But one did.

Heath.

The image of his handsome face surrounded by those ribbons of dark hair lifted her leaden lips into a smile. Thinking of his lean, smooth body and the wickedly delicious things she'd done and still wanted to do with him stirred a warmth deep inside her to which no fire could compare. Closing her eyes, she imagined the sensation of his brawny arms around her and how he made her feel safe and cherished.

Wrapping her arms about her body, she hugged herself close, rocking gently to the sounds of the window latch bumping in the whipping wind.

The room was three stories up, so there was no need for bars, thank heavens, but Warden Newman insisted that the shutters remain closed. Not a bad thought considering the chilly temperatures outside.

Still wrapped in her arms, she spun for another turn. She needed to stop thinking about her pitiful state and start focusing on how she was going to get free. She wondered how Heath had fared with Reynolds. How did Reynolds react to the news that she was in prison? Tess frowned. Probably with irritation. He had little patience when things didn't go exactly as he wished.

Lord, how she hoped Wheaton was back in Town. The man might be a viper, but he was on her side and wouldn't forsake her.

Or would he?

She stopped mid-step. Wheaton was the kind of man who cut his losses without a backward glance. Was she too much of a danger to him now that she could be exposed?

Tess swallowed, then shook her head. No, she'd done a lot for Wheaton, and was still of use, for the moment, at least.

She began pacing once more. Oh, how Tess wished she'd gotten more intelligence on the countess!

Could the countess be behind Fiona's murder? Why? What threat could Fiona pose?

Fiona. What had she meant by what she'd said in her letter?

More importantly, *to whom did Fiona write that letter?*

Tess's paced quickened. Who was the "sir" who'd told Fiona that Tess was not as she appeared? Who was the mystery man that Fiona had wanted to meet? Had that meeting occurred? If so, perhaps it was *that* man who had harmed Fiona?

And what terrible thing had Fiona wanted to share? *What did I do to inspire such condemnation?*

Guilt and shame and frustration warred within Tess.

Why should I feel guilty? What have I done?

Fiona had to have seen something upsetting. But what? Informing on people? It just didn't seem as horrific as Fiona's words conveyed.

Aggravated, Tess grabbed one of the pieces of wood from the pile she'd been rationing. She suddenly had no patience for being practical.

She knelt before the grate, hammering the poker into the wood, trying to position the lumber, her motions jerky, her anger steeping. *What have I done to turn a woman that I care about, one whom I trusted, into a snitch?*

Tess did recall that Fiona had said that she was doing as the man asked out of concern for Tess's safety. But still, Fiona was telling this "sir" any and all matters pertaining to Tess. It was despicable. No matter that Tess had informed on people, she'd always been circumspect about what she'd shared.

Tess stabbed at the wood as the fire crackled.

"Where's yer mistress?" a deep voice called.

Tess started. As she turned, her breath caught. A hefty man with dark curly hair tied back with a bit of rope and a black beard stood near the closed door. He wore rough street clothes and scuffed brown leather boots that had seen better days.

"You frightened me." Pressing her hand to her chest, she tried to calm her racing heart.

"Where's yer mistress?"

He thought she was a servant. And no wonder, she wore her serviceable work gown, an old shawl, and was kneeling before the grate.

Still holding the poker, Tess stood, suddenly glad for his mistake; every hair on her body was raised in alarm.

The man's meaty fists curled and uncurled as if he was nervous, and his eyes darted about the room and behind his back, as if fearful that someone might be coming.

Her heart began to pound so loudly, her ears roared. She hadn't heard a peep from the guard outside. Anna was gone. It was just she and this man, alone in a scary place where a scream wouldn't seem so out of place.

She swallowed, feeling as if tiny needles pricked her skin with terror.

She needed to start using her head and the opening that God had given her. Her hand tightened on the poker.

Clutching her shawl around her with one hand, she lifted her chin and mimicked Anna's mother, "Me mistress went ta see the warden. And what's yer business with her anyway?"

Holding her breath, Tess waited as her pretense hung in the air between them.

After the longest moment, the man's lip curled and frustration flashed in his dark gaze. "I've a message for her."

Tess swallowed. "I'll pass it along if ye like."

"It's just fer her."

Licking her dry lips, Tess nodded. "Suit yerself. But she's not here."

"That I can see."

The silence grew thick.

So what's it to be? It's your move.

Her palms grew sweaty and the scents of metal and sweat filled the air.

Finally he snarled, "I'll be back."

Tess nodded, involuntarily taking a step backward.

As her skirts swooshed about her feet, the man's eyes flickered to her expensive kidskin shoes.

Tess's heart skipped a beat.

His smile was full of malicious intent. "Ta the warden's, eh?" Never taking his eyes from her, he reached behind him and closed the door.

Raising the poker, Tess ran to the shuttered window screaming, "Help me!"

The brute charged across the room.

Tess lifted the poker but he swatted it out of her sweaty fingers as if it were a feather.

Screaming, she ran behind the table and tossed a chair down in his path. He stomped the chair as if it were made of sticks, his meaty hands reaching for her, grabbing her curls and yanking her back and off her feet. She landed hard on her back, knocking the wind out of her.

Slamming his knee into her chest, he pinned her down on the floor. She scratched at his arms and kicked at his legs.

He punched her in the face. Pain speared her jaw, and she saw stars, tasting blood. She pushed away the pain, raising her fists and fighting him.

He yanked off the twine tying his hair and looped it around her neck. The rope tightened, slicing into her throat, cutting off her air. She gagged. Her hands scratched at the cord, catching nothing but her own flesh. Gurgling sounds spewed from her mouth, and inside her head she heard screams.

Chapter 30

Heath didn't think, didn't call for help; his body simply *moved*!

Barreling forward, he slammed into the man, knocking him off Tess and into the far wall with a bone-jarring crash.

Heath roared, fists pummeling. Bone cracked, blood splattered, and Heath's fists grew slick with sweat and blood. The bastard kicked and punched, landing blows that Heath didn't feel, his mind an empty slate of hatred.

Arms grabbed Heath, lifting him off the bastard, but Heath fought and kicked, lunging forward.

"Bartlett!" a voice bellowed as the arms held him at bay.

A familiar face swam before Heath's vision. "Bartlett!" It was Warden Newman.

Heath's head cleared. "Tess!"

"She's alive, thanks to you," Newman offered.

His knees almost buckled with relief.

"Let him go," the warden ordered the two guards holding Heath.

Released, Heath spun.

She was sitting up, her face was battered, her lip bleeding and her eyes wide and frightened. Her neck was a bloody mess. She looked up, reaching for him.

Heath fell toward her, grasping her hands and pulling her close.

She quivered in his arms, and his heart wept for her anguish. He held her gently, no matter than he wanted to squeeze her so hard and never let her go. He was filled with a violence that shook him to his core.

Two beefy guards lifted up the assailant and headed toward the door.

"He's not going anywhere!" Heath snarled.

The warden turned, stepping forward. "He's going in the lockup. I have a few questions for him."

Heath shook his head.

The warden held up his hand, his eyes hard as nails. "I need some answers and don't feel that I ought to be asking for them here, in front of the lady. Not the way I ask 'em."

Heath hugged Tess tighter to him, torn.

"I swear he'll pay for what's he's done." The warden's lip curled. "But not until I have my answers."

There was naught Heath could do; this was the warden's domain. And Heath wasn't about to leave Tess, no matter how badly he wanted answers and vengeance.

Mutely, Heath nodded.

"I'll send for the doctor," the warden offered, then as an afterthought, "I'll pay."

"No quacks!" Heath demanded.

The warden scowled. "Now see—"

"Do you know Dr. Winner?"

"Nick Redford's friend?"

"Yes. I want him. Only him." Heath trusted Dr. Winner and knew that Tess did, too.

Nodding, the warden sniffed. "As you wish. And I'll set two guards before the door and one in front of the residence. No one else will be bothering Lady Golding. "

"Bothering?" Heath roared. "Is that what you call it?"

"I don't know what happened to my guards, but I assure you I'll find out and it won't happen again."

"That's not good enough!"

"I'm sorry. What more can I say?" Then the warden was gone.

The window latch banged in the stone-cold silence.

Looking down, Heath scanned her bloodied face and neck. The marks were hideous, but they seemed superficial. Was there more damage he couldn't see? Should he check her or wait for the doctor?

Gently Heath lifted Tess and carried her over to the bed. Except for the quivering, she was limp as a rag doll. His heart pinched with fear and worry.

Her eyes were open, her gaze fearful, yet clear.

"Can you breathe?" he asked, voicing his biggest worry.

She nodded. "I'm all right," she croaked. "I'm alive."

He gritted his teeth, fear, guilt, and grief over what

might have been scorching him like lightning. He needed to do something, to act, to help.

Sitting down beside her, he busied himself with the basin of water, dipping a cloth.

Her hand grasped his, arresting his movements.

Their eyes locked.

"You saved me," her voice cracked. "I'm all right . . . thanks to you." Her crystal blue gaze was full of gratitude. "I'm . . . all right."

Tears suddenly burned the backs of his eyes. She was reassuring him! He couldn't believe that after he'd left her alone, had allowed the bastard—

He grasped her hand and squeezed. "I shouldn't have left you."

"Don't be a dolt," she whispered.

He shook his head.

"You're going to argue with me? I'm wounded." She gave him a weak smile.

He exhaled, feeling slightly reassured. If she was teasing him she had to be all right. Right?

She swallowed and made a face as if pained. "Water?"

He jumped, feeling like an idiot, and reached for a mug.

Swallowing looked terribly painful, but she pushed through it, handing him back the mug and lying down. "Thanks," she mouthed.

Carefully he set the wet cloth on her wound and wiped away some of the blood. It was a nasty wound, but it could have been so much worse if he hadn't come when he did . . .

His mind veered away from that possibility.

He needed a dressing! Some kind of ointment!

"Lie down with me?" she asked. Her eyes looked so vulnerable, his heart squeezed even more.

Carefully he lay down beside her, wrapping her in his arms and hugging her close.

She sighed. "Cabbage."

"Huh?"

"We're like cabbage leaves."

Oh, we're lying pressed together. "Oh."

Smiling, she closed her eyes, and astoundingly, her body relaxed. She was probably exhausted from her fight with the attacker.

He lay staring at the paint-peeled ceiling, feeling wound tighter than whipcord. The violence was still fresh in his fists, the blood still staining his hands. Even now he felt the residue of the strength surging through his muscles, the blinding rage . . .

The last hour washed over him. The anticipation as he neared her chamber, ready to see her, to kiss her, to hold her sweet, lavender-scented body in his arms.

Not like this.

Not with the odor of blood and sweat and fear clouding the room. Not with the terror of near tragedy so fresh.

The nightmare he'd seen upon opening that door.

He closed his eyes, unable to grasp it.

"It's all right," she whispered in his ear.

Opening his eyes, he looked at her. Her face was swollen, her neck a bloodied mess. "How can you be so brave?" he asked with wonder.

She smiled. "We're together."

I love her.

The insight caught him like a bullet to his heart; it was so powerful, he could hardly think, he could hardly breathe.

I love Tess. More than my life. More than . . . anything. If anything happened to her . . .

Fear gripped him so powerfully, he shivered.

Her hand squeezed his forearm, reassuring.

She was so strong. She'd faced her husband's betrayal, weathered unjust scandals, and dealt with the Reynoldses of the world as she worked to protect her country in a time of war.

Well, it was time for someone to protect her. Time for someone to put her well-being first.

Heath knew he was the man for the job.

The only question was whether Tess would allow him to be that man.

Chapter 31

Hours later Tess awoke to the sound of voices, her every muscle feeling as if it had been hammered with a mallet.

"She's fine," a male voice soothed. "Her breathing is regular and her pulse is steady."

"You're sure?" Heath's voice sounded distressed. "There won't be any lasting effects?"

"Not physically, but many have difficulties with nightmares and anxiety after such an attack, and understandably so."

"I survived," Tess murmured, opening her eyes. "I can handle a few nightmares." Her throat was still sore, but her voice didn't seem to be harmed.

A healthy fire flamed in the hearth and the sun shone brightly through the open windows, warming the room. A new stack of firewood lay piled nearby. Obviously small consolations from Warden Newman. Pigeons cooed outside, and the air smelled oddly of flowers and olive oil.

"You're awake!" Heath rushed to her side. Shadows bordered his beautiful cocoa brown eyes, his clothes were wrinkled beyond repair, and his boots were badly scuffed.

"You look like hell." She traced her hand across the rough fuzz grazing his beloved cheeks. "Did you sleep at all last night?"

Smiling, he shook his head and kissed the palm of her hand.

Dr. Michael Winner stepped forward. "How are you feeling, Lady Golding?" He was a tall, portly fellow with kind eyes and loose lips that usually slipped easily into a smile. Today his mouth was set in a line and his brow was furrowed with concern.

"I ache. But I'm all right considering the circumstances. Thank you for coming."

"I would have been here sooner. But I have a difficult case, a young lad with the mumps, and only just received the message from Warden Newman." Dr. Winner frowned, scratching the tuft of brown hair ringing his receding hairline. "From what Mr. Bartlett tells me, you had quite a close shave."

Upset, she looked to Heath. "What ever happened to—"

"Warden Newman took him to the lockup for questioning. I haven't heard anything." His constancy was unspoken; the dear man hadn't been willing to leave her to find out.

Sighing, Dr. Winner shook his head. "I confess, I never expected to treat you here, Lady Golding. What, pray tell, is going on?"

"Lady Golding has been falsely accused of murder," Heath explained.

Winner's brown brows knitted. "First Beaumont and now this? Is there an epidemic of false murder charges these days?"

Eyeing Heath, Tess changed the topic, "Is that your special ointment I smell, Doctor?"

The good doctor nodded. "You have quite the nose for scents. Olive oil, calendula flowers, and a few secret ingredients. If you will allow me, I would like to dress that wound and examine you more fully."

"Yes, thank you."

Holding out his hand, Dr. Winner turned to Heath. "Perhaps you can excuse us?"

Heath shook his head.

"It's all right, Heath," Tess interjected before he could argue. "Dr. Winner will take good care of me, and I would like you to find out what happened with . . . that man. I want to know why he attacked me."

Winner frowned. "You think he had a motive?"

Tess shook her head. "He asked for me." Remembering, she closed her eyes. "That man wanted me dead."

Heath laid his hand on her shoulder, reassuring. She opened her eyes. "I'm all right."

"How can you be so calm about it, Lady Golding?" Dr. Winner's face was distressed.

Heath grasped her fingers and kissed them. "Tess is no ordinary lady."

Tess smiled up at Heath, trying to ignore the ache in her jaw. "Please find out for me."

He nodded. "There are two guards stationed outside the door and another in front of the building. You send for me if you need anything. I won't be gone long." He stood, releasing her hand and turning to Winner. "Don't leave her alone."

Dr. Winner's smile was warm. "She'll be fine. Don't you worry."

The examination was completed in a trice and Tess was relieved that the damage was as minimal as it was. Notwithstanding a lot of aches and bruises and her neck injury, she would be perfectly fine in a few days.

Snapping his black medical bag closed, Dr. Winner nodded. "The wound shouldn't even scar. Just keep applying the ointment and change the bandage every other day or so."

"Thank you, Dr. Winner." Tess sat up, gingerly touching the bandages on her neck. The scents of olive oil and flowers made her stomach growl. "I'd give a lot for a piece of toast with butter right now."

"Hunger's a good sign. I'll be sure to have a word with Warden Newman about getting you some breakfast."

"Step aside!" a woman's voice commanded. "We have leave from the warden."

A heartbeat later Janelle swept into the room, Ginny and Lucy following in her wake.

"Oh my God, they've beaten you!" Janelle shrieked, tossing her white spotted ermine muff onto the table.

Turning to Lucy, she wagged a finger. "I told you we should have come sooner!"

Lucy's doe-like eyes were awash with distress.

Ginny was wringing her hands so hard they shook. "How could they have done that to you? Oh my dear!"

Tess was deeply touched by their concern, but simultaneously mortified that they had to see her here, as a prisoner at Newgate. Standing, she straightened her wrinkled gown as best as she could, then pulled a scarf from a portmanteau and tied it around her bandaged neck. "I must look dreadful."

Lifting her hands heavenward, Janelle cried, "How can you be so vain when the guards have attacked you? Did they knock the sense out of you, too?"

Tess's cheeks warmed. "The guards didn't beat me, Janelle. And it looks worse than it is. I'm fine. Just ask Dr. Winner."

Janelle's eyes narrowed. "A quack."

Dr. Winner smiled. "Hello, Lady Blankett, good to see you again, too." Turning to Tess, he asked, "Since your friends are here . . ."

"Please go. I know you're anxious to check on that boy. He's quarantined, I presume, so none of the other children at Andersen Hall become ill?"

"Yes. That's always the biggest fear."

As he squeezed her shoulder, Dr. Winner's eyes were filled with warmth. "I'll be back to see you in a few hours."

Janelle shot Ginny a glare, interjecting loudly, "I'm sure Lady Golding doesn't need that kind of attention. You said yourself that she's fine."

Janelle nudged Ginny with her elbow.

Ginny blinked. "Oh yes. Isn't it better to check on someone in the morning, anyway?"

Scratching his head, Dr. Winner frowned.

"Morning would be better." Janelle nodded vigorously, shepherding the good doctor over the threshold. "We'll see you then." She slammed the door closed behind him.

Janelle turned and with a determined look in her eyes, motioned wildly for the ladies to join her in the far corner of the room.

"You're being a bit theatrical, don't you think?" Ginny suggested, limping to follow.

"Shhh," Janelle hissed, gesticulating for her and Tess to join them huddled in the corner.

Crossing her arms, Tess eyed the three women warily. "What's going on?"

Janelle waved her hands. "Lower your voice!"

"All right," Tess whispered. "What's going on?"

Janelle's sharp, catlike gaze moved from Tess to Ginny to Lucy, and back to Tess with dramatic aplomb. Then her lips twisted into a satisfied smirk. "We're breaking you out."

Tess's mouth dropped open.

Lucy grabbed Tess's hand and squeezed, her eyes earnest as she nodded.

Ginny leaned forward. "I confess I had my doubts about this harebrained scheme, but seeing what they've done to you . . . We can't get you out of here soon enough."

Sudden tears burned the backs of Tess's eyes, and she sniffed.

"Don't be so easily overset." Janelle's lips firmed into a disapproving line. "Stiffen your backbone; you can't afford to be weak and rattled."

Reaching up, Tess wrapped her arms around the three women and hugged them close. They smelled comfortingly of heliotrope and rosewater, and as they held Tess, she sent off a prayer of gratitude for such loyal friends.

But if they knew the truth about her spying, they wouldn't trust her so easily. Nor would they be putting themselves at risk. And who could blame them . . . The doubts squeezed at Tess's heart, and her head ached from anxiety.

After a long, sweet moment, Janelle pushed away. "You know how I loathe sentimentality." Still, she took a linen and wiped her teary eye. "The mold in here is abominable."

"I am so grateful." Tess bit her lip. "But I can't let you do this."

Reaching into the folds of her skirts, Lucy pulled out a piece of foolscap and handed it to Tess.

Tess read, "'Plan of Escape. One: Tess and Lucy exchange clothing. Two: Lucy takes to Tess's bed, pretending to be Tess and feigning ill.'"

"There'll be no trouble with credibility with your treatment here," Janelle interjected.

Tess continued. "'Three: Tess leaves with Janelle

and Ginny. Four: Aunt Sophie comes to visit Tess and the switch is revealed to the warden. They can't hold Lucy for taking a nap and so Lucy and Aunt Sophie leave.'"

Ginny placed her hand on Tess's. "It's the mourning attire. Men usually don't look past it. You wear a big black bonnet and a veil and we all walk out of here."

Janelle lifted her brows meaningfully. "A good plan if I do say so myself. Your aunt wanted to come now, but we couldn't afford to raise any suspicions by having a relative involved. When Sophie arrives later we do want the cat out of the bag, so it works perfectly."

Tess's vision blurred with fresh tears and she smiled. Reaching for Lucy, she squeezed her and Ginny's hands. "It *is* a good plan. And would probably work, but I can't allow you to do it." She swallowed. "I was attacked last night—"

Janelle waved a hand. "Lucy won't even be here an hour and we've sent for Bills to stay with her."

Tess's eyes widened. "Bills is involved in this?"

"Not that he's aware of, yet." Janelle sniffed. "But he won't rat us out, not with Lucy implicated."

"You are good." Tess shook her head in amazement.

Crossing her arms, Janelle smirked. "I know."

"Still, I cannot allow it. Fiona is dead, God bless her soul. Murdered, and so young . . ." Tess swallowed as grief overwhelmed her, followed by resolve. "I was almost killed last night. The dangers are too great. I will not place anyone else at risk."

Funereal silence enveloped them.

Pressing her hand to her eyes, Tess groaned. "I fear that this whole mess is my doing. I have brought this upon us—"

"How so?" Janelle asked.

Exhaling, Tess bit her lip. "I work for the Foreign Office."

Janelle raised her brows. "And . . .?"

Tess blinked. "And? I work for the Foreign Office . . . as a spy."

Waving a hand, Janelle sniffed haughtily. "We already knew that."

A breath escaped from Tess as she counted her racing heartbeats. One, two, three. "You knew?"

"From the moment you applied for membership to the society."

Ginny raised her finger. "Not the very moment, but pretty shortly thereafter."

Tess's mouth fell open. "How?"

Ginny shot Janelle a worried glance. "We promised not to say . . ."

Ignoring her friend, Janelle lifted a shoulder. "Sir Lee Devane told us."

Tess blinked. "The man who used to run the Foreign Office knows about me? The man's practically a legend."

"Yes."

"But I thought he was long retired. And how do you know him?"

"He's Edwina's grandfather-in-law," Ginny explained. "And he and Janelle . . ."

Janelle's cheeks tinged pink. "We are friends, simply friends."

Ginny smiled adoringly at Janelle. "It's so nice to see you happy for a change."

Lucy winked at Janelle with a knowing look on her face.

Scowling, Janelle looked away. "Please don't think that just because I allow the man to take me fishing that I grant him any kind of liberties . . ."

"I thought he was in his seventies . . ." Tess wondered aloud.

"And quite fit for his age," Ginny added with a teasing smile. "It was actually his idea that someone keep an eye on things at the society."

Janelle raised a finger. "It is designed as a place to share information and influence others, so it's not illogical to be concerned that when we are at war it can be put to unintended uses. Sir Lee was right to be careful about certain elements using the society for despicable ends."

Crossing her arms, Janelle sniffed. "But that Wheaton fellow wouldn't hear of any of us doing the intelligence gathering. No matter how good a spy I would make. He wanted his own person."

Tess pressed her palm to her racing heart. "Me."

Ginny nodded. "Yes. And we're quite satisfied with the choice, especially since you've enough backbone in you to stand up to that Wheaton fellow."

Tess's eyes widened. "You know about my reports?"

Ginny smiled sweetly. "Sir Lee says that you've

taken very good care to guard our privacy. Thank you."

Shaking her head, Tess moved over to the chair. "I need to sit down." She lowered herself into the seat and pressed her hand to her temple, trying to grasp the truth of it. "You knew. And you didn't mind."

Ginny eyed Janelle. "We weren't all content with it, but when the countess applied for membership, we were very glad to have you around and on our side."

"You knew about the countess, too?"

Ginny made a face. "I can't believe that she and that Gammon woman thought we'd do anything that might possibly harm England. The nerve!"

Squatting, Lucy picked up the piece of foolscap from where it had fallen and brought it over to Tess, her dark eyes urging.

Tess set it on the table. "I can't put you at risk. Especially not now."

The door opened and Heath stepped inside the room. Tess's heart skipped a beat and she was overcome by an emotion so powerful, she felt awash in radiant sunshine. Without thought, her hand stretched toward him, seeking his comforting touch.

His eyes met hers, and she could see the relief inside them, and a tenderness that warmed her to her toes.

"Out!" Janelle hissed, rushing toward Heath and flapping her hands like a crazed stork. "We'll have no turncoats in here!"

"Turncoat?" Heath held up his arms to ward off her attack.

"How dare you lead Tess on while you're engaged!"

Tess stood. "Engaged?"

Stepping forward, Ginny wagged a finger at Heath. "Shame on you! We saw the *Times* this morning!"

"The *Times*? What about the *Times*?" Heath demanded, sidestepping Janelle to avoid her flying hands.

"You're engaged! To Miss Penelope Whilom! You lying snake!"

Chapter 32

"**E**ngaged?" Heath cried, disbelieving, and lowering his arms.

"Yes, engaged!" Janelle smacked him on the side of the head. "To Miss Whilom!"

Heath didn't even feel the blow as he looked over to Tess. Her face had washed white. "I didn't send the notices! I swear! I had no idea!"

"You must have had some notion!" Bills stepped into the room, a folded newspaper under his arm and an angry look on his face.

"No. Of course not!" Heath shook his fist. "I was here all night."

Janelle smacked him again.

Heath pointed a finger at her, fury and fear lashing through him. "Don't do that again!"

"Or what will you do?" Janelle sneered. "Go get engaged to someone else? Polygamy is a crime, you know. Mayhap you need to be the one locked up at Newgate!"

"How could you do this?" Bills demanded, shaking the broadsheet in his hand.

Heath gritted his teeth. "I didn't. I can only guess that Lord and Lady Bright heard about Tess's arrest and then sent out the notices last night."

Tess blinked. "You said that Lady Bright was pressing for the investigation . . ." Her face crumpled with hurt and betrayal. "Oh my . . . your engagement was contingent on my arrest!"

Guilt and anger clutched him in a viselike grip. "No . . . no . . . it wasn't like that . . . not really . . ."

Janelle grabbed the newspaper from Bills's hand and popped it open with a crackle of pages. "The facts speak for themselves."

Hugging herself, Tess moved to the window as if unable to look at him. "I can't believe that I trusted you."

Striding over to her, he grabbed her hands and pressed them to his heart. "I made a mistake, Tess."

"Obviously." She looked away, the anguish on her face killing him.

"I'm talking about the engagement! I can't marry Penelope! I love you."

Removing her hands from his, she turned. "Don't confuse lust with love. I've made that mistake before, and it doesn't end well."

His anger steeped. "I know the difference between love and lust! I'm not your bloody husband!"

"Mr. Bartlett!" Ginny chided.

Tess looked over her shoulder, her crystal blue gaze filled with sorrow. "No, you're not. And you never will be."

The pronouncement hit him like a ball of lead in

his heart. "You can't think that I had any idea . . . that I wanted this . . ."

Holding open the broadsheet, Janelle sniffed. "Isn't this the 'young lady of a very respectable family of the *ton*' that you were courting? *Courting*, mind you. It's not like she just fell into your lap."

Clenching his fists, Heath looked at the angry faces around him, unable to grasp the nightmare unfolding before him.

At the look on his face, Ginny bit her lip. "Maybe this isn't too terrible . . . Engagements have been broken . . ."

Janelle shook her head. "You can't do that to that poor girl! Think of the scandal."

Scowling, Bills shook his head as if disgusted. "Miss Whilom would be ruined."

"Go ahead and marry your perfect Miss Whilom." Tess's voice was so dead it was frightening. "Have your perfect wife, your perfect life . . ."

Smacking the broadsheet closed with a crackle of pages, Janelle straightened. "Enough of this sentimental rubbish! We have a prison break to execute!"

"Oh, what a funny jest, Janelle!" Ginny jerked her chin toward the open doorway and the guard hovering outside.

Setting her fists to her hips, Janelle glared at Heath. "Now see what you've done! We had a perfectly good plan until you showed up. This is all your fault, Bartlett!"

The injustice of it all pierced his soul, mixed with

no small sense of hurt. He'd just told the woman of his heart that he loved her and she told him to go marry another woman.

Bills picked up the sheet of foolscap from the table and read it. Looking up at Lucy, his face hardened. "You weren't really . . .?"

Lifting her chin, Lucy shrugged.

Tess stepped toward the bed, her movements wooden. "If you don't mind, I'd like to lie down."

Concern pinched at Heath's chest. "Are you all right?"

Lying down on the bed, Tess curled into a ball with her back to the room. "I'm fine. Just tired." Her voice was flat.

Heath stepped forward, fear, heartache, and love tangling him in knots. He got down on bended knee and reached to touch her back, but his hand hovered, uncertain. "Can I get you anything?"

"No, I just want to sleep."

Heath dropped his hand.

Ginny stepped forward. "I think you'd better go. We'll stay with her."

He was unable to move; his legs felt almost as leaden as his heart.

"Come along, my friend." Bills urged. "The guards are here, her friends are here. She doesn't need you now."

Heath was overwhelmed by his own inconsequence. Tess meant everything to him; she was the spicy sweetness in a world that was so bland, the vibrant color to his empty canvas. He hadn't known how barren his life had been until she'd filled it with her courage, her grace and her wild beauty.

He felt as if he couldn't live without her, and she didn't need him. Or want him. *She just told me to marry another woman.* His heart ached so powerfully, he could hardly breathe. His head dropped and his shoulders fell as he was overcome by a sorrow so black, he was defeated by it. *How could I have been such a fool?*

Helping Heath to rise, Bills led him out the door.

"I agree with your theory that Lord and Lady Bright must have been so delighted by Tess's arrest that they sent the notices straight off to the papers." Bills sipped his beer and sighed. "I wonder if they even know that the charge has nothing to do with the alleged thefts."

Heath sat hunched on the stool, his gaze dull, his glass sitting untouched before him on the bar. He was in a dark haze of grief so overwhelming he could hardly move. "Tess told me to marry Penelope . . . she told me to go ahead with it."

Sighing, Bills set down his drink. "That had to hurt. I'm so sorry, old boy."

Heath looked to his friend. "I don't understand how she could do that. If she was supposed to marry another man I'd—I'd . . ." His throat constricted as jealousy and fury and hurt pierced his soul.

"Mayhap she thought that she was doing you a favor? You said yourself that Tess doesn't wish to marry."

"But I don't want to marry Penelope!" Heath barked, drawing the barkeeper's penetrating gaze.

The man stopped cleaning the glass in his hand and whipped the cloth onto his shoulder as if ready to take steps. "She should know that," Heath hissed.

Bills waved to the barman that all was well, and the man resumed his cleaning once more.

Resting his palm on the bar, Bills faced his friend. "Let us look at it from Tess's point of view. She spends the night with you and the next morning learns from the broadsheets that you're engaged to someone else."

"But—"

"Stop and listen to me for a moment!"

Heath blinked at the sharp tone.

Adjusting his coat, Bills raised his hand. "The poor woman finds out that you've been courting a young woman whose family wants to see her hang badly enough that they'll wager an engagement on it."

Heath gritted his teeth. "You're really lifting my spirits . . ."

"Her husband almost ruined her, her father cut her off, and now you? No wonder the woman doesn't wish to leg-shackle any man."

"But I'm different. I really love her!"

Bills made a noise of disgust. "You have a very odd way of showing it."

Slouching, Heath shook his head.

At the look on Heath's face, Bills's features softened. "If it's any consolation, Tess seemed pretty upset about the engagement, before she knew the other part."

"You think so?"

"And then did you see her when we left? She seemed about as low as one gets."

Heath looked up, hope stirring inside him. "If she's upset . . . well, then that means that she actually cares."

"Of course she cares. Like I said, she probably feels pretty betrayed right now . . . But I'll bet she's pretty torn up about losing you."

Heath wrapped the hurt around him like a funereal cloak. "I find that hard to believe. She just told me to marry Penelope."

Bills's eyes took on a determined light. "Have you ever considered that she told you to marry Miss Whilom because she thinks it's what you want?"

"What?"

"Remember how she asked about her friends first when inquiring about the investigation?"

"Yes."

"If there's anything that should be clear as day to you now, it's that Tess sacrifices her own needs for those she loves."

"But—"

Bills raised a hand. "Hear me out, old friend. Today, did she say, 'I don't love you'?"

"No, but—"

"'I don't want you'?"

"No."

"'I don't need you'?"

"No."

The barman set his fists on the counter. "Do you two want to be alone?"

Bill waved a hand. "We're talking about the lady he loves."

"Oh." Removing his fists, the man relaxed.

Motioning for the barman to refill his glass, Bills explained, "The poor woman is in prison, charged with murdering her friend, and he's upset that he's engaged to someone else."

Blowing out a gust of air, the barman smirked. "You need to be counting yer lucky stars!" He topped off Bills's drink.

Heath scowled. "She didn't kill anyone. And someone is trying to kill her!" He straightened, feeling as if a lightning bolt had just blasted through him. "Devil take me!"

"What?"

Heath jumped from the stool. "I was so caught up I forgot all about Pernel!"

The barman leaned forward. "Who?"

"The bugger who attacked Tess last night!"

Bills stood. "Tess was attacked? Where the hell were the guards? Where were you?"

"I arrived just as . . ." Clenching his fists, Heath swallowed. "We caught him."

"So that's why her face was banged up. I didn't want to ask . . ." Bills shook his head, his face troubled. "So what happened to this Pernel fellow?"

"Warden Newman interrogated the man. He named the man who'd hired him. It was Reynolds! Reynolds tried to kill Tess!" Tossing two coins on the bar, Heath moved to go, glad for the opportunity to do violence. "I'm going after him! He'll not get away with this!"

Laying his hand on Heath's arm, Bills shook his head. "Getting yourself locked up, no matter how justified, won't do anyone any good!"

Heath shrugged him off. "No court of law will arrest Reynolds based on the word of a tortured criminal. Justice demands—"

"That you see him pay for his crimes," Bills interrupted. "But we need evidence!"

"The man works for the blasted Foreign Office. He disavowed Tess. Now he's trying to prevent her from asserting the connection. The only way to stop him from hurting Tess is to stop him, *permanently*."

Heath moved toward the door, but Bills stepped in front of him. "Move aside, Bills, I don't want to hurt you."

"Think, man! Think! If Reynolds's superiors sanctioned the attack, then you're doing her no good." An odd light flashed in his gaze as Bills wagged his finger. "But what if they didn't? What if he's gotten out of formation; what if he's as much of a threat to *them* as to us?"

Heath hesitated. His thoughts were colored by the thirst for violence, the need to make Reynolds pay. But what if Bills was right? Then there were other options, and ones that might better help Tess. "What are you saying?"

"If the man's operating outside the lines, then his own people might help us stop him."

"Go on."

Pressing his finger to his mouth, Bills narrowed his eyes. "That Wheaton fellow and anyone he answers to will be displeased with Reynolds if he's connected to attempted murder. But why would he take that risk? Why would he want to silence Tess? What else has the man been up to? What else . . . *Confound me!*"

"What?"

"What if Reynolds is the 'sir' that was meeting Fiona Reed? What if he was the one who convinced Miss Reed that Tess was in danger and needed watching?"

"You think he killed Miss Reed?"

"I'd bet my last farthing on it. And I'd bet my boots that his superiors have no idea that he's going around killing English damsels."

Frustration, anger, and fear coursed through Heath like a torrent. "We don't have time for this! You're right, there's more to this than we can understand right now, but we don't have time to sit around discussing the what-ifs! Reynolds might go after Tess again. But if this came from higher-ups, then if I get him, then she still might be in danger! I can't allow anything to happen to her!"

"I know! We need more time. But—"

Heath smacked his fist into his palm. "We need to get Tess out of Newgate! That's what we need to do, and quickly!"

"That would be a perfect solution to buy us more time. But her hearing is not until next week."

"We can't wait for the legal system to grind to resolution. We need to get her out, now!"

"First you're planning murder and now a prison escape? When you go full force, my friend, you pull out all the stops. But even if the guards didn't overhear enough today to be suspicious, after the attack John Newman is going to be vigilant. He won't allow anything a hair outside the law."

Tapping his fist to his lips, Heath's mind churned. "Who says it has to be outside the law?"

"What are you proposing?"

"I'm going to enter a nolle prosequi. It will stop all judicial proceedings against Tess."

Bills straightened. "I don't care that it's within the special powers of the Law Officers of the Crown to enter it, Dagwood won't do it."

Heath shook his fist. "The nolle prosequi is exercised in cases where the interests of justice do not require that the defendant be brought to trial. It fits this situation perfectly! And it's the only way to keep Tess safe!"

"It's rarely used, but aside from that, after that terrible mess-up with the Beaumont affair and now Lord and Lady Bright, and him catching you kissing Tess, Dagwood won't do it. He's a smart man, brilliant actually, and it makes no sense to enter a nolle prosequi."

"Justice demands it!"

Bills shook his head. "You can argue with him until you're blue in the face, Dagwood won't allow it to be entered at this point in the proceedings."

"I'm not asking him."

The air grew quiet.

Bills laid his hand on Heath's arm. "If you do this, it's all over. Your career, your respectability, everything."

"I've been a little too fixated on my career and my status. Love, Tess, it's all more important than any job or what anyone has to say about me." Heath's brow furrowed as realization dawned.

"What is it?"

"I'm more like my father than I'd ever thought."

"Tess isn't a married woman."

Heath shook his head. "It's just that he was always willing to chase the dream on the chance it might lead to happiness. He knew great love with my mother and he's spent every moment since she died searching for another taste of it. No, I don't agree with all of his choices, but I finally understand him a bit more."

"Well, I hope you get a chance to tell him someday and aren't locked up for breaching your fiduciary duties."

Heath slapped his friend on the back. "With you representing me? I doubt it." Energy coursed through him as Heath realized with perfect clarity what he needed to do. "Go to Newgate, get Tess ready. I'll send word as soon as it's done. I want her away from there as quickly as possible. Take her to Andersen Hall. Reynolds will not want to be connected to Miss Reed, so he'll stay away from there. Tess should be safe for a short while at least."

Bills nodded, his face stoic. "And where will you be?"

"After it's done, I need to see Dagwood."

"You're going to tell him?"

"He should hear it from me. I owe him that much at least."

Nodding, Bills exhaled. "Just so you know, I could always use a partner in my legal practice. We make a bloody good team, you and I."

Heath pursed his lips as he tried to contain his emotions. "Thank you, Bills."

Bills sniffed, his eyes suspiciously shiny. "Don't get all sentimental on me. You haven't heard my terms yet. Besides, I can be a bugger of a taskmaster when I put my mind to it."

Heath clutched his friend's shoulder. "I won't forget this."

Rubbing his nose, Bills stepped aside. "Get out of here already before the barkeep thinks we're going to start dancing. Go. Tess needs you."

Bills always knew exactly the words Heath needed to hear.

Chapter 33

Heath followed the liveried servant to Solicitor-General Dagwood's private study. The man motioned for Heath to go inside. "Mr. Dagwood will be with you in a moment."

"Thank you."

Stepping into Dagwood's inner sanctum, Heath straightened his neck cloth and tugged on his silk waistcoat, suddenly glad that he'd worn his Sunday best.

The chamber was an imposing testament to all that Dagwood had accomplished in his legal career. Parchment certificates in gilded frames lined the walls, awards with commemorative engravings sat on a mantel, and inside a special glass case rested the notice declaring Dagwood the Solicitor-General of England, Law Officer of the Crown.

The walls were lined with legal treatises, and the scent of old books was like a comforting friend to Heath as he moved to stand before the window to wait.

The rear garden was barren and unkempt. Dagwood spent most of his waking hours at work; he likely had little care for the part of the house that he didn't use and that visitors rarely saw. He had no children to run in the grass, no wife to tend a garden. It must be very lonely. For the first time ever, Heath felt a little sorry for his superior. Not that Heath had any of these things. But he hoped . . .

"Hello, Bartlett."

Heath turned.

Dagwood strode across the room with that authoritative air that Heath had tried to emulate when he'd first come to work for the solicitor-general. "Congratulations! Lady Bright sent me a note last night and then I read the announcement in the *Times* this morning. Well done!"

Dagwood pumped Heath's hand vigorously and patted him on the back. "A drink is in order, my friend!"

Moving over to the sideboard, Dagwood poured each of them a generous portion of brandy. Heath recalled the very first time Dagwood had brought him into this study and they'd shared a drink. Heath had just secured the repayment of a ten-thousand-pound debt on behalf of the Crown. The debt had been outstanding for five years and Heath had succeeded where his predecessors had failed. He'd made it happen not by using threats or sanctions, but by helping the debtor structure his payment so as not to lose the lands that had been in his family for generations, the key sticking point in the deal.

It had been a triumph that he'd savored, all the more gratifying because Dagwood had been pleased.

Dagwood's usually stern face was creased in a wide smile as he pressed a glass into Heath's hand. "Here's to your fortuitous marriage. May you and Miss Whilom share many prosperous years to come."

Nodding, Heath took a sip. It tasted like vinegar, and Heath knew it wasn't the brandy that had soured.

Dagwood's sharp dark gaze was assessing. "What's troubling you, Bartlett? You should be on top of the world, and instead you look as if your best friend just died."

Setting down the glass, Heath straightened. "I want to thank you for everything, sir. You've been only generous to me—"

Waving a hand, Dagwood stepped behind his great mahogany desk and sat. "There's no need to get sappy now, Bartlett. Everything I did for you was for my own ends. Every general needs good lieutenants, and you're one of my best."

A large oil portrait of Dagwood was on the wall behind the desk, and Heath felt as if he was facing two Dagwoods. The Dagwood in the painting was resplendent in court attire, and the artist had managed to capture the hint of gray at the temples of his raven hair and the intelligence gleaming in Dagwood's coal black eyes.

"Thank you, sir. That means a lot to me, sir." Heath swallowed. "I hope you always feel that way."

Dagwood's eyes narrowed. "There's something

amiss. Are you concerned about the guest list? Or the wedding preparations? That's for Lady Bright to worry over. Not you."

"I . . . ah, well, there's no easy way to say this, sir . . ."

"You, the exemplary barrister, at a loss for words? Mayhap marriage isn't so good for you after all!" Chuckling, Dagwood reached into the box on his desk and selected a cigar. He held one out to Heath, who shook his head. Dagwood busied himself with the cutter and used the candle on his desk to light it.

Puffing white clouds of smoke, Dagwood narrowed his eyes and considered Heath through the haze. "So, what is it then? Concerned about your father meeting the Whiloms?"

Heath gritted his teeth, ashamed that he'd told Dagwood about his father's indiscretions. He'd been lashing out at his father for far too long. He'd been acting like an adolescent, self-involved and without concern for the damage he was inflicting on his father or their relationship. He realized that he had some fences to mend. But they would be easier to repair now because Heath had finally stopped wanting his father to be someone other than who he truly was. Heath could finally accept his father and love him without judgment or shame.

Heath lifted his chin. "Nay, sir. My father is quite the gentleman and can carry himself well, no matter the company. He is not the problem." Reaching into his coat, Heath pulled out a sheet of heavy vellum. He slipped it onto Dagwood's desk.

"What's this?" Dagwood asked.

"My resignation."

Dagwood stilled, then leaned back in his chair and puffed on his cigar. Smoke surrounded him in a cloud. He did not touch the paper. "Did you accept the offer from Benton and Williams?"

"You knew about that?" Mr. Isaac Benton had been courting Heath for two years, and Heath had taken pains never to let his superior know about it. Heath hadn't wanted Dagwood to hold it against the law firm, and he'd never had any intention of accepting the position. Now Heath doubted that Mr. Benton would offer him so much as a drink after what he'd done. Again, the generosity of Bills's offer warmed Heath's heart.

Dagwood grimaced. "I never figured you for the private sector, Bartlett, but appreciate that you might feel the need for more funds now that you will be wed. I can see about a raise in salary, but you know there's only so much I can do. Staying with me offers more than simple compensation, as you well know. "

"I'm not asking for an increase in salary, sir. I'm resigning. And if you read that letter you will understand why."

"Hmm." Blowing out a line of smoke, Dagwood lifted his quizzing glass to his eye and peered intensely at Heath.

"Aren't you going to read it?"

"I'm sure it's quite poetic, but I'd rather hear you say why you're resigning after all I've done to help you."

Heath swallowed. "I do appreciate all you've done for me, but I have no other option."

"There are always options, Bartlett." Dagwood's smile was self-satisfied. "If we don't have one, we craft a new one. We're lawyers; we define the rule of law."

Heath shook his head, thinking of how brave Tess was. She'd stepped outside the little box that the world had placed her in, and instead had become an agent for England. She lived by her own code of ethics, safeguarding those she loved. He, in contrast, had gotten mired in legalities and caught up in his "position," somehow losing sight of his values in the process. Her example inspired him.

Heath rubbed his eyes. "I can't remember when I started seeing things less as 'right and wrong' and more as 'win or lose.' I can't count the number of times when I justified an unjust result by saying it was how the system operated or was the way of things." Dropping his hand, Heath frowned. "I can't remember the last time I did something for the greater good that didn't somehow further my ambitions."

Dagwood stopped smiling. "Pray tell me you're not going haring off to the country to teach snot-nosed children their numbers."

"No, sir. I have no idea what I'm going to do." *Or who I'm going to do it with.* But he had a hope, a dream . . .

Dagwood straightened in his chair. "I can't believe that you're quitting now, after working so hard and rising so high. It makes no sense."

"I don't want to quit, but—"

"Then don't."

"I have to, sir. After what I've done you will no longer want me in your employ. I've filed a nolle prosequi in the Golding matter."

Dagwood's quizzing glass dropped from his eye as disbelief shone in his dark gaze. "Pray tell me why you would do such a stupid thing?"

"Lady Golding is in danger."

"Is that what she claims?"

"She was attacked last night and almost murdered. If I hadn't come in when I did, she'd be dead."

Leaning back in his chair, Dagwood stared at the ceiling. "So you were there last night. With her, in her rooms, at Newgate Prison."

"That's not the point, sir—"

"I could press charges, you know. Breach of fiduciary duty. You do recall that little pledge you made regarding the Crown?"

"Believe it or not, sir, I am keeping my promise to uphold justice—"

"By setting a murderess free?"

"Lady Golding didn't kill anyone."

Dagwood straightened. "And you know this, how? Because she told you so?"

"She works for the Foreign Office, sir. She's an agent for the Crown. The very same Crown that we work to safeguard, too!"

"It's very convenient that you tell me this *after* your insubordination."

"I couldn't take the chance that you'd say no. Or

that you'd try to stop me." Dagwood would have considered the political ramifications, the pros and cons. Heath couldn't accept any compromise on Tess's safety. It had been the first time that Heath had realized that Dagwood might not be the perfect model for him after all. He needed to carve his own mold, true to himself and his own code of justice.

Heath squared his shoulders. "I came here because I wanted you to learn it from me. I'm sorry to disappoint you, sir. I will never forget all you've done for me."

Heath turned and walked out the door, leaving his career and everything he'd worked for in shambles behind him.

And he didn't mind in the least.

He felt good, at peace with his decision and with the rightness of his actions. The law was sacred, and protecting its virtue for the woman he loved was the most gratifying thing he'd ever done.

As Heath made his way toward the front door, he sent off a prayer of thanks. For sending him Tess to help him find his way.

A liveried footman stepped forward. "This just arrived for you, Mr. Bartlett." The man held out a folded note.

"Thank you." Opening it, Heath read,

Mr. Bartlett,

I received your message regarding the attack on Lady Golding and am glad to hear that she was not too badly injured. Regarding the nolle prosequi, you certainly know how to make my job easier. I would dearly like to know how you managed to get S.G. Dagwood to agree to it, and if he'd be willing to consider it more in the future.

Please call upon me if any additional services will be required. I am at Lady Golding's disposal.

Sincerely,
D. Bernard.

P.S. If it's still pertinent, Wheaton is back.

"Yes!" Heath crushed the note in his hand. Wheaton was back. Tess was safe. It was time for Heath to make the Foreign Office do right by her. Wheaton would do it, for Heath was going to give him no other alternative.

Chapter 34

The scents of leather, old parchment, and dust filled the air of the library as Tess traced her fingers along the smooth spines of the volumes lining the walls. It was evening, and she was physically exhausted by all that had transpired at Newgate Prison and the trip to Andersen Hall. Yet she was restless, and the events of the last few hours had her thoughts spiraling in dangerous directions.

Heath had executed a stunning stroke to protect her. The nolle prosequi was the only means of getting her out of Newgate legally and quickly. She would be eternally grateful to him. But what would it cost him? How would Heath's superior react to the news of his unilateral action? Would Heath lose his position? Would his career be destroyed? Bills had refused to answer her questions, giving her the sense that Heath's act had been a mighty sacrifice.

And how would Heath's fiancée respond to the fact that Heath had helped her? What about Miss Whilom's parents? Tess felt ill every time she considered Heath in their company. But she had to face the reality that he was engaged to another woman, no matter how utterly demoralizing it might be.

"This is an extraordinary collection." Nearby, Bills slowly scanned the chamber, his raised candelabra sending shadows dancing across the shelves.

Pushing all distressing thoughts from her mind, Tess turned. "Headmaster Dunn likened his books to the orphaned children he helped. They each had a unique story to offer and a distinctive place in his heart."

"How did you meet him?"

"At a lending library. I was there to examine some comparable volumes to help me assess the value of some books I was selling. When Headmaster Dunn learned of my business, he immediately wanted to talk with me about books. The newest ones he'd found, his old favorites, the latest trends." Unbidden her lips lifted. "He was no highbrow; anything on the written page interested him; from great poets to horrid novels, he loved them all. He had such a passion for the written word."

Remembering the inspiring man, Tess sighed with sadness. "Headmaster Dunn taught me to love books and to experience the joy they could bring. He helped me turn a business that was meant to be a façade into a real calling. And for that I will be eternally grateful."

"What's this?" Bills pointed to the table.

Tess's heart pinched with grief as she saw the quill,

ink, and record, still waiting for Fiona to return and finish her cataloging. "It's Fiona's worktable. We were sorting the collection." She shook her head. "I still can't understand why Reynolds would kill Fiona. It makes no sense."

"Perhaps I can explain that," a raspy voice answered.

A thin, gray-haired, wizened chap with a gold-topped cane and a jaunty air stepped into the library. His black buckled shoes tapped loudly on the wooden floor.

Bills moved forward, but Tess shot him a look not to worry for her safety. By his craggy face and hunched stature, Tess guessed that the man had to be well past seventy. And given his cheerful mien and relaxed pose, he did not appear to be a threat.

His old-fashioned dove gray coat and knee breeches with white stockings pronounced him an "older gentleman," and therefore, Tess dipped into a curtsy.

The gentleman bowed with a flourish. "Sir Lee Devane, at your service, Lady Golding."

Straightening, Tess involuntarily lifted her hand to her bandaged throat.

"So you've heard of me, eh?" His craggy face split into a smile. "Lady Blankett, I presume? She finds it hard not to talk about fishing, I know."

Tess dropped her hand, understanding how this man might have charmed his agents into feeling like a family, instead of a haphazard collection of recruits. "Actually, sir, I've heard a bit about your days when you headed the Foreign Office." *And have wondered what it might have been like to work for someone a shade warmer than frost.*

Tess motioned to Bills. "May I present my friend Mr. Smith."

Bills nodded. "A pleasure to make your acquaintance, sir."

Sir Lee's green eyes twinkled. "Of course, Lucy's friend."

Bills's cheeks flushed, but he squared his shoulders. "Janelle was a bit vague. I'm curious what you did at the Foreign Office."

"In my glory days, I was the man in charge of intelligence on every suspicious foreigner in England. It was my privilege to serve my country and was as rewarding a position as one could ever hope for."

"Do you miss it?" Tess asked, suddenly wondering what life might be like if she stopped working for Wheaton. She loved what she did, but could she live without it? Memory of Heath's demand that she quit her work still caused a swell of anger within her. But thinking of all he'd sacrificed for her scattered that resentment like leaves in a windstorm. That tempest swirled inside her, buffeting her emotions until she didn't know which way to turn. All she knew for certain was that she longed to be with Heath.

Sir Lee leaned on his gold-topped cane. "Ah, that I do. I miss the thrill of the chase, the challenge of outwitting my opponents and struggling to think one step ahead of everyone. It was dashedly exciting." He shrugged. "But one must make room for new blood; it's the way of things. And besides, I have a great-grandchild on the way and soon will be too busy teaching him how to ride a horse."

Tess couldn't help the smile from lifting her lips. "I daresay you'll not be setting the babe on a horse too soon. How is Edwina?"

"Abed, as the good doctor ordered. It's my grandson who is really suffering; he's as nervous as a hen. One would think that a child's never been born before this one."

Bills shot Tess a questioning glance. He was as curious as she as to why Sir Lee had suddenly turned up. "If I may be so bold . . . why are you here, sir?"

"I'm here regarding a special matter with Solicitor-General Dagwood. We are both on the board of trustees of Andersen Hall, you see. It's a fascinating affair actually, with murder, dangerous secrets, and a love story that would break your heart." Sir Lee's eyes crinkled at the corners and his smile was mischievous. "But that's a story for another time."

Sir Lee's gaze moved pointedly to Tess. "Given this opportune encounter, I am greatly interested in your situation, Lady Golding. I would very much like to know how things stand. Have you spoken to Wheaton yet?"

Nervous, Tess licked her lips. "He's back?"

Sir Lee nodded. "He and I spoke a short while ago. Please be assured that he did not know about what's happened with you, nor did he sanction Reynolds's actions."

Clasping her hands before her, Tess braced herself. "What do you know?"

"Managing agents is a delicate task. One must take risks, and inherent in any gamble are the inevitable mistakes. Reynolds was one of them."

Bills made a noise of disgust. "A bit of an understatement, don't you think? He murdered a young woman and tried to kill Lady Golding!"

Sir Lee held up his hand. "This is a nasty business, and sometimes even the most level-headed man cracks under the pressure."

Wrapping her arms around herself, Tess shuddered. "Reynolds was never level-headed. He's sick."

"The facts do speak for themselves," Sir Lee agreed.

"What are the facts? Why did he kill Fiona? Why did he try to kill me?"

"Miss Reed was working for him."

The betrayal tasted bitter on Tess's tongue. "So it's true that Reynolds was the mysterious 'sir' that Fiona was meeting."

"Yes. If it makes you feel any better, he told her and another employee of yours, a footman named Paulson, that you were in danger and that keeping an eye on you would help keep you safe."

Recalling Paulson's words when Heath had stormed her carriage, "Your safety is my only concern!" Tess did feel a little better. But if Fiona and her footman Paulson worried over her safety, why didn't they simply ask her about it? Why did they have to sneak about?

Tess gritted her teeth, knowing that some questions might never be answered. "But why did Reynolds set my employees to watch me? Did he think I'd turned? That I was working for the French?"

Sir Lee's lip curled. "Nay, that would have made sense. It seems that Reynolds had developed an unnatural fascination with you."

Tess raised her hand to her chest, appalled. "With me? I never even liked the man!"

"As I said, Reynolds was not stable. I'm sure that there was nothing that you did to invite such interest, but it grew, nonetheless. Neither Miss Reed nor Paulson knew of your connection to the Foreign Office, by the way. Their orders were purposefully vague. Reynolds simply asked them to keep an eye on you and to recount anything at all that pertained to you. They reported to him every third day."

Tess scratched her arm, feeling violated. "On what? What I ate for breakfast?"

"That, too. But apparently, when Miss Reed reported certain goings-on between you and Mr. Bartlett . . . Well, Reynolds did not take that intelligence too well."

"Not too well? Fiona was beaten to death!"

Sir Lee scratched a craggy cheek, his green eyes sad. "I know. Reynolds had cracked, and in a fit of rage killed the messenger, so to speak."

Bills shook his fist. "Why didn't anyone notice he was round the bend before this? Who put this man in charge?"

"I assure you, Mr. Wheaton is quite torn up about it all."

"Why, because he has a mess to clean?" Tess didn't

bother to hide her disgust. "Is he going to try to kill me, too, now? Just to keep things tidy?"

Sir Lee pinched his nose as if distressed. "No one is going to try to harm you, Lady Golding. The attack at Newgate Prison was another of Reynolds's mad schemes. He wanted you to take the blame for Miss Reed's murder and simultaneously wanted to keep you from making a connection to him at the Foreign Office. Stupid plan, actually, since it would have brought more attention to your claims, but that's neither here nor there."

Crossing her arms, Tess shook her head.

"So what happens to Reynolds?" Bills asked.

"Reynolds is finished. You will not see or hear from him again."

Bills's eyes narrowed. "Finished? That's it? No indictment, no trial . . ."

Opening his hands, Sir Lee shrugged. "It wouldn't serve anyone at this point."

"Nay, can't have anyone know what a brilliant bungle the Foreign Office made of things!" Bills scoffed.

Sir Lee motioned to Tess. "Lady Golding would not fare well if news of this got out. And at this point all actions are predicated on the goal of making things right."

"Right." Tess's laugh was mirthless as she pressed her hand to her suddenly aching head. "A young woman murdered. People reporting on what others eat, with whom they sleep, where they go, what they say, and in whom they confide. I'm having trouble making the correlation between these foul deeds and safeguarding our beloved country. And I'm not just talking about the things that Reynolds did." Although this wasn't the first occasion that Tess had questioned her work, it was the first time she was actually tempted to leave it all behind her.

What would it be like to have a normal life? No more spying, no more juggling Wheaton's demands and her own wishes. No more reports. A normal life.

With Heath.

Her heart ached with longing and she blinked back tears. She wanted Heath. By her side. Forever. She wanted to bear his children, desperately and with a yearning that stole the breath from her throat.

The idea of life without him . . .

Hugging herself, she shivered, thinking of the long, lonely years without the man she loved by her side. Watching him marry another would be worse than Newgate. The only escape she would have would be death. And without Heath, she wondered if she'd welcome it.

Tess dropped her face into her hands as grief pierced her heart. *Oh, dear Lord in heaven, what have I done?*

"Are you all right?" Bills moved beside her.

Swallowing, she looked up. "I'm fine." But she wasn't; she was dying inside.

"You're white as a sheet. Perhaps we should return to the guest house? You've had quite a time of it."

"No, no. I'm fine."

"I'm curious . . ." Sir Lee stepped forward. "Would you please tell me how you got out of Newgate

Prison? I know from Janelle that her escape plan was never executed. How did you manage it?"

Tess bit her lip, overwhelmed by Heath's sacrifice to help her. No one had ever given up anything for her. No one had ever loved her the way that he so clearly did.

And I told him to marry Miss Whilom!

"Oh God, I feel ill." Pressing her hand to her middle, she groaned.

"Tess, sit down." Bills grabbed her arm and led her to the chair.

She sank into it, distantly wishing that it was a shallow grave. *I can't live without him. And I sent him away . . .*

A sob escaped.

Sir Lee thrust a handkerchief into her hand. "Please don't tell me! I'm sorry I asked about the prison."

Pressing the handkerchief to her mouth, she shook her head. *What have I done?*

"You really love him, don't you?" Bills's tone was gentle.

Sniffing, she nodded. "And . . . I . . . I told . . . him . . . to . . . marry . . . her!" A dam broke within her and tears gushed forth. Howling, she sobbed into the handkerchief, her shoulders shaking. Her heart ached so badly, it was like a knife spearing her chest.

Leaning down beside her, Bills laid a hand on her back. "Then fight for him, Tess! He loves you."

Tess wept harder.

Sir Lee leaned forward. "Whom did she tell him to marry?"

Bills explained, "Miss Penelope Whilom. Bartlett's engaged to her."

A sob burst from Tess's throat as she pressed her palms to her eyes so hard they hurt.

A hand shook Tess's shoulder. "Lady Golding."

She curled forward, wanting to be left alone with her despair.

The hand shook her shoulder harder. "Lady Golding! Janelle told me that she sent you a note at Newgate, but you must not have gotten it!"

Sniffing, she looked up. "A note?"

Sir Lee's face was animated. "Janelle is quite the spy when she sets her mind to it. She found out that last night Miss Penelope Whilom ran off to Gretna Green with her dance instructor!"

Tess blinked as the words sunk in.

She didn't realize that she'd stood until she saw her hand gripping Sir Lee's lapel. "Tell me!"

"According to Janelle, after the notices were sent to the papers last night, Miss Whilom got into a terrible row with her parents. Then, just before dawn, her dance instructor climbed into her bedroom and the two took off down the servants' stairs. The scullery maid spied them and reported the goings-on to Lord Bright. He scrambled to give chase, but was slow to rally and—"

"Is she married or not?" Bills demanded.

Tess's heart was racing, her mouth dry as dust. *Is it too much to hope? Too propitious to be believed?*

Sir Lee's mouth split into a smile. "Miss Whilom and her instructor are on their way to Gretna Green and Lord Bright abandoned the chase. The deed is done."

Swallowing, Tess released Sir Lee's lapel and sank into a chair, her mind a jumble. "Heath can't marry Miss Whilom?"

"Of course I can't marry Penelope!" Heath strode into the chamber, his dear gaze seeking hers. "As I tried to tell you before, I love you and I'm not about to let you tell me who I should or shouldn't marry. I know you're upset about the notices but—"

Jumping up, Tess ran into his arms, hugging him so tightly as to never let him go.

"Ah, I'm glad to see you, too," he murmured in her hair, holding her close. "I suppose this means you're no longer angry with me?"

She looked up at his beloved face. "I thought I'd lost you."

He placed his palms on her cheeks and drew her lips close to his. "You can't get rid of me that easily." His heady kiss banished any remaining doubts from her mind. As she melted into his embrace, Tess was filled with a heavenly joy so profound, she wondered if her feet had left the ground.

"Congratulations, old chap!"

With obvious reluctance, Heath broke the kiss but did not release Tess from his close embrace. Tess's cheeks burned and she knew that she should be embarrassed about her display in front of Bills and Sir Lee, but she was so happy, she was finding it hard to care.

Bills stepped forward, beaming. "You owe me one

hundred and fifty pounds! But consider it my wedding present to you. Congratulations!"

Breathless, Tess blinked. *Wedding?*

Bills motioned to Sir Lee. "This is Sir Lee Devane, by the way. Janelle's friend who used to work at the Foreign Office."

Sir Lee bowed. "Mr. Bartlett."

"He was just telling us that that bugger Reynolds is no more."

Heath nodded. "So you know."

"You don't seem surprised."

"I met Wheaton. The man's a cold-hearted snake, but I managed to get the whole sordid tale." Shaking his head, Heath looked down at Tess. "I don't know how you deal with those—"

Stopping, Heath pursed his lips. "I'm sorry, Tess, I know you love your work. I know it's important, and I'm terrifically proud of you for doing it. But I couldn't bear it if anything happened to you. It's grossly unfair of me to ask you to give it up. But I must."

Furrowing his brow, he went on, "I'm not telling you what to do. It's not an ultimatum. But I'm *asking* you, as the man who loves you more than anyone else in this world, would you please consider it, for my sake?"

Exhaling, Tess looked deep into those cocoa brown eyes and saw his love and his vulnerability. He was afraid for her, and for their future. She understood *exactly* how he felt. "I choose you." The words came easily because it was what she wanted.

His mouth fell open. "You do? You can give it all up, for me?"

"You sacrificed your career to save me."

"But I don't want you to feel indebted. I want it to be your choice."

Tess's heart was filled with gladness and love for this wonderful man. "I love my book business and will miss it terribly. But the spying . . . I'm ready to move on to other things. What I really want—what I really want is a family. With you."

Heath expelled a breath as if amazed. Then his handsome face transformed to a look of glowing happiness. He wound his arms around her and hugged her close. "I love you, Tess," he whispered in her ear.

"I love you, too." Tess closed her eyes, cherishing his strong embrace, his generous heart, and the way he made her feel so treasured. She inhaled his earthy scent that had grown so dear. "I want to marry you, Heath. Can we . . . will you marry me?"

"What the blazes are you doing here, Bartlett?" Solicitor-General Dagwood walked into the room. "Lady Golding?"

Reluctantly Tess pulled back, her heart racing, her unanswered question still lingering in the air.

Sir Lee waved his cane. "Ah, you're finally here, Mr. Dagwood. Thank you for responding to my request."

Mr. Dagwood's sharp dark gaze traveled to each person in the room and finally settled on Heath. "I take it by the woman in your arms that you've heard the news."

Heath's brow furrowed. "What news?"

"About Miss Whilom running off with her dance instructor."

Heath's smile widened. "No, I hadn't heard. But I can't say I'm displeased!"

Exhaling, Mr. Dagwood tilted his head. "It seems that my marriage advice to you was wide of the mark, Bartlett."

Disengaging from Tess, Heath stepped forward with an outstretched hand. "You were only trying to help me, sir. And I greatly appreciate all of your efforts on my behalf."

Moving closer, Dagwood clasped Heath's hand and shook it. "It seems I was mistaken about Lady Golding as well. Today I received a visit from a Mr. Wheaton." Turning to Tess, Dagwood bowed. "My apologies for how I treated you, Lady Golding. In my defense I can only say that I had no notion of your true character and had no idea that you work for the Foreign Office."

"Worked. I am no longer in that position." Tess's gaze met Heath's, and the love she saw within filled her with a happiness that brought tears of joy to her eyes.

"They sacked you over this?" Dagwood asked.

"No, I'm quitting." A flicker of disquiet breached her gladness. "Although I don't know how I'm going to convince Wheaton to let me go."

Heath's fists curled. "Oh, I'll convince him."

"There'll be no need for that." Sir Lee stepped forward, swinging his gold-topped cane. "There comes a time when we need to give our thanks and allow our friends to live the very lives that we work to protect. Besides, Wheaton wants the whole Reynolds business to go away quietly. He won't cause a problem."

"But can you keep your book business?" Bills wondered aloud.

Sir Lee's lips dipped. "I don't see why not." He turned to the solicitor-general. "Now, Mr. Dagwood, our meeting is in the next room and we should be moving along."

Dagwood bowed to Tess. "Lady Golding." He nodded to the men. "Mr. Smith. I'll see you in the morning, Bartlett."

Heath straightened. "I'm not sacked?"

Waving his cane, Dagwood frowned. "I thought we took care of all that. What else do you want? A raise?"

"Ah . . . That would be nice."

"Hmm. We'll discuss it tomorrow."

Sir Lee's green eyes twinkled with mischief. "Lady Golding. Mr. Bartlett, Mr. Smith. If not sooner, I'll surely see you at my great-grandchild's christening. When that fortuitous day finally arrives, *all* of the members of the Society for Enrichment and Learning will be invited."

Bills's eyes widened. "We made it? We're actually members?"

Sir Lee winked. "You didn't hear it from me. Janelle

swears I can't keep a secret." Chuckling, he and Mr. Dagwood left the room.

Bills raised his fist in triumph. "Yes! Lucy is going to have to eat her words!" Grinning, he wagged his brows. "If you don't mind, I'm off to the society. I have some crowing to do."

Tess gave Bills a big hug. "Thank you, Bills. For everything."

"I wouldn't have missed it for the world." Straightening, he slapped Heath on the back. "I couldn't be happier for you, old boy. And yes, of course, I'll be your best man. Now I'm off!"

Quiet descended on the library.

Heath pulled Tess back into his arms. She was soft in all the right places as her body molded to his as if made for him. They were perfect together, exactly as they were. No longer the master's daughter or the tutor's son, they had grown up into very different people who'd come together to be as one.

As he held her close, Heath felt as if every step he'd taken in his life had brought him to this moment. And he thanked the heavens for leading him here.

Leaning her head on his shoulder, Tess sighed.

Heath inhaled the familiar scents of leather, old books, and the lavender bouquet he'd come to adore. "I love you, Tess."

She smiled up at him, her beautiful face so radiant that he knew she was as happy as he. "And I love you, Heath."

Furrowing his brown, he hid his smile. "What was that question you asked me, again?"

Playfully she punched his chest. "I don't like it when you tease me."

"Liar." Then he kissed the spy who'd stolen his heart.

Next month, don't miss these exciting new love stories only from Avon Books

The Duke's Indiscretion by Adele Ashworth

An Avon Romantic Treasure

Famous soprano Lottie English has a secret . . . and when Colin Ramsey, Duke of Newark, asks her to be his mistress, Charlotte must think quickly or she will lose everything. But when she is threatened, will they be able to find true love in the face of grave danger?

One Night With a Goddess by Judi McCoy

An Avon Contemporary Romance

Chloe is the Muse of Happiness—it's going to take more than a year on Earth to bring her mood down. Thriving as a wedding planner, Chloe never expected love to come her way. But handsome doctor Matthew Castleberry is everything she ever wanted—if only she could find a way to overcome that pesky issue of immortality . . .

Wild Sweet Love by Beverly Jenkins

An Avon Romance

Teresa July is ready to make amends for her past, and a job with one of Philadelphia's elite is the perfect start. When she meets her boss's far too handsome son, Teresa is faced with the one thing she always desired and never thought she could have—a future with the man she loves.

The Devil's Temptation by Kimberly Logan

An Avon Romance

To unmask her mother's murderer, Lady Maura Daventry must turn to the one man who could prove to be a threat to her vulnerable heart: Gabriel Sutcliffe, Earl of Hawksley, the handsome and seductive son of the very man once accused of her mother's death.

AVON TRADE *Paperbacks*

978-0-06-083120-2
$13.95

978-0-06-057168-9
$13.95

978-0-06-082536-2
$13.95

978-0-06-117304-2
$13.95 ($17.50 Can.)

978-0-06-114055-6
$13.95 ($17.50 Can.)

978-0-06-085995-4
$13.95 ($17.50 Can.)